FIGHTING FATE

SCARLETT FINN

Also by Scarlett Finn

GO NOVELS
GO WITH IT
GO IT ALONE
GO ALL OUT
GO ALL IN
GO FULL CIRCLE

TO DIE FOR...
TO DIE FOR TRUTH
TO DIE FOR HONOR
TO DIE FOR VIRTUE
TO DIE FOR DUTY
TO DIE FOR LOVE

KINDRED SERIES
RAVEN
SWALLOW
CUCKOO
SWIFT
FALCON
FINCH

MCDADE BROTHERS NOVELS
ALL. ONLY.
ONLY YOURS

THE EXPLICIT SERIES
EXPLICIT INSTRUCTION
EXPLICIT DETAIL
EXPLICIT MEMORY

LOVE AGAINST THE ODDS STANDALONE COLLECTION
SWEET SEAS
HEIR'S AFFAIR
RESCUED
MAESTRO'S MUSE
GETTING TRICKY
THIRTEEN
REMEMBER WHEN...
RELUCTANT SUSPICION
XY FACTOR

WRECK & RUIN
RUIN ME
RUIN HIM

MISTAKE DUET
MISTAKE ME NOT
SLEIGHT MISTAKE

THE BRANDED SERIES
BRANDED
SCARRED
MARKED

RISQUÉ & HARROW INTERTWINED
TAKE A RISK
FIGHTING FATE
RISK IT ALL
FIGHTING BACK
GAME OF RISK

NOTHING TO...
NOTHING TO HIDE
NOTHING TO LOSE
NOTHING TO DECLARE
NOTHING TO US
NOTHING TO SAY
NOTHING TO YOU

EXILE
HIDE & SEEK
KISS CHASE

LOST & FOUND
LOST
FOUND

THE FORBIDDEN NOVELS
FORBIDDEN DESIRE
FORBIDDEN WANT
FORBIDDEN WISH
FORBIDDEN NEED

ONE

IDIOTS.

The word kept going around in Ivy Dune's mind. Five men sat on velvet couches in the rounded window of the Vegas high-roller suite. Idiots.

Seven women danced and drank with the idiots. Either the females were stripper-hookers or hooker-strippers. With the fondling and oral on top of the floor show, they had to be one of the two.

When she took on the role of private attendant at the GoldSpring Hotel, she'd expected glamour. Those illusions were shattered pretty fast. The physically demanding role required a lot of running around, lots of stairs, and ample heavy lifting. Anything the customer wanted, they got; that was her job.

This brand of idiot was more common than glamorous starlets or millionaire businessmen. Though, of all the idiots she'd pandered to, this gang took the cake. They snorted cocaine from the ample selection of fake boobs and took tequila shots from generous cleavages, leaving chaos and carpet stains in their wake without a care or consideration in the world.

Everything that happened there stayed there. It was

Vegas after all. So long as no one was brandishing a weapon, anything went, that was the basic rule. At her post, by the door, inside the suite, she was on hand for client convenience. Her shift ended in less than an hour and she couldn't wait to get the hell out of there.

The idiots drank more and more, their intoxication increased by the second. All except one. The black-haired male closest to the window held a heavy crystal tumbler on the high arm of the couch with his fingertips. The Scotch in it had barely been touched. None of the others noticed his disinterest or cared he wasn't indulging like they were.

The black-haired male had glanced her way a few times earlier and now openly stared. Yeah, keep dreaming, Hotshot. Ignoring him, her focus was supposed to stay straight ahead. Except her eyes insisted on sliding back to his. What was wrong with her?

His electric blue eyes were so crisp and clear, she could absorb their intensity from the other side of the room. Something about them was fascinating. What was their fascination with her?

The worst of the bunch, the sandy-haired idiot, next to the black-haired man, snapped his fingers at her. "You! Maid!"

Ivy crossed the room. "Yes, sir?"

"Have a drink," he said, raising a bottle of tequila, sloshing it on her shoes.

"No, sir, thank you."

"Coke then, come take a line."

"No," she said, maintaining her neutrality. "I'm still working."

"What time do you finish?" he asked, then waved. "Doesn't matter, I'm the guest, I'm always right. Take your shirt off."

"No, sir."

"Don't be a drag," he said, grabbing her arm, hauling her toward the couch. "I've always wanted a naked maid."

She stumbled, landing on top of the sandy-haired idiot, her face in the lap of the black-haired man. The sandman smacked her ass, then grabbed the hem of her skirt.

Scrambling away before he could pull it up, she found her feet and started to retreat. "Hands off what doesn't belong to you," Ivy said.

The others laughed.

"Can you believe that shit?" Sandman declared to his posse before addressing her. "Do you know who I am? I'm Trystan Stark. I have more money in my wallet than you'll make in a lifetime! I own anything I want to own!"

An angry, disrespected man, high on drugs, and with an audience, was volatile.

"Just take your shirt off," one of the girls chirped as if it was no big deal

If she was going to take fashion advice, it wouldn't be from a woman wearing only a trail of playboy jerk drool over her nipples.

The other girls began to jeer along.

Trystan turned to the black-haired man. "Can you believe her?" he asked. "Seriously?"

The black-haired man looked at the wristwatch under his shirt cuff. "Her shift ends in thirty-eight minutes. If you want me to do something about her attitude, it'll have to wait until her colleagues think she's gone home."

Making a threat without using a single negative word was quite a feat. He'd achieved it without even bothering to look at her.

"No," Trystan said. "No, Dax, I don't need you to do a fucking thing. I'll do it myself."

Launching up, he snatched hold of her to wrestle her onto the couch. Flailing around, fighting for freedom, her efforts were futile. With his body, he pinned her down, and forced his mouth onto hers. Wailing in resistance, she turned her head to escape the kiss. The fucker took that as an excuse to give her a hickey.

His friend, at the end of the couch, was no help. He moved to immobilize her ankles, resorting to sitting on her feet, screwing her real good.

"You're going to like me," Trystan said. "Yeah, you are. No one says no to me and gets away with it." Snatching the tequila bottle, he poured alcohol on her sealed mouth, soaking her in the potent liquid that burned when it ran up her nose. "You want a drink, don't you?"

He held her nose for long enough to force her mouth open. The searing alcohol flooded her tongue, drenching her gullet until she choked, spraying it over them both.

By what she heard, the others, thought it was hilarious, and goaded him on.

"Now you're in the party mood," Trystan said.

Blinking alcohol diluted mascara from her eyes, she missed his action of switching both her wrists into one hand until it was too late. Her shirt was ripped open. Buttons flew. She screamed as white powder was scattered across her breasts. Burying his face in the mess, the fucker snorted the dispersed powder and laughed, looking to his friends on the opposite couch for approval.

Her shrieking was ignored. Her legs were still trapped. And everyone else laughed.

"You want some?" Trystan asked, rubbing a moist finger over her breasts then forcing her lip up to smear the grit over her gums. "Yeah, see, you like that. We're going to be up all night you and me. You're in for a real treat. Tonight is your lucky night. It's time for some real fun. Want me to fuck you now?"

"No!" she spat out.

"Yeah?" he said. "You asking me to fuck you? You all heard that, right?"

His troupe chorused in agreement.

"No!" Ivy tried again.

"Open those legs for me, Lucky," he said, lifting his hips to undo his belt.

His buddy, Dax, held her ankles apart for Trystan to settle between her thighs and grind himself on her. Her struggling didn't make any difference. The strength at the end of the couch forced her to do its bidding.

"Got some roofies, want 'em?" someone called.

Trystan licked her face. Sick fuck. "No," he said, digging his teeth into the back of her jaw until pain fired through her. "I don't need 'em, she wants it. Oh, she's going to want me bad."

"No," Ivy said, bucking and thrashing, trying to shove him off.

He whooped. "Oh, yeah! She's riding."

More shouting ensued. Everyone's cheers motivated him to keep going. She wouldn't give up fighting. No. Never. She wouldn't let him take what she didn't want to give. He got her skirt up, his friend still held her legs. This could be it. Her fight could be for nothing.

When Trystan's attention switched to laughing with his friends, she jolted her head up, sinking her teeth into his cheekbone, biting down until she tasted blood. Skin came loose on her tongue, and he roared out, releasing her.

Not hesitating for a heartbeat, she scrambled away and ran at full speed for the door.

"You bitch! I'll fucking kill you!"

Better dead than violated. She ran out of the suite to the employee elevator and headed straight for her manager's office.

TWO

HER MANAGER LISTENED and then left her alone, without calling the cops, to talk to the people in the suite. The frown he wore on his return couldn't be a good sign. He came to sit at her side on the couch, without meeting her eye.

"Are the cops on their way?" she asked.

"Ivy," he said. "I saw what you did to him."

"In defense of myself! I don't care about him, I was assaulted!"

"They say nothing happened you didn't instigate; that it was you who got rough with him."

"That's crazy! That's a lie!"

"That may be, or not, but he says he's going to the police."

"He's not going to the police," she scoffed. "Did you see the drugs up there? Guys like him don't go to the police for retribution."

"All the more reason you shouldn't visit that on yourself," her manager said, examining her and the concealing towel over her chest. "You took those drugs yourself, and you stink of alcohol. Who would you believe, Ivy? He's a good customer. He comes back a couple of times a year and spends a fortune. We all answer to someone, and my supervisor wouldn't—"

"What? Who cares about money? I wasn't partying, he did this to me! I demand that you call the cops!"

"He says he'll press charges against you, and sue the hotel, unless…"

"Unless what?"

"I'm sorry, Ivy. You're fired."

"What?"

How the hell could he be taking the pervert's side instead of hers?

"It's his word against yours, and I'm sorry but a man with that kind of influence and charisma… You've only been here for a month. Take my advice, don't pursue this, go home and forget about it."

"Forget?"

"No one will believe—"

"Not after my boss fires me and takes that bastard's side," Ivy said, standing up, tossing the towel at him. "You're as bad as him! Fucking men!"

Marching away, she cleared out her small locker of her jacket and purse. Talk about the night from hell. Unless she got another job pronto, she'd struggle to make rent. Least things couldn't get any worse.

Getting out of there, fast, was her first goal. Shoving out of the staff exit into the alleyway, she started thinking about where could be hiring.

"You should be more careful."

She stopped. The disembodied voice came from the other side of the alley. As she peered through the darkness, a figure emerged from the shadows.

The black-haired man.

The one Trystan called Dax.

"You should take your own advice, stranger. Hanging around in dark alleys to beat on single women could get you in trouble."

"If I was here to beat on you, you wouldn't have seen me coming."

"Said the voice of experience," she said, folding her arms. "Are you proud of tonight?"

"Heard you got yourself fired."

"No, your buddy got me fired. He's a bully with an overinflated sense of entitlement. One day he'll get what's coming to him."

"Not while I'm around to stand in the way," he said. "You should watch yourself. You pissed off a very influential guy tonight."

"So I've already been told," she muttered.

"Mr. Stark doesn't like to be disrespected, and he's been known to hold a grudge."

"Doesn't have anything better to do?"

"You better hope he finds something. If he gets tonight stuck in his craw, you're gonna be a very sorry little girl."

"I can take care of myself."

She turned to go, but he got in her way. "Not against me. You'd have no defense if I came for you."

"I see that gratuitous ego syndrome is contagious, or at least common in your circle of friends. Just how close are you and your buddy?" She pouted. "Does someone have a little crush?"

His intimidating height came closer. Despite the wall at her back, she didn't shrink in the shadow he cast over her.

"Do you think you're a tough girl?" he asked. "You have no idea what you did tonight; no idea what I'm capable of. Never piss off a man with no conscience."

"Is that why your buddy Trystan keeps you around?" she said. "I don't know who you are or your connection to each other. But threatening me won't win you points with him. If you're hoping this little intervention will get you between his sheets—"

"You don't know when to quit," he sneered, bearing down on her. "You couldn't keep your eyes off me tonight. Is that why you're obsessing about my bedroom?"

"Obsessing—"

Urging her back to the wall, he blocked her in with his forearms on either side of her head. "Is that why you fought Tryst so hard? Were you disappointed I wasn't the man above you?"

With what little space she had, she managed to bring her hand across his face in a half-force slap. His lip curled to betray perverted satisfaction.

Jerking forward, he snatched her hands and slammed them to the concrete at her back. "You want to get physical with me, Minx, you better be damn sure about it."

"Get off of me," she protested, trying to wrench herself free.

"Mr. Stark likes a show," he said, her feeble struggling doing nothing. "Should I take you back upstairs and show him how compliant you are when you're getting what you want?"

"What I want is for you to let me go," she spat.

"You're lucky you're not my type."

"Oh yeah? And who is? The only women you probably get near are the unconscious ones your buddy is through with after about thirty-five seconds."

"Women like you deserve every damn thing they get," he said, pressing himself against her, making no secret of his arousal that imprinted itself on her belly.

The disgust upstairs at Trystan's violation wasn't replicated with this guy. He should repulse her... yet the verbal sparring and earlier's lingering glances provoked her curious hormones, sending them into overdrive. Angry and intimidated? Yeah, maybe. But afraid? No.

Long ago she'd learned how to quash ineffectual fear and channel useful adrenaline into fight rather than flight. Bullies only won if victims lost their wits, and she never would, not again.

"And men like you eventually lose their power. When your physical strength fades, you'll be left with nothing. That vulnerability will ruin you; you'll self-destruct."

"Said the voice of experience," he said, then shoved away. "Think twice before you insult people more important than you."

"Thanks for the advice," she said without concealing her disdain.

"You better hope you never hear of the Starks again. If Trystan decides to come after you, to punish you, nothing'll save you."

"Like I said, I can take care of myself."

"Hope so, because on my side of the fence, there's no mercy."

"I'm shaking with fear," she said with no sincerity.

"You will be."

The liquid ocean of his eyes coated her figure, sending a shiver through her. He turned and stalked away. A few seconds later, he was out of sight.

Men rarely intrigued her anymore, not in the way Dax had. The fantasy of mystery surrounding him would never live up to the reality. Nothing ever did. Just the company he kept was evidence enough he wasn't sane or reliable. At twenty-nine, she was too old for adventures of the heart with bad boys. For a while, that had been her life. The sheen came off the adolescent illusion of romance a long time ago.

FACING HER ROOMMATE wasn't going to be fun. If she could skip it, she would. Unfortunately, it was unavoidable. Their one-bedroom apartment was in a rough area not too far from The Strip. It smelled of mold and sweat. The windows were covered with lengths of material pinned to the wall in their corners. It had been the same since she'd moved in. The rent was cheap, and the neighbors kept to themselves. The streets were filled with gangs, and hookers, and drugs, sure, but she was used to it.

The tension of the day expelled from her lungs as she sank onto the couch.

Trudi bounced out of the doorless bedroom, hooking a shoe onto her foot. "That was quick," she said. "How'd you get home so fast?"

Her head dropped onto the back of the couch. "I got fired," Ivy said, spreading her hands.

"Oh, shit," Trudi said. "You wanna take a shower and come out with me?"

"No."

"I know a guy who'll look after you."

"How many times have I told you not to tie yourself to a pimp?"

"You don't know what it's like out there," Trudi said. "It's dangerous these days."

"I know it's dangerous," Ivy said. "But you don't need anyone taking your money away from you."

"Not now that my roommate has lost her job. You think you can live straight, but you can't. It's no way as easy as that. You held onto that job for a month; the one before that was two weeks. You've lived here nine months, and you've never had a job for more than two months."

"Not your problem," Ivy said. "I've never missed rent, have I?"

"We're in Vegas. Girls like us, from the streets, we make money one way. You're no better than the rest of us, Ivy. I know you try to stay legit, but…"

"I am not walking the street, Trud. Things haven't got that bad."

"Maybe not yet," Trudi said, scooping condoms out of the drawer under the coffee table. "You know where I'll be if you change your mind."

Trudi was a pretty girl who'd made some bad life choices. Her drug habit was moderated by the various men who came and went from her life. Despite her chaotic existence, Trudi was upbeat and was already singing as she headed out the door. How could the beauty be so happy going out to sell her body?

In her own life, Ivy had travelled from city to city and done just about every job there was. Streetwalking was a last resort she'd managed to avoid so far.

Just once she'd like to catch a break. Her private concierge role at the GoldSpring had been a great job with great tips. Without it, she was back to square one. She didn't need fame and fortune; she just wanted to belong, to know that she would be okay and that she wasn't alone. That dream got more distant every day.

THREE

BEING TRYSTAN'S MINDER wasn't a job Dax requested. Despite his efforts to delegate the babysitting, somehow the role fell to him way too often.

Trystan, the youngest Stark son, lived at the Stark mansion with his father and brother. Plenty of staff ran around pandering to him, which was probably why he'd never grown up.

For most of the night, he'd been in Trystan's private drawing room, listening to him go on about Vegas being a bust.

Dax glanced toward the window. "You're letting it get to you," he said. "It's been a week, forget about it."

"No," Trystan said, refilling his Scotch. "That's what she wants. It snowballs, you know that. My father always taught us—"

"Disrespect is the greatest enemy," Dax muttered.

Over the years of cleaning up Trystan's messes, he'd gotten used to the brat fixating. Usually, his obsessions were linked to getting his own way. Trystan just couldn't keep his nose clean. He didn't realize the attention he brought on the family affected the business. The last thing they needed was anyone in law enforcement looking too closely into how the family made their money.

Owing the Starks like he did, making sure Trystan didn't get himself into too much trouble, obvious trouble at least, had become second nature. Seemed like the least he could do given he wasn't blood, but Maurice Stark treated him as family.

"Women don't say no to me. Do you know how long it's been since one turned me down?"

Did it fall to him to point out that most of the women in Trystan's life wanted to use him for his family connections, or were paid to enjoy his company? Sometimes both. No way those women were going to say no to him.

"You should think about settling down," Dax said, though he was a year older than Trystan and it was the furthest thing from his own mind.

Trystan snorted and collapsed into the wingback chair opposite his. "You sound like Mauri. He said the same thing last night."

"It's not a bad plan," Dax said. "You get yourself hitched then you've got a woman who'll never say no to you, or disrespect you."

"Yeah right, a wife would probably be worse!"

"Not if you get the right one," Dax said, allowing a smile to twist one corner of his lips. "And train her right."

Trystan swirled his drink then took a long gulp. "The only woman I'll marry is one who'll let me keep partying."

"Who will let you screw around and sample the Stark family product? There are a bunch of women who would put up with that to get a taste of the high life."

"I don't want a cheap whore," Trystan objected. "She'd have to be faithful and obedient. I don't want some whiny bitch on me all the time. She'd have to keep her mouth shut while I treat her like shit but serve me and put out when I'm on a come down."

Was that too much to ask? Geez. He tried not to shake his head or roll his eyes. "Mauri could hook you up."

"An arranged marriage? I don't think so," Trystan said. "But it would get the old man off my back for a while if I knocked-up some girl and left her at home to bring up the kids. Dad thinks that kids will straighten me out."

Trystan with children was difficult to imagine; he didn't have much wise, worldly wisdom to pass on.

"Maybe it will, Mauri knows how to solve every kind of problem."

"Think I'm a problem?" Trystan asked, teasing.

The way the playboy gazed out of the window betrayed he was cooking up a scheme.

"What are you planning?" Dax asked.

"To kill two birds with one stone," Trystan said, knocking back the rest of the liquor and pouncing to his feet. "Wait here, I'm going to talk to Mauri, then we'll hit the clubs."

Great. Trystan left the room and Dax closed his eyes. He couldn't be bothered with nightclubs and had hoped for a night off. He should've known better. Trystan had a way of sensing when he was getting fed up with him and, at that point, he'd push to have him around more often. The guy just couldn't take a hint.

To say Tryst held a grudge was a massive understatement. Making others unhappy for his own benefit was Trystan Stark's greatest pleasure and achievement.

FOUR

AFTER DOING THE ROUNDS, the only job offers on the table were the usual ones… in strip joints. Vegas attracted young, beautiful women like a magnet. Every day the airport and bus station spawned new hopefuls. In the world-famous city, there was no shortage of spritely females in need of money, and that meant there weren't always enough jobs to go around.

Strip joints offered good money, but she left that circuit years ago. Being there meant basically admitting you were only as good as the breasts on your body. She didn't want to be employed simply because God had graced her with a generous pair.

After paying what was due, her savings were gone. If she didn't find employment, next week's bills wouldn't be paid.

Poring over the newspaper on the coffee table, she circled possibilities and would trek to the payphone on the corner after checking all the ads. Exercise didn't scare her, anywhere within walking distance would get a personal visit.

Trudi burst into the apartment waving a flyer, which she came over and slapped down on the coffee table.

"What's this?" Ivy asked, picking up the yellow paper

to read the advert for a swinger's club. "Uh, there's no way—
"

"Not that. On the back," Trudi said, sitting on the couch to tug off her boots.

An address, phone number, and another number were handwritten on the back.

"What is this?"

"I had a client last night and—"

"I'm not interested in hooking, Trud—"

"I know," Trudi said and tsked. "His boss is looking for a live-in housekeeper. It's the real deal. I could never put up with that kind of crap, the 'yes, sir, no, sir,' stuff. But you could and look at the starting salary!"

"I don't know," Ivy said, tempted by the number at the bottom. "What kind of place is it? Maybe they'll expect extras, you know? If his employees use your services…"

"Please," Trudi scoffed. "Have you ever met a guy in Vegas who doesn't use sex services? I don't think so. This is just perfect for you. You should be grateful I thought of you."

She and Trudi hadn't seen eye-to-eye much, especially recently, but she hadn't thought the woman was eager to kick her out.

"I guess I could call and see what it's about. The address isn't too far so I'd still be in Vegas."

"Right," Trudi said, standing to begin shedding her clothes as she headed for the bathroom. "And Carlos says I could start seeing clients here at home, that would help with the rent. I mean there's only one bedroom, so it would be cool to live alone, right?"

Trudi didn't wait for an answer and went into the bathroom to turn on the shower.

Reading the newspaper ads and the back of the flyer side-by side, she considered both. There wouldn't be any harm in calling and finding out more about the housekeeping role. She gathered everything and headed out to use the payphone.

Getting a job and more importantly, getting paid, was her only priority. Unless it was linked to something sinister, she'd happily take a job with a salary and somewhere to sleep into the bargain. If it was as good a deal as Trudi said, a bunch of people would apply. Hopefully, Trudi had given her an inside edge, she had a personal connection, and maybe got the tip before the job was available everywhere.

In the blazing heat, she picked up the pace. The housekeeper job would be her first call. Could this be the lucky break she'd been waiting for?

FIVE

TRYSTAN HAD GONE OFF TO EUROPE. For around two months, he'd be on another continent. The news bred a sigh of relief.

Vegas hadn't provided the rest and recuperation Trystan felt that he deserved. His vacation time was valuable, the jerk took it seriously.

So two weeks after Vegas, a week after their conversation in Trystan's drawing room, the playboy was on a plane over the Atlantic on his way to party across another land mass.

Dax wasn't going to Europe. Maybe without Trystan around, he could get back to the serious work.

Maurice Stark had two living sons, Trystan and Brad. Brad, the eldest, followed in daddy's footsteps and was a chip off the old block when it came to the family business. All Trystan wanted to do was spend the money his father and brother made. He was spoiled, but they seemed okay with that—as long as he stayed out of trouble and didn't draw attention to them.

At thirteen years old, Dax had been caught stealing from Mauri. He'd been forgiven the slight on the condition he start working for the Starks. Twenty years later, he was still part of Mauri's crew.

As was usual at the start of the month, he and a dozen privileged guys sat in Mauri's office at the mansion, waiting for updates and instructions. Bruno came in to spout assignments, getting rid of half a dozen guys, who went off to do as told. In his late fifties, Bruno, Mauri's right-hand man, had worked with the Starks since his grandfather ran the operation.

Brad was next to appear. He updated them on the expected shipment and handed out jobs.

Eventually, Dax was the only one left with Bruno and Brad. "What's going on?" he asked from the high back chair near the double doors of Mauri's office.

"We've got a special assignment for you, Dax," Bruno said, finishing up something at the desk.

Being the unofficial third son, Dax had done everything the old man had ever asked of him and knew more family secrets than Trystan could dream of.

Whatever was about to be asked of him, he'd do it. "What is it?"

"We're going away together," Bruno said. "Alone."

He never worked alone with Bruno, this had to be big. "Keep going," Dax said.

"It's Tryst," Brad said, coming over to pull up a chair opposite him. "Dad wants him married and straightened out. He's getting messed up in too much shit."

"Tryst told me. Do you think there's a woman alive capable or that would put up with him? I heard his demands."

"We came to a compromise," Brad said. "He'll get married if we make sure his pick won't give him an earache."

"He wants to party, sleep around, and carry on as usual," Dax said, recalling their conversation.

"My father thinks having kids will teach him responsibility," Brad said, his tone conveying he wasn't convinced.

"Where will you find a woman to do that? Put up with a cheater who'll abuse her? Have his kids and toe the family line? You'll have to pay her a fortune."

"Not pay, train," Bruno said. Leaving the desk, he

came over and rested a hand on the back of Brad's chair. "Trystan said you put the idea in his head. Him and Mauri made a deal. Trystan will get married like Mauri wants him to, if the wife will do what she's told without a fight."

"If Mauri can't promise the girl will capitulate, Trystan gets out of the marriage?"

"It's win-win for Trystan," Brad said. "I guarantee that's what my brother is thinking. He doesn't think dad can pull it off."

"He wants to humiliate Mauri?" Dax asked.

Mauri didn't take being made a fool of lightly. Trystan would be on shaky ground if he set the old man up.

"No," Brad said. "He just doesn't want to settle down. If the girl does what she's told, then he gets to order her around and give her shit. If she doesn't, he doesn't have to marry her."

"Win-win," Dax muttered. "If Trystan is sure he won't have to do it, why is Mauri pushing for it?"

"Dad is sure that having kids will change Trystan's outlook."

Both father and son were as arrogant as each other.

"Each is sure of their own position," Dax said.

"Trystan's been pissed off for a couple of weeks," Bruno said. "You know why."

"Because Vegas didn't end how he wanted it to," Dax said.

"My father had to call in favors to pull Trystan out of a sticky situation… again. If that girl had gone to the cops—"

"I spoke to her," Dax said. "She wasn't going to the cops."

"Maybe not. But dad likes the reputation he has at GoldSpring. He likes the treatment we get; it's why he insists on all of us using the place whenever we're in Vegas."

That and Mauri had done some business with the owner in years gone by.

"It's a decent place."

"Yeah, but Tryst once again drew attention to the family and dad is sick of it."

"He told Trystan if it happens again then he's out, that Mauri will cut him off," Bruno said.

Mauri was renowned for never making hollow threats; it was one of the first things Dax had been taught by the old man. Never bluff in life. If you're playing a hand, then you're either in or out. He would never say anything he didn't mean.

"Trystan wouldn't go quietly," Dax said.

"Dad obviously doesn't want to do that, which is why they came to the agreement. Trystan will get married."

"It was that or start working for a living," Bruno said, he was privy to all the family's comings and goings. "That was never gonna happen."

There wasn't a person alive Mauri trusted, or valued, more than Bruno.

"If he can be something other than a shallow playboy fuck up, maybe we can go a day without diverting cops or paying off witnesses."

More often than not, it was the other way around. He'd done his share of scaring witnesses into amnesia where Trystan was concerned.

"He gets married, makes a good show, and the world thinks he's a decent guy… who doesn't need to do a hard day's graft—"

"Because he's so busy providing the family with heirs."

Not only was he expected to marry, but he was expected to reproduce right away. "And you think you can find a woman to train into putting up with Trystan?" Dax asked, wanting to end the statement with the phrase, "*good luck with that.*"

"We've already found her. Trystan picked her out himself, it was another of his terms," Bruno said, going to a side door to haul out a blindfolded, gagged, and bound woman. "Meet the newest member of the Stark family."

The dirty, shaking woman wasn't a stranger. Now faced with her, he wasn't surprised. Typical that Trystan should make his demands and fuck off to another country to have fun while everyone else did the hard work. If he and

Bruno were going away, this woman had to be coming with them, because someone had to teach her how to stay in line.

HE'D RECOGNIZED HER IMMEDIATELY. Trystan had been told to pick a woman and he'd picked her. He should've predicted this. Trystan hated to be disrespected more than anything. By refusing and embarrassing Trystan, she'd disrespected him in the worst way. Their altercation left him making excuses to his father, causing him more embarrassment. Now the woman would pay by dedicating the rest of her life to the man she'd disrespected.

Dax drove and Bruno rode in the passenger seat. Their packed bags were in the backseat because the female was in the trunk. She'd been silent for most of the journey. Whenever she started kicking and moaning Bruno turned up the radio.

Conversation hadn't been flowing. Bruno was happy to talk to himself, he didn't really care what was said in return, so Dax didn't say much. Being away from the city might be good for him. Maybe. He wasn't used to doing nothing and didn't know how he would enjoy spending his days at the beach house with no possible end in sight. His days were usually filled with checking on operations and following up leads for Mauri with those who needed some extra special persuasion. On his rare night off, he did what he enjoyed most. Though his favorite hobby was something few people understood, it made perfect sense to him.

At least this job gave him the chance to get closer to Bruno. They'd done jobs together before, but Dax had never warmed to the guy. Bruno was too hasty; he preferred a more patient approach. This time together could teach him more about Bruno and give them the chance to see things from each other's perspective.

Back in the day, Bruno had advised Mauri against trusting Dax, he knew that, though he wasn't supposed to. A quiet, unspoken animosity existed between the two of them. In recent years, Bruno seemed to have lightened up but was prone to bouts of rage. That would need monitoring, though it wasn't like he was worried. If he had to defend himself, he'd own the guy without breaking a sweat. The only concern was how he'd explain the mess to Mauri.

The Stark California beach house was perfect for their requirements. Set on an isolated clifftop peninsula with the sea on three sides, the land boundary was walled off, gated, covered by cameras and half a mile from the house. They weren't visible from the road.

He parked and set to work taking the bags from the backseat while Bruno dealt with the difficult cargo. Bruno's reputation was ironclad. The legend was a man to be feared, and he made no secret of the lives he'd taken.

Another part of that reputation? Bruno wasn't known for treating women well. His long line of girlfriends ended up bloodied and bruised at some point. Probably why he'd never been married, the women never stuck around for long. Stories of illegitimate children flared every once in a while, in various corners of the world, but he'd never met any of them to verify their existence.

The true glory days of Bruno's heyday were gone. Years of drug and alcohol abuse left the geezer impotent and slow. Not that anyone would say that to his face; not unless they had a death wish.

While dumping the luggage in the bedrooms upstairs, noise of scuffling and muffled screams came from downstairs, accompanied by Bruno's rumbling deep voice. Dax went into his shower room and stripped to step under the cool spray. He'd wash off the day, then go for a swim and maybe barbeque afterwards. Bruno loved the grill and Mauri had his crew stock the house before they arrived. They'd be living in luxury for a while.

Trystan's European excursion gave them sixty days to whip this woman into shape. Having never trained a woman before, Dax would follow Bruno's lead. No sweat, Bruno had experience in everything.

THEY GRILLED STEAKS, drank Scotch, and smoked cigars as the sun went down. As a kid who grew up on the streets, fighting other street kids in a ring for money, access to opulence still didn't feel real. He'd earned it and reminded himself of that all the time.

After the sun was gone, they went to bed.

Neither of them were small talk types. So the next day they pursued their own shit until they eventually ended up on the couch watching television.

Twenty-four hours after arriving at the beach house, Bruno turned off the TV and sat up. "Okay, let's get started."

"What's the play?" Dax asked.

"You just watch and learn, son," Bruno said and slapped his knee then headed to the basement door.

The three-bedroom property had a basement gym. Despite it being dark down there and basically underground, it was a favorite spot. That morning he'd gone down and discovered a corner had been walled off. A cell for their captive? Convenient, but he hadn't been interested enough to check it out.

He stayed on the couch, waiting for Bruno to retrieve the woman. From the basement stairs, a gasping scream, obscured by a gag, got louder when Bruno dragged her into the living room. Her hands were bound, and a blindfold blocked her view.

Her hands were secured at her back. Tied tight too because her jugs were thrust forward. With her blindfolded, he could examine her figure as much as he liked, she would never know it. Her skinny jeans were ripped, her grey top had probably once been white, yeah, she was a mess. Grease, muck, blood, on her clothes, on her skin. Dried blood cracked on her hairline, neck and around her nostrils, but the injuries were superficial, cuts and bruises. She'd taken a beating somewhere, but no serious or permanent damage.

Bruno threw her down onto the rug in front of the TV and went around behind her. Chipped red nail polish on the toenails of her bare feet was almost the color of the blood. She had a tattoo on her foot above her arch. Interesting.

"I'm going to take this off and give you some answers, okay?" Bruno said into her ear. She nodded, huffing out sharp breaths through her nose, her only available airway.

"Keep quiet or it goes back on."

He took off the blindfold, bindings, and the gag, then came around to sit down. Dax remained static in the corner of the couch, one ankle propped up on his knee and his arms spread along the back and arm.

"Where am I?" she croaked, blinking into the bright sun shining through from the floor to ceiling windows behind them.

"Here's what's going on," Bruno said, the epitome of cool. "All you have to do is what you're told. Don't ask questions, just follow our orders and you'll be treated well, very well."

The corner of one eye was blackened, both were blood shot, and make-up was smeared from her eyes down her cheeks. She took the time to examine them both, then fixed on him.

"I know you," she said and exhaled. "You're the Vegas guy… you were with that pervert."

"He is Dax Harrow," Bruno said, glancing back. "He is your new owner."

This surprised him as much as it did her, but Dax kept his practiced eyes narrowed, assessing her with apathy as though he did this all the time.

"My… my—"

"Your owner dictates your actions. He tells you what to do and where to go. He makes all the decisions about your life."

"Are you sick?" she asked, in a surprisingly strong voice. "Is this a sick joke? Why would I ever—?"

"Because if you don't, you'll spend more time in our basement. You'll spend your life down there. We have all the time in the world. We'll keep on going with this until we get bored, and you don't want that to happen. So you choose, do what you're told and have a good life, or don't and we'll leave you down there to die. Do you get it? Let's start with something simple, would you like a drink of water?"

"Yes," she whispered.

Oh, that cost her a lot.

"Sit on the floor," Bruno said, and she lowered

herself down. When she was there, Bruno took a bottle of mineral water from the cooler next to the couch, pulled off the cap, and got up to hand it to her. She gulped it down. "Sip."

How long had she spent at the Stark mansion? If she'd been deprived of food and water for a few days, her stomach would be weak.

"Why are you doing this?" she asked and looked straight at him. "Is this to score points with your buddy? Where is he? Is he here?"

"No, he's not," Dax said. "I did warn you that you would be sorry."

"He got this in his craw?"

"Yeah, he did."

"He's crazy. I didn't go to the cops. I kept my head down and let it go… not that he deserved to get away with what he did to me."

"Are you sorry, little girl?"

"You're perverted friend needs help," she spat. "This isn't going to solve anything. I'll press charges, I'll—"

"You don't speak unless you're spoken to," Bruno said, getting up to approach her.

Without responding, she returned to the drink, getting halfway down the bottle before Bruno took it away and capped it again. "See how well that worked? I told you to sit, you complied, and you got a reward." Her frown formed slowly. "Do you want to eat?"

"Yes," she said in reflex.

"Good," Bruno said with an audible smile. "You're good at this; what a good girl you are. Take off your shirt."

She faltered. "What?"

"Take it off and we'll feed you."

"No! No, I won't do that," she said.

Clambering back to her feet, she stumbled back and caught the entertainment center to balance herself.

"One more chance," Bruno said. "Take it off and we'll forget your insubordination."

"Go to hell!"

"Your choice," Bruno said.

Grabbing hold of her, he dragged her back the way they'd come.

The screams lowered in volume as they descended the stairs. Dax reached for the remote and turned on the TV again.

SIX

THEY TRIED AGAIN TWO DAYS LATER with similar results. When Bruno took the girl back to her shackles in the basement, Dax joined them. Her determination was admirable. She had to be terrified but wouldn't show it, not in real terms.

It came down to one simple task: remove your shirt.

She wouldn't do it. Maybe it was pure stubbornness, or maybe she was uncomfortable with her body. More likely? her apprehension was the next command. If she complied once, there would be precedent. Where would she draw the line? He got it. And probably would be as defiant in her position.

"Give me a minute," Dax said to Bruno as he locked the cage with the woman inside.

Bruno nodded and left him alone.

She didn't say anything, just regained her composure and crawled over to seat herself on the foam mattress. Two chains reminded her of her place, one around her wrist, the other connected to her ankle. The manacles gave her freedom to roam throughout the full caged space but reminded her in no uncertain terms just what her situation was.

"If you do as you're told, no one will hurt you," he

said.

"Go to hell," she grumbled and scratched under one of the shackles.

"You'll draw blood and get an infection if you keep picking like that."

"Now you care?" she snapped, her vengeful eyes burning into his. "What's the fascination you and your friend have with seeing my breasts? You can pay women for that treat you know, or there's always the internet."

"Sass won't keep you alive," he said. "Argue, fine, that's cool. The only person you're hurting is you. What we're doing has a purpose, can you say that about what you're doing?"

"I give in and then what?" she asked.

"Why don't you try it and see? If you don't, there's no chance of getting home to your mommy and daddy."

"I'm sure they'll be disappointed," she said with a flare of ire then lay down on the bed.

"If you want to spend the rest of what will be a very short life down here alone with your bitterness, go ahead. You'll die alone and no one will know where to look for your body. There's a big ocean on our doorstep, Minx. If that doesn't remind you of your insignificance, maybe a few more days down here will."

Ready to walk away from her prison, he was surprised to hear her laugh.

"Still trying to impress that buddy of yours with your willingness to do anything for him?" she asked. "Does he appreciate you?"

"Back to that obsession you have with my bedroom? I'll show you where it is right now if you're ready to bow down."

"Is that what it will take?" she asked. Her eyes became slits. Either she was struggling to hold onto her sanity or her consciousness. "It's a shame, because you are sort of hot. But I'm damn sure you'll never get the chance to disappoint me between the sheets."

"Don't be so sure about that," Dax said. "When I want you, I'll have you."

"I thought I wasn't your type."

"You're not. But I think you're long overdue a lesson."

"What lesson is that?" she asked. "That bullies get their way if they're strong enough to overpower you? Is rape what gets you off?"

"You haven't seen me try it yet, have you?"

"You were happy for your friend to do it."

"Trystan isn't my friend, he's a colleague," Dax said, not planning to reveal his personal connection to the Starks. "And it's because of him that you're here, that we're having this conversation."

"That much I had figured out," she said. "What is the plan? To keep me locked up forever? To turn me into some sort of slave or something?"

"Or something," he said. "Spend your time down here thinking about what you want from your life, what's left of it. Do you want to be angry and bitter or have a future? What we're offering isn't gonna do you any harm unless you are difficult."

"What are you offering?"

"A better life. A better future. You won't have to worry about paying bills or finding your next meal. We'll take away your worries and look after you. In exchange, you follow orders, that's it."

"A simple exchange in your eyes maybe," she said. "But my body isn't for sale."

"We're not looking to buy, we're looking to win, and your compliance is the prize. Think about it, Minx. You can have every material luxury you ever dreamed of, or you can starve down here. Another missing person. Another statistic." Backing toward the door, he watched her eyes close. "Be smart."

Only time would tell if his words had cracked her exterior. She wouldn't make their job easy, but there wasn't an easy one ahead of her either. A few more days to reconsider things might be enough; that was all he was willing to give her.

LEFT ALONE IN HER BASEMENT CELL, three days went by. Knowing she wouldn't last long without water, Bruno went down periodically to give her some, but he didn't speak to her.

On the third day, Bruno brought her upstairs and made the same demands. No dice. As headstrong as ever, it looked like she'd never give in. The screaming, struggling, and sarcasm decreased. She'd be weakening, but that mettle remained steadfast.

Four days later, Bruno retrieved her again. Immediately, it was different. The struggling and screaming had stopped; her ability to resist was lessening. As he usually did, Bruno released her when they got onto the rug. Instead of staying on her feet, she collapsed in a heap. Bruno wasn't worried, he came back to the couch and took a handful of popcorn from the bowl beside him. Stuffing it into his mouth, he crunched loudly.

From the way she barely moved except to blink and twitch, he'd say she was on the cusp of giving in… or death, one of the two. All of her decisions so far had been wrong, in his opinion, because they hadn't yielded results.

"You got water downstairs," Bruno said past the popcorn mulch in his mouth. "If you want to eat, take off your top."

Bruno could go over there and remove her top, or all her clothes. Her weakened state meant she wouldn't put up much of a fight. But what Bruno was doing wasn't about getting her naked. It was about getting her to do something she didn't want to.

"Okay, your choice," Bruno said, wiping his hand on the couch. "Back downstairs."

He snatched her up to her feet and she objected. "No," she said.

Bruno stopped.

With meagre strength, she locked her eyes to his and lifted the hem of her top to take it off over her head. It fell from her fingertips to the floor.

"Good girl," Bruno said, "and now we'll feed you. Don't move."

When Bruno turned his back on the girl to head for the kitchen he winked, Dax didn't acknowledge the exchange.

The kitchen door clicked shut, signaling Bruno's departure. She might have had difficulty focusing her eyes, because she didn't seem to look at any specific thing. Eventually, her attention dropped to the floor.

Her cans were incredible, not that she seemed aware of them. Showcased in underwired once-white cotton and lace, the display made quite a picture. Ribs were almost visible beneath, the definition in her abs told him she worked out and probably hadn't weighed much to begin with.

Her legs were long, but he'd only put her at a height of five six. The tattooed black symbol above her instep interested him.

"What does it mean?" he asked. Her head only swung on her neck. "The tattoo on your foot, what does it mean?"

"Who cares," she grumbled.

"I do," he replied. "Answer my question, or the basement will be your home for the rest of the week."

"Don't fight fate," she said. "It means, don't fight fate."

"Sort of fitting."

"I don't think that this is my fate," she said.

"Probably last week you didn't think that you'd have your tits on show in my living room, but here you are."

"You're as sick as him, aren't you?"

"You'll get to like Bruno. He's not a conventional guy, but there's plenty of time for you two to get to know each other."

"How long do you plan to keep me here?"

"Haven't decided yet," he said, although the truth was, he didn't know.

"Why are you doing this to me?"

"Why doesn't matter, you're here now, and you're here for a reason."

"What reason?" she asked.

The whisp of desperation in her tone was well hidden, but he still managed to catch it.

Every encounter he'd had with this girl since the night

they met reinforced his belief that she'd fight oppression for as long as she could. After spending so much time captive in the basement, her resolve was cracking. She'd lasted a lot longer than most would, something to be proud of.

"Did you get another job?"

"Is that supposed to be funny?" she snapped.

No, and he had no idea why her reaction was so strong. Upholding a façade of cool indifference made the cruelty she'd endured, and would endure, more severe. If the people surrounding her didn't value her, saw her as worthless, hope would swirl down the suckering drain, unable to cling to anything that might mean salvation.

"My humor's subtle," he said.

Her eyes, already filled with impotent rage, narrowed further. "If you're worried people will notice I'm gone," she said. "You should be."

"I'll bear that in mind," he said, unconcerned. Mauri's men were thorough. "No one will find you here, they can look all they want."

Another light of hope extinguished within her. With his indifference and Bruno's expertise, this woman would be eating out the palms of their hands soon enough. A part of him, a tiny part, wanted her to fight.

Something about her demeanor hinted that life had been a struggle. Surrendering to them would sort of put that toil to shame. Having spent his own life waging war just to survive, he had an affinity with others who hadn't had it easy.

Bruno came out of the kitchen with a bowl of lukewarm soup that she ate slowly, as instructed. They watched her consume every mouthful. Then drink a little water.

"Time for a bath, I think," Bruno said. "You'll want to clean out those cuts and use a proper toilet instead of a bucket, won't you?" She nodded. "Say yes. We want to hear the word. You answer every question you're asked aloud, it's the only time you'll have permission to speak."

"Yes," she said.

"Follow me," Bruno said, walking towards the stairs.

Instead of going down to the basement, he took her

up the stairs. Only thing up there were the bedrooms.

The girl was slow, unsteady on her feet, but got there in the end.

A few minutes later, Bruno came back down alone and took the TV remote out of his hand before the set was even on.

"You left her up there alone?" Dax asked, not really caring about the TV.

"Where's she gonna go?" Bruno asked. "Anyway, she can't walk the length of herself. She's a fucking mess. Your bathroom doesn't have windows, she's stuck in there."

"She's in my bathroom?"

"Sure. She's your property."

"Mine?"

"I'm showing you the ropes, kid. Mauri likes you and Brad trusts you, neither's an easy get," Bruno said, scooping up more popcorn.

"I thought we were doing this for Tryst."

"We are, but someone's gotta own her. She's a slave for fuck's sake. She's gonna believe she's all yours until we gift her to Tryst, then he'll be her owner. He's not gonna take the time to beat her into submission, that's our job. There's a lot riding on this. Mauri wants it done and they're already planning a wedding. Mauri wants them down the aisle quick, as soon as Tryst is back. Before the little prick tries to back out."

"You'll do a better job than I will." Dax couldn't be bothered with a woman giving him grief. "You take her."

"This will be the greatest experience of your life. We're gonna whip that girl into shape; she'll be the best fuck of your life. She'll do any damn thing you want, any minute of the day."

So he was here for sexual purposes, that should've been obvious. Bruno couldn't do the honors, which left it up to him. "What d'you know about her?"

"Mauri's guys took blood and piss from her and tested her for everything, she's clean. They gave her the injection thing too. You're good to ride bareback for the next two months... it lasts three so we're still good even if we run over."

Getting her to agree to the sex wouldn't come easy if her reaction to Trystan in Vegas was any indication.

"I'll be the one to break her. You watch and learn," Bruno said. "Once we've got her dancing to our tune, you'll take over."

"You want me to fuck her?"

What a waste of time to go to all this effort for a quick roll in the hay.

"No, kid, you're missing the point. You're not gonna just fuck her. You fuck her in every way you've ever thought of. You make her fulfil every dirty, depraved fantasy you've ever had and make her beg for more. Push her further than you've ever pushed a woman. She can't say no to Trystan, not ever, that little fucker made a deal with his father. He'll marry her and stay out of trouble if, behind closed doors, he gets away with anything that he wants. The minute she complains, or refuses him, that's it: deal's off."

"Two months to make her into a Stepford wife."

"Fifty days," Bruno said, "to make her into a slutty Stepford wife."

In his experience with women, he'd yet to find one he could trust. Sure, they were good for a night or two in the sack, but show one weakness or confide in one? Not a chance. Playing with the uptight Vegas chick might be fun. If she could keep Trystan on the straight and narrow, he'd have fewer messes to clean up. For a break and a laugh, Dax was up for the challenge. If she decided to fight and resist, at least he'd be occupied and entertained. Sitting on his ass doing nothing wasn't his style.

"Give her twenty minutes, then you go up there. Now let's talk about how to play the game."

They ended up talking for close to half an hour. In his time with the Stark family, Dax had done his share of enforcing. It was one of his favorite tasks. Manipulating the woman would be easy, she was pliable enough now. He'd put good money on her realizing that being holed up in the basement limited her options.

If he was in her position, the first thing he'd want was

a lay of the land. He'd want to take a measure of the people holding him too. Neither of which could be done from the basement. With a plan in place, Dax entered his bedroom and closed the door.

Tugging off his tee-shirt, he tossed it into the corner on his way to his private bathroom. He couldn't hear water or movement, so on opening the door he wasn't surprised to see her sitting on the floor motionless, wrapped in a blue towel.

"Move," he said, bobbing his head back into the bedroom.

Backing up, he went to sit on the edge of the bed, facing the bathroom door, waiting while she pulled herself onto her feet and came into the bedroom. She stopped a couple of feet from the bathroom.

"Close that door, then come stand here," he said, pointing to a spot on the floor near him.

Her velvet brown eyes simmered with seething frustration. She closed the door and came to him as indicated.

"We start here, forget who you were before and everything that happened to you. This is the moment your life begins. As your owner, I have a responsibility to you. I'll take care of your wellbeing, your food, shelter, and necessities. You'll live in luxury. I can give you anything and everything you could ever want."

His own personal money had accumulated from his work with the Starks. It didn't amount to anything close to what Trystan had. Everything around them belonged to Maurice, but she didn't need to know that.

"You can't buy me," she said. "You've got the wrong girl if you think I'll fall for that."

"Do you think we're gonna have you turning tricks?"

"I make my choices," she asserted. "The only thing I have to do is what I choose to do."

"You have a clean slate," he said. "You'll never fear enemies while you belong to me. Being my property has its advantages."

"I don't see any," she said. "Let me go home."

"I am your home," he said, pouncing up from the bed to loom over her. "You'll do exactly what I tell you without question or I'll make you regret every minute you breathe. You're gonna become so dependent on me, you'll forget how to live without me. Being apart from me will cause you physical pain."

"Never! I won't ever surrender my free will."

Smiling down at her, the growl of perverse pleasure in his gut came from the knowledge he'd break that fiery spirit. He would own her wrath and direct it as he saw fit.

"You've already lost it," he said. "Your life belongs to me. I have the power of life and death."

"You'll kill me if I don't comply?"

"What other use do I have for you?" he asked. "Drop the towel."

"Not a chance."

"We can play this game, but you know I'll win. Do you want to go back to the basement for five days? It makes no difference to me if you rot down there."

"Drop my towel and then what? You'll force me to have sex with you?"

"No one has forced you into anything. Everything you've done so far has been your choice."

"It wasn't my choice to be bound in your basement."

"It was after day one. I don't know what being down there achieves, but it was your choice not to follow instructions. That decision resulted in you going back down there. You were given a chance to make the right decision."

"I won't have sex with you," she said. "I won't."

"You are the only person who's mentioned sex," he said. "All I want you to do is drop the towel. When you behave, you'll be allowed to sleep out of the basement, that means sleeping in my bed. When you are in my bed, you'll be naked, unless I say otherwise."

"You're sick."

"You've never been naked for a guy before? I find that difficult to believe."

"I've been naked for men I'm attracted to."

"And you're not attracted to me?"

Taking hold of her wrist, he ran her fingertips over his steely abs. "What are you doing?" she asked, trying, and failing, to pull away.

"You are attracted to me, and you know it too. You were attracted to me in Vegas."

"Your ego is showing again," she said, but she wasn't trying to pull away anymore.

When he loosened his grip just slightly, her fingers continued to drift up and down of their own accord.

"I noticed you in Vegas," he said, keeping his naturally husky tone soft.

"You kept staring at me," she said.

Her eyes flitted down, but he pushed her chin up with a finger, joining their gazes again.

"You noticed me too."

"Your eyes are electric blue," she said. "I didn't think their glow was natural."

"I'm all real," he said. "Are you?"

"I don't wear contacts," she answered.

"I wasn't talking about your eyes."

Far as he could tell she didn't see his hand coming, so when he took a handful of her breast and squeezed, she jumped back. "Don't touch me!"

"You've touched me."

The declaration confused her. Disorientation and bad decision making would be influenced by the lingering effects of her starvation and dehydration.

Her confusion gave him scope to maneuver. "I didn't... I..."

"Drop the towel, show me that body, and you'll have a reward. Would you like some more food and something to drink?" She nodded. "You know the rules. Let me hear your answer."

"Yes."

"Then drop the towel or its back to the basement." He prepared himself for the latter. "I'm getting bored." After three tense beats, her hands fell, and the towel dropped. "You're a clever girl," he said, stepping back to check her out. "Maybe this will work out between us."

Her tits were high and round with dark, dusky nipples that lilted up toward him, in perfect placement for his mouth.

Her hunched shoulders told him she wasn't proud of the oversized beauties, but the vibrating pressure building in his groin was damn proud.

"Push your shoulders back." She did a half-hearted job. "Unless you want me to touch you, get them all the way back." She did as told and thrust her chin up at the same time. "Better."

He took his time examining the abs he'd already seen and allowed his focus to descend to her pussy where there wasn't a hair in sight.

"Your friend gave me cream and told me to take it all off, I assume you're into that."

Though there was contempt in her tone he didn't care.

With narrow eyes and a gnarled smile, he answered. "I do. You better keep yourself groomed all the time."

Walking around to check out the rest of her, he took his time, feeling her bristle. Why did he enjoy setting her off-guard? Taking his time to look his fill of her pert ass, he wanted more than he should. Way more.

Before he could think about taking it, the door opened, and Bruno came in. The girl ducked intending to retrieve the towel but missed because he was faster. He tossed it toward the bathroom, allowing Bruno to check her out too.

His colleague's perusal made her prickle. They were doing her a favor; she better get used to guys leering. Fast. As Trystan's girl, she'd be expected to be naked in front of his friends, associates, and family members as well. The youngest Stark never cared about protecting his woman's modesty. Tryst liked to boast about what he had by putting it on show. She'd spend most of her married life topless at least. From what Dax had seen, she'd be a prized exhibit, Tryst had a lot to be proud of.

"You're a lucky fucker, Dax," Bruno said. "Twirl around."

Defiance burned from her. Was she going to comply?

"Do as he says," Dax said.

Though she growled at him, she did a three sixty.

Bruno whistled with approval. "I've got a long list of

ideas for that. You got your hands on the cans yet?"

"Not yet."

"Mind if I do?" Bruno asked him.

Dax shook his head, so he started towards the girl.

She ran to the corner and grabbed his discarded tee-shirt to yank it on. "I won't let you touch me!"

"Oh now, that's insubordination," Bruno said, not deterred. "You still don't get it… You need some more time to think about it."

When he got within reaching distance, Bruno snatched a handful of the girl's hair and yanked her off her feet to drag her, screaming and scrambling, back to the basement. The deeper into the bowels of the building they got, the quieter the feminine cries became.

He sat on the bed to unlace his boots. He'd spend the night alone… with that image of her killer body imprinted in his mind.

SEVEN

After another four days of isolation, even opening her eyes was a struggle. What was the point in trying?

Putting up a fight, resisting these men, was going to kill her. She had to get out of this room. Out of the cage. Living in the dark was demoralizing, but not as detrimental as the sapping of her energy through lack of food and water. If these men abandoned her, she'd die. If they brought her upstairs, and a chance of escape presented itself, she wouldn't be strong enough to take it.

Getting upstairs, living upstairs, even if it meant being nude twenty-four seven, was her only hope. Survival instincts kicked in. The drive to see the sun and be free was overwhelming. Her life couldn't be over. There was too much she still wanted to do.

Escape was vital. It might take time, days or weeks, maybe months. To be ready to grab the first available opening to get out, she had to be there, upstairs, strong.

Letting them touch her, or have sex with her, would be a high price, but one worth paying if it meant keeping her life. Her tears were done. In the first week, she'd pitied herself. The following three days were dedicated to anger. Now, she was weak, broken, and alone. She needed to detach herself, to switch off and build a shell around the truth. For now, while regaining her strength, she'd be what they wanted. When back to full power, she'd form a plan.

She'd known hookers and roomed with them on and off for years. Once or twice, the street had almost become her workplace. In those times, her hooker friends coached her on how to switch herself off, on how they were able to give their body to even the most disgusting of men. Luckily, she'd scraped by without taking the final plunge. It was bad enough that in her younger years she'd swung herself around a pole or two, but stripping was not the same as hooking, not even close.

Despite her decision to play along with her captors, telling herself to comply was easier than doing it. It would be a fight not to let the truth of her personality come out. If she wanted to survive, she'd have to quash her naturally rebellious nature. Become a robot, go through the motions, and obey until the moment was right.

All she could do was wait to put her plan into action. Someone came down once a day to the gym, in the basement beyond her cage room. With nothing better to do, she'd tried to time how long the person exercised for. Sometimes it seemed to be an hour. Other times, much longer. Like way longer.

Dax had to be the one working up a sweat. She'd suspected his fitness, but now she'd seen his torso, it was undeniable. Her fingertips had touched his solid six pack and she'd seen his defined pecs. Oh, yeah, he worked out.

His thick arms were tattooed. The left one had a tribal pattern with Celtic elements covering him shoulder to elbow. On the other arm, a dragon emerged from tangling vines. The black ink made his already foreboding form even more menacing.

The kicker was, much to her shame, he'd been right. In Vegas, before the incident with Trystan, she had noticed Dax. One look and she'd thought: sex. Learning the truth of his associations dowsed his appeal. In physical terms, he was ripped, hot by outward appearance. If she was going to be forced into anyone's bed, better his than Bruno's.

Bruno was rough and liked to manhandle her, he liked slapping her around giving the sense he enjoyed exerting power over her. Four days ago, when Bruno last caged her, he'd smacked her around just for the pleasure he got out of it. She winced against the tender bruises; enough was enough. If she ever wanted to be free again, there was only one route out. Letting them win in the short term was the only way to guarantee her future.

Eager to get away, out of this space, every creak and squeak intrigued her. Anticipating Dax's arrival in the gym, the wait was excruciating.

The unmistakable reverberation of footsteps coming down the stairs kicked in her adrenaline. Relief came too, so much that her ears rang. This was it. Time to sell the performance.

Licking her lips, she prayed he wasn't wearing earbuds. She needed to be heard. Doing her best to sit up, she coughed to clear her throat.

"Dax," she said, fighting to put strength in her voice to get volume. "Dax." It wasn't enough. "Dax!"

A tense score of seconds passed. Had he heard her?

She wasn't sure until the lock clicked. The door took its time to open. Eventually, a topless Dax came in, wrapping his hand with a long strip of narrow fabric. He took his time observing the cage, the bare concrete floor, the single foam mattress, and the bucket, also known as her toilet. After absorbing the details, he examined the chain on her ankle and the one on her wrist.

"I didn't say it before," he said, finished wrapping his hands. "But it's a helluva place you have."

"Minus the chains, I've actually lived in worse," she said.

His expression flickered like he hadn't expected a response. "What do you want?"

"I'll do what I'm told."

"You will?" he asked, leaning against the doorframe, folding his arms.

"Yes."

"You've got another day to think about it."

He began to turn away.

Panic forced her onto her knees, jangling the chains in the process. "No, Dax, please. Don't leave me here."

"Not so easy is it," he said, peering over his shoulder. "To admit when you're wrong."

"Me staying down here isn't getting any of us anywhere... I know now that..."

"You know now, what?" he asked.

The sinister curl of his lip made her want to lash out. That wasn't the plan. If he left her there again, it could be days before he was back. The basement was making her ill. Just being there was a symbol of her fragility. Goddamn, she resented that humiliation. Fighting for her freedom meant sacrifice. Letting this depraved duo believe they'd broken her would be worth it if it got her freedom.

Good sense didn't match years of conditioning; she bit back her impulse to curse at him. To spit and swear and tell him where to get off.

It took some time to gather the will to respond. In that time, his focus switched to the exit.

"I know now that I was wrong," she forced herself to say. "You have the power here. You have power over me and I'm asking you to please let me out of this room."

"What do I get?" he asked, without turning to look at her. "You get free and what do I get?"

"Anything," she said. "Everything you want."

When he turned, his new victorious smile said it all. "Now you've got it."

DAX GAVE HER A BOTTLE of water to drink on their ascent of the basement stairs. From there, she was allowed to eat at the kitchen table while the men lurked in the sliding glass doorway out to the covered deck.

When they decided she'd eaten enough, she was commanded to clean up in the kitchen. From the looks of things, neither had washed a dish or cleaned a surface since their arrival. Yet, they'd somehow managed to lock away every knife and sharp utensil in a drawer.

Her movements were sluggish, partly through her condition and partly because she was in no hurry to get to their next demand, whatever that may be. Throughout her stint doing the chores, one or both of her captors supervised… without a word. At least not until they were issuing instructions for her to do the work over again, under the guise it hadn't been completed to their satisfaction.

Her dreaded fear became reality when Bruno led her upstairs and told her to wash herself in Dax's bathroom. This time the letch remained there, leering through the clear glass shower screen, ogling her naked form in the shower.

Being observed in such a vulnerable position was unnerving. She sped through her grooming, but on emerging wished that she hadn't. Bruno produced a string bikini and told her to put it on.

"You've got a killer body," Bruno said while she tied on the tiny scrap of material that made a pathetic attempt to cover her. "You keep in shape like that to make men want you."

"I don't," she said.

"Are you arguing with me?"

"No."

"You want men to want you. You can't blame a guy for looking at you and thinking about sex, can you?"

The intent glare he burned into her expected only one response.

"No."

"So if a guy wants it," he said, "you're going to give it to him, aren't you?"

"Yes."

"You'll fuck any guy who asks for it, you get me?"

"Yes," she said, responding because he wouldn't accept non-verbal acknowledgement.

Dax came into the bathroom just then, poised to say something to Bruno. On catching sight of her, he stopped to absorb the view.

"What's he thinking about?" Bruno asked her.

"Sex," she responded, lowering her gaze to the floor.

"And whose fault is that?" Bruno asked.

"Mine."

"Apologize for distracting Dax. And look at him while you do it."

Bringing her eyes up to his, she was overwhelmed by shame. "I'm sorry for distracting you, Dax."

"You should refer to him as Master," Bruno said.

"I apologize, Master."

"I need to talk to you," Dax said to Bruno, apparently over the visceral response his body had to hers.

Bruno went toward the door after Dax exited. "Turn that shower on as cold as it goes and get back in. You need to cool off," Bruno said to her and left.

Get back in? She'd freeze!

The dark basement. Refusing would put her back there.

She went straight back into the shower and turned on the icy spray.

EIGHT

WHEN THE SHOWER WENT ON, Bruno closed the bathroom door.

"Master?" Dax asked.

Bruno grinned, coming over, rubbing his hands together. "You are welcome, buddy. She's gonna be begging to swallow your cock by the end of the week."

Sex was great. He loved getting laid… not that it was hard for him to pick up women. The opposite actually. One thing he could say with certainty: he'd never had another guy so geared up to provide pussy for him.

"I've gotta head into town," he said before the moment could get any weirder. "Have you got this?"

"Yeah, yeah, but do me a favor. Pick me up some, huh?"

Bruno was already wide-eyed and hyped. He'd thought it was the situation that had him amped… maybe the energy was chemically enhanced. "Since when are you using again?"

"I'm not. I'm not. I just think we might have a party with this girl."

Maybe Bruno had a few dozen strong blue pills to get through. From what he'd heard of Bruno's ability to get a hard-on, it would take more than that. Some of Bruno's exes got chatty when the alcohol and powder flowed. Women talked to him, they opened up, probably because he wasn't a talker. Most women did the circuit of Mauri's crew and often went around for another shot.

Once a woman chose to ally herself with a specific syndicate, the others were suspicious of her. That left her stuck moving in the same social circle. If she was cast out, she was vengeful, dangerous, and often recruited by enemies for the secrets she held.

"Okay, you want roofies?" he asked, heading for the bedroom door.

"E, coke, whatever you get your hands on," Bruno said. "Let's get her high and see how she parties."

"Got it."

Once he was gone, Bruno would go back into that bathroom to torment their captive some more.

Experience excused a lot of sins. Being something of an old-timer, Bruno deserved respect. He'd done it all, including time in prison for the Starks and never once ratted out a fellow comrade.

Sometimes Bruno grated on him, sure, that didn't mean anything. Everyone grated on him. Dax could sit in the company of all kinds of people. Even if they were jerks, like Trystan, he'd just ignore them and interact as little as possible. Seething in silence was his art form… and the reason he pounded the shit out of the punching bag at least once a day.

He was no rookie. From a young age, he'd witnessed cruelty and depravity. Switching off, going through the motions, was a way of life. How he survived. Empathy was for the weak. Showing it would get you stabbed in the back. Mercy was a failing likely to get you killed.

Ignoring cries for compassion, he'd beaten up his share of lowlifes and learned to shut off emotion while he did it. It wasn't something he took pleasure in, and he didn't share Bruno's sadistic side. If the job needed to be done, he'd take care of it like any other responsibility. In contrast, Bruno relished the suffering.

Although Bruno claimed his role was that of mentor,

he'd guess that Maurice wanted confirmation his unofficially adopted son had the stomach to perform even the most depraved of duties.

Dax had never said no to Maurice Stark and never planned to. He owed the family a lot and wouldn't disappoint them. Definitely not for the sake of a gorgeous brunette with tapered Bambi eyes and full pouting lips he imagined whimpering for him. No, this was Trystan's girl. Trystan's. In order to prepare her for life with the youngest Stark, he'd have to go to the extreme.

DARKNESS SHROUDED THE BEACH house when he got back. He grabbed a bag out of the backseat and headed inside. Bruno was on the couch with a beer, watching sports on TV.

The girl was kneeling in front of Bruno. Plastic stripper heels joined her bikini, the spike of them jutted out underneath her neat little ass. Her hair was up in high bunches. Maybe clichés were clichés for a reason.

"Hey, get everything?" Bruno asked.

Dax came further into the room to see that the girl was giving Bruno a foot massage. "Yeah, I did," he said, tossing the bag to the floor. "I'll get the rest of the shit out the car in the morning."

"No need, our little slave here will do it for us," Bruno said. "It's the least she could do what with flaunting those boobs at us all the time. We never get a break."

Destroying a person involved certain behaviors, like contradicting them and constantly reminding them everything was their fault. It was how cult leaders recruited and got otherwise sane human beings to do their bidding. Guilt and shame were a brainwasher's best friend.

"Whatever," Dax said.

"You'll do that for us, won't you?" Bruno said to the girl.

"Yes. Should I do it now?"

"You're busy now," Bruno said, pushing his toes into one of her breasts, rubbing in circles.

The fondling went on and on. She said nothing, just continued with the task at hand as if the violation wasn't happening.

What would it be like to touch such luxury and have no reaction in his dick?

Bruno exhaled in bliss, his head sank against the back of the couch, and his eyes closed. She just kept massaging... as did Bruno. Maybe she was closer to... Her eyes came around to his. Determined. Aware. Completely detached from her actions. Her body did what Bruno wanted, but the blank resolve in those chocolate eyes didn't suggest defeat. No, it was survival. She was doing a job, what needed to be done. Who the hell was this woman before she met Trystan Stark?

Bruno's toes hooked the edge of her bikini top and peeled it back to expose one of her nipples, which he tried to pinch by curling his toes.

"Upstairs!"

Everyone in the room was startled by the bellowed command. Even him and the word had come out of his own damn mouth. The girl scrabbled to her feet and, walking on those heels at an impressive pace, she did exactly as he'd demanded. Why had he ordered her upstairs?

Bruno laughed. "No need for a party tonight, you gonna put her through her paces already?"

He and Bruno had agreed to take their time in breaking the woman. Full compliance had to be guaranteed. Knowing that had been their plan made his outburst even more mystifying, but he wasn't about to show his indecision.

"If it's gotta be done, might as well just do it."

"I've told her that her place is to kneel at your feet until you give her a command. If you're not here, I take your place, if you get me."

"Whatever," Dax said, wondering where Bruno came up with these rules.

"You're a lucky dog," Bruno said. "Not a tough job you've got, is it?"

"I'm still not convinced it will work. If this is the assignment, I'll do it. But keeping her out here and expecting her to—"

"Trust me," Bruno said. "All you've gotta do is keep it up for a month and a half. We do the job and get back to the city. Then we're off the hook."

"Yeah."

He and Bruno were off the hook as far as the girl was concerned, but her nightmare would be just beginning. She was going back to Trystan and was expected to dedicate herself to him… not that she knew that yet.

"Better get up there, you've got work to do."

"Goodnight," Dax said, not addressing the innuendo.

He had the amount of time it would take him to go upstairs to his bedroom to figure out what the hell he was going to do with this girl.

NINE

ON THE ASSUMPTION that *"upstairs"* meant the bedroom, Ivy had gone straight there. Getting away from Bruno the Letch was a reprieve. At least the worst thing she'd had to touch were his feet, anything more intimate would've made her puke. Literally.

Before closing the bedroom door, she'd overheard the men talking downstairs. A month and a half was what Bruno had said. Judging by his tone, Dax was no happier about being there than her. If he was somehow indebted or being coerced into this, he too was a prisoner, just in a different form. He wasn't being deliberately cruel through choice; it was a necessity.

When they stopped talking, she closed the door and hurried further into the room.

Less than a minute later, Dax stalked in and slammed the door. Why was he so tense?

"Take it off," he said. The order didn't immediately make sense. "The bikini, take it off now."

Any hope that sleep was the only thing on the agenda went out the window.

She stripped off. "What are you going to do?"

"We're going to pick up right where we left off," he

said, closing the space between them, fogging her hair with the heat of his moist breath. "You've been good today, haven't you? Following all the rules."

"Yes."

"And you're gonna keep doing that all night long, aren't you?"

"Yes."

"Take that ridiculous shit out of your hair," he sneered, but didn't give her an inch of room to pull the bunches out.

He stayed there, right on top of her, crowding into her personal space. The musky male scent of him permeated around her. When her hair was down, he grabbed the hair-ties and tossed them away.

"Lose the shoes too."

Slipping them off, she kicked them behind her. The knot in her abdomen tangled in a thicker web of adrenaline and hormones when she literally shrank down into his shadow.

"Get on the bed."

He didn't ask questions. With him, there was no choice, only commands. Non-compliance didn't occur to her, not that she planned to make the night easy for him.

"Lie right in the middle," he said when she crawled onto his mattress. "On your back and look at me."

Her heart had beat so fast that her skin throbbed. Her guts became so heavy that they seemed to sink down through the bed. Nausea became speckling anticipation that speared from her waist to her hips. So much going on. What to think? What to do? Go along with it? Play along. Anything to stay out of the basement.

He took off his shirt and her mind cleared. The evidence that this guy was capable was chiseled into his form. If he wanted to hurt her, to overpower her, it would take nothing, he wouldn't even break a sweat.

Shit, she was hot. Watching him strip everything but his jeans, her feminine reaction altered the flow of adrenaline from anger and fear to arousal and anticipation. Shit. Looking at him was a treat, not a punishment. What would come next?

Whatever it was, she had to think weak, meek, obedient. He wanted her to be intimidated, so she'd give it her best shot. Didn't take long to get there.

Intimidation slammed her when he dropped his jeans. The weight of his thick erection bobbed to aim straight at her. Could she accommodate that monster? Where was he planning to put it? If her throat—

"Open your legs," he muttered. She slid them apart. "More!" That insistence answered her question. "Get them nice and wide."

Her view was stolen when he lunged down on top of her. The heat of him, the proximity. Damn, this wasn't going to be easy. Bracing his forearms on either side of her head, he held himself above her so none of his skin met hers.

"You're a clever little minx, aren't you?" he said. The bubble of desire in his eyes was too knowing for her to be comfortable. "You've got Bruno fooled."

"I don't know what you—"

"Yeah, you do. You're not fooling me…"

His mouth opened over hers, but he didn't let them touch. Their breath merged in a sensual, invisible kiss that separated her lips further as though accommodating more of him. It was an illusion, an unrealized fantasy.

"I recognize that look in your eye," he breathed in a sneer. "You're down there playing 'yes sir, no sir.' But you know exactly what you're doing. What age were you when your mom kicked you out?"

"Why would—"

"Enough of the innocent princess act. What were you? Twelve? Thirteen?"

Okay, well fuck. Maybe it took one to know one. Fooling him apparently wasn't possible. Didn't matter how switched on he was, being made still pissed her off.

"Thirteen," she said, loosening out of the scared, tense virgin pose. Their naked forms warmed each other. "My mom didn't kick me out, my stepdad got too close, I left."

"Group home?"

"A few."

"Hooker?"

"No, never," she said, feeling claustrophobic in the enclosed space. "Fuck me or move."

"Which would you prefer?" he asked.

"You could go and fuck yourself."

"I'll let you play your game for a while, it's interesting to watch, hot even, but don't think about yanking my chain. Bruno and I have a job to do, and we will get it done, no matter how hard you fight. No matter how smart you think you are, you're not fooling me. I am smarter and I am stronger. You belong to me and pretty soon you're gonna love it."

"What job is it that you're doing? Is this just about me?"

"You don't ask questions; you do what you're told."

"Which I'm guessing is gonna include me doing you and your buddy at some point," she said somewhat grateful of the opportunity to display her disgust.

His face came even closer, blocking everything else out. "I will never touch you sexually on the same day another man has," he said.

The snarl in his voice betrayed the statement was one of propriety not common decency.

"Lucky me."

"You might think you're a tough chick, Minx, but you haven't met a man like me. I guarantee it. By the time I'm done with you, I will own every inch of you. You'll beg to surrender that fuckable body to me, to do whatever I want with it. But I'm gonna get bored of you and when I do, I won't look at you twice again. To me you're disposable, but I'm gonna be your whole goddamn world."

"Keep dreaming, Master," she said, spitting out the moniker like it amused her.

"I guarantee it, Minx. I guarantee it." He vaulted off her to one side of the bed. "Get on your own half and stay there."

The defined muscles of his back might be alluring but she had no intention of, or interest in, touching him. Dax had seen through the façade she used to regain the strength needed for escape. She should be annoyed or disappointed;

instead, she was intrigued. How had he known she was playing them? To improve her technique of disguise she'd have to find out how he'd figured it out. It was more than a guess. Something in him recognized something in her and when it did, she saw it look right back.

TEN

MUCH LATER, the steady sound of Dax's rhythmic snore revealed he was sound asleep. Bruno had made a lot of noise going to bed more than an hour ago. In the house of unconscious jailors came an opportunity for escape. Maybe not the safest opportunity, but an opportunity nonetheless.

Naked, clothes were the first concern. The bikini wasn't a smart choice in the middle of the night, so whatever she could lay her hands on…

Rolling off the bed, she crawled around to snag Dax's tee-shirt and boxers from the floor. Still in a crouch, she crossed to the door and opened it with deft, quiet fingers to slink out.

Keeping moving was key, relief could come later. While descending the stairs, she put on the clothes and got as far as the front door. Locked. The damn thing was locked.

Spinning around with the intention of seeking out the key, she gasped and staggered back against the door when Dax's looming form materialized from the surrounding gloom. He kept on coming, without a word, until she was pinned between his body and the door, unable to move.

For half a minute, he said nothing. Just stood there glaring into her.

Nothing. Waiting. His breath and hers. Into the night and out. In. Out.

Moving fast, he grabbed her neck to yank her from the door and jerk her along. He didn't speak and she stayed quiet, fearful of waking Bruno. He took her upstairs. Oh, thank God! Not the basement. She couldn't have handled that again… and it wouldn't be so easy to persuade him of her compliance if she found herself in that predicament.

Dax threw her against the bedroom door then turned the handle to thrust her forward onto the floor. Slamming the door, he came to her before she could stand and hoisted her up to catapult her over the bed's footboard. She bounced on the mattress and tried to stabilize herself to get up, except there was no time.

Dax was on top of her. "Think you could sneak away?" he growled.

She tried to kick, but his pelvis locked down on hers. "Get off me" she said, punching out, failing to make substantial contact. Dax got hold of her flailing wrists and trapped them on the bed, locking her bent elbows against her ribcage. "Get off!"

"Oh, you don't want me to yell, Minx. You wake Bruno and you're going back to the pit."

"Let go," she snarled through gritted teeth.

The glow in his eyes was so intense, it illuminated the humid space between them. "You don't want me to let go."

"I want you off me. Get off!"

"I give out the orders, did you forget?"

"I'll never give in," she panted. "I'll never stop fighting."

"You want to die? You'll fight your way into a coffin." She kept trying to wriggle and struggle, never willing to surrender. He pulled her arms up and slammed them down again, demanding her submission. "Listen!" Huffing out, she kept on panting but loosened. "Be smart. You want to survive. You have to survive, nothing else matters."

"I don't know your story, street rat, but it's not the same as mine," she spat. "I don't want to just survive. I want more than that."

"More?" Anger spilled out and with his iron grip, he slammed her wrists on the bed again. "There is no more. You breathe in, you breathe out, that's it."

"You don't fight hard enough," she said. "You're a hypocrite. You tell me to fight, but you're the one who's given up. Why are you here, Dax? Why are you doing this to me?"

His response wasn't immediate. The lowering of his brows dimmed his glittering eyes. "Why?"

"Yes, why are you doing this to me? You, why are you here? Not them, not why they're doing this. You. Why are you doing this?"

"Because I was told to."

As she absorbed that ridiculous answer, he did too. His grip relaxed and she gave up her resistance. They lay there, still, panting through the revelation.

Now upstairs, she didn't want to go back down. An ally above ground could help her escape. Dax had proven he could bend the rules by not immediately revealing her deception to Bruno.

Gaining Dax's favor could lead to her convincing him to let her go sooner than the deadline. The sooner she could get out the better. Maybe manipulating Dax into caring for her was a way to make that happen. Sex might not have been his ultimate goal, but he was attracted to her. Using her body to create a connection between them might save her life.

"You're a lapdog. I thought you were a big shot," she said. "I'm supposed to fear you, Master? I don't think so."

Her attempt to shove him off failed. His fingers constricted, crushing her bones.

Struggling again, she wanted to be free of the pain. "Get off me," she cried, her own anger branded itself into her diaphragm.

This guy was a grunt. The cool, intimidating exterior was bullshit. Maybe she could use that to her advantage.

"You're here to learn your place," he said, "to learn respect. You're gonna do what I tell you because I'm in control."

Her laugh was ironic, belittling him was a bonus to making her point. "You're not in control of anything."

To prove it, she lifted her head and grabbed his mouth with hers. The thrum in her pussy built until the spear of delight in her gut made it impossible to ignore the fury of their attraction.

If they were going to get physical, it would start on her terms, not his. Their power play wouldn't end with their kiss; the snarling war of their tongues proved that. Her writhing for physical control provoked him to exert his superior strength.

Grumbling her frustration into his mouth, he snatched his away in a mocking laugh. "Horny, Minx," he said, forcing his already probing erection down on her pubis. "What's your game?"

"This is what you want, Master," she said, returning his gesture by grinding herself up, matching his stimulation.

"You take my direction, Minx. You will learn your place."

"Oh yeah, which is where?"

The beat of his unyielding chest made her breasts grow, the compressed weight of them fueled the spill of hormones sensitizing her core. Her arousal had begun in the Vegas suite when the laser precision of his vision met hers. It was in one of those seconds that awareness between them hooked into their uncontrollable attraction.

"Right where you are," he growled, "under me."

Their next kiss was so consuming she struggled to breathe. But she didn't care. The pressure of his mouth pushed her head deep into the mattress. He slid her captive wrists upward until they were far above them, their bodies flush. The weight of him crushed her but she met the full force of the ferocious kiss.

The inferno numbed every part of her that wasn't connected to him. Her world became her wrists, her chest, those broad concrete thighs fixing her in place as he rubbed his naked dick into the damp cotton between them.

His grip faded, giving her hands freedom to explore. Instead of pounding his shoulders, she stroked them. Investigating the width and definition of his tattooed arms, she maintained the momentum of their starving mouths.

When his head went this way, hers went that. She countered each of his confident maneuvers with her own.

His actions suggested he wanted her out of his clothes, but that would mean depriving her fingers of their prize, her touch from its expedition over his incredible body. Though resistance came first, he didn't tolerate the defiance, and forced the tee-shirt up, taking her objecting arms with it. Getting it to her wrists, he twined it around, locking her limbs out of his way. Ignoring her objections, he descended to her exposed breasts, tasting and fondling them with blatant entitlement.

"I thought you wouldn't touch me on the same day another guy had," she seethed.

"It's after midnight," he said, continuing his molestation. "I can claim you today."

"No. Get off me."

She argued, because it fit the role, but his deep, exhaling kisses penetrated the mounds of perceptive flesh, and her body rebelled, rising to relish the indulgence.

Quiet, indecipherable words spilled from him, the motion of those lips tantalizing her nipple. He swirled and sucked on her, savoring the receptive peak until it seared with the over-attention. But the pain became pleasure in the ecstasy he delivered.

He bit into her so hard a yelp of agony escaped, but he didn't react to it. He kissed down the center of her abdomen, sealed his mouth around her belly button and sucked. Dipping his tongue into the groove, he tantalized her with ideas of how his mouth would feel if he practiced the same act further south.

Except she didn't get that pleasure, he flipped onto his back and took himself in hand.

"Get on," he murmured before she had time to wonder what was going on.

"What?"

"You're gonna ride yourself dry tonight."

"I don't think so," she spat, turning her face away from the sight of him stroking himself.

"I know what you want," he said. She didn't

appreciate his wry amusement. "I know what you want, and I've got it right here."

"You're kidding yourself."

In truth, her whole body was alive with the fantasy of doing exactly what he asked.

Although she didn't look, she felt the bed move. The head of his erection poked her outer thigh before he hooked an arm under her leg to part it from the other, locking it between his.

"You've soaked right through your underwear, Minx. That doesn't lie."

The underwear was his, but that didn't change his point. Her arousal was in overdrive, there was an obvious damp stain at her core.

Still, her defiant eyes remained on his mocking ones. "I can keep control of myself."

He kept one of her thighs trapped between his and shoved the other away to widen the distance between her legs.

"Why don't you let me control you, Minx," he said, his hand pushing under the waistband of her shorts. "You'll be happier when you realize I'm all you'll ever need."

His fingers slid down through her juices. Trapping her clit between his knuckles, he carried on down to massage it with the ball of his hand. With the increase of her heart rate, her chest rose and fell faster until her panting razed the air.

By the time he descended to kiss her, his amusement was gone. "That a girl," he breathed, rubbing harder, faster. "I'm gonna give you everything you need."

"No," she said, trying to hold onto her fading defiance.

"Think about it," he said and speared her with his finger.

Unexpected orgasm slammed into her. The force of it stalled her breathing, her sense, her world. He gave no reprieve and kept working his finger in her.

"Dax," she whimpered, hating the weakness that trailed her voice.

"You want it to be my cock in you. I know it. I see it in you. You're thinking about how I'd feel right here." Pushing his finger deep, he wiggled it, stimulating her in ten places at once, stealing air from her again. "It's okay, all you have to do is say it. You want my cock inside you. You want me to fuck you. Nothing else in the world matters to you right now except my cock."

"You've got some ego."

Undeterred, he nuzzled his mouth nearer to her ear, and joined his first finger with a second. "I know it will feel good in here," he said, parting his fingers to expand her. "My cock will slide in real slow, you're gonna squeeze me tight, Minx. You're gonna work hard to please me, you think about how good it will feel to have my spunk fire up, deep inside you. Medicine to soothe that ache, Minx. You're gonna get addicted, one taste and your pussy will start to crave it. She'll want a new hit every day and then once won't be enough. Think about it."

She would never admit how the fantasy worked for her. Oh, fuck, it worked too well. The undulation of his fingers was countered by the instinctual move of her hips and the pressure of climax built again. The apex was just out of reach when his fingers withdrew, and he closed her legs to take off the shorts.

Tossing them aside, he lowered to kiss her clit, then lapped the length of her to collect her juices. He came up to kiss her, bestowing on her the taste of what he'd sampled.

"Don't deny your body what it wants. My angry little plaything has enough resentment in her already."

"I am not angry," she protested.

Having freed her arms from the shirt, she took her chance to shove him away. Instead of running for the door, her leg followed over him and she did what he'd asked… on her terms.

Positioning herself over him, she sank down onto the pleasure he promised. The ensuing sting threatened to make her immediately withdraw, but he took her hips, preventing her from rising. Did he mean to soothe and reassure? No, shit! He drove his hips up in one scathing action that could have ripped her in half, but her cry of pain made him snicker. Damn him.

"You're gonna get used to living most of your life exactly where you are. I'm making sure you never forget the minute your obsession with me started."

"Get over yourself," she said, trying to pry his hands away.

With the strength of his arms, he moved her up and down, using her body like his own private sex toy. "Mm, it is tight in here," he groaned, increasing his pace.

"Let me go!"

"You started this, we're gonna finish."

"Let me do it myself, would you?" she protested. "At least give me a chance to see if I can get you off."

The reasoning for her request hadn't formed in her head before she said it. As much as it startled her, it amused him.

"Go ahead, Minx," he said, letting her go. "Show me what you've got."

Without his guiding hands, she took a while to find her rhythm. Once she did, it was easy, soothing and stimulating. His member, there, impaled within her was familiar, yet she'd never experienced anything like it. Closing her eyes, she blocked out everything except their point of contact.

As he moved with her in opposition and unity, they sped the journey to orgasm. When he took her hips again, she didn't object. He gave her what she needed. Everything and more.

Yelling out her exhaustion, her body spasmed around his, but he didn't let her sag, he kept on driving up into her, using her body to wring out his own pleasure. A subdued growl came from him as a tortured huff, and he curled up clenching his abs. After three pants of climax, he wrenched her up off his body and tossed her onto her own side of the bed before collapsing back with a hand on each pec.

Yeah, she didn't need to be told he wasn't the type to cuddle. She needed time to come to terms with the truth of what they'd just done herself so was happy to say nothing at all.

Mismatched exhales became her focus. Her eyes

closed. Guilt wouldn't change what had happened. Sleep, she needed sleep. Maybe by tomorrow she'd have her sense back. Because seriously… what the hell?

Apparently, Dax wasn't of the same mind. His arm channeled between her back and the mattress to scoop her up over his lap, face down on the bed.

"Hey!"

When she tried to get up, Dax brought his leg around to pin it over the back of her thighs, holding her down. Before she could object anymore, he thwacked her ass with an open palm. The buzz of his spank stunned her still for a split second. The next smack goaded her into action. She tried to fight, but his arm came down on her spine to trap her tight and he spanked her again.

"What do you think you're doing?" she called.

"You were a naughty girl, Minx. You don't get away until I tell you."

He spanked her three more times. Though she yelped at each, and the pain of his force increased, the tingling continued to the still engorged center he'd just penetrated.

"Stop," she protested but arched her ass up a few inches.

His palm smoothed over the flesh he'd just bruised then he smacked it again. "You're a bad girl. When you break my rules, you need to be disciplined. My female does what I tell her to."

"I am not your female," she said. His next smack was enough to make her squawk. The insistent line of his erection prodded into her belly. "You're not gonna use that."

"I'll do anything I please with my female, and that's exactly what you are, Minx. I own you."

"You do not control me."

Her wriggling was useless, so she slackened, and he whacked her ass again before tossing her aside.

Clambering away, she shifted to sit for the split second it took to realize her stinging ass cheeks wouldn't allow that and settled for lying on her side. He pushed her onto her front and threw a leg over her, holding her down as he stroked her butt.

"You'll learn to be a good girl for me, Minx. That spirit of yours will belong to me, just like the rest of you. Now get some sleep, you've got more work to do. I'm not done with you yet."

He rolled over. Sleep time? No. A drawer rolled on its runners, and he turned back to sit up. Something plastic tightened on her ankle. She tried to see it, then he linked another one through it. The sound brought clarity. He'd used two zip ties to link her to a footpost.

Brushing her hair aside, he pressed a condescending kiss between her shoulder blades. "Close your eyes, Minx," he said, patting her butt.

"Keep your hands off me, jerk."

Rubbing his face in her hair, he whispered in her ear. "I will until that body of yours craves mine again. You want me and I'll do anything I want with you. You can't say no. You're too cock hungry. Go to sleep."

This time when he turned over, he remained in place with his back to her. Eventually, he started to snore. Lying on her chest wasn't a comfortable position. Her breasts were so squashed they ached, but with the tie around her ankle she couldn't get to her back.

Reaching for a pillow, she tried her best to get comfortable. For now, she was stuck and needed her rest. It had been a long time since she'd seen a bed. Despite despising herself for giving in to her overload of hormones in the presence of this asshole—this domineering, arrogant, hot as hell asshole who'd just been the best sexual experience of her life—she closed her eyes and relaxed into slumber.

ELEVEN

DURING THE NIGHT, Dax woke her three times to demand further satisfaction. Her stubborn nature obliged her to protest, but each time she'd given in. Each encounter was more intense than the last. Something in her seemed to tame something in the wildness of him; though he battled the instinct to be calmed by her.

Being that she was still recovering from her stretch of incarceration in the basement, where necessities like sustenance were rare, Ivy was tired and stiff that morning. Though the stiffness more likely came from Dax's demands that she do all the physical work in bed. She would be quite happy to stay there in their sullied sheets all day recovering from the past few weeks.

When she cracked open an eyelid and saw Bruno towering over her, she came awake quickly.

"Shower time," he said. "The men are getting hungry."

The last time Dax strapped her ankle to the footpost she'd been on her back. So at least she could sit up. Dax wasn't there, the bed was empty. The covers had been tossed aside, exposing her to the room. Either the draft, or the violation of Bruno's ogling, must have woken her.

On the tip of her tongue was a question. Where's Dax? She didn't voice it and kept her lips sealed. Bruno freed her ankle and escorted her to the shower where he once again watched her wash and directed her grooming. He didn't loiter over the process. When she was dry, he gave her another bikini, told her to don the stripper shoes and tie her hair up in the absurd bunches.

In the kitchen, she was expected to prepare breakfast, yet there was still no sign of Dax. A while later, as she fed Bruno his honey slathered toast, Dax came in and poured himself a coffee. Tracking his solid form with her eyes, she waited for acknowledgement.

Coffee in hand, he crossed to the kitchen table to sit opposite her and Bruno. He turned over the newspaper Bruno perused earlier and read the back page as though he was alone in the occupied room.

"Where should you be right now?" Bruno asked her.

Snapping herself out of her mental fume, her role was to capitulate not decapitate. If any other guy blanked her so blatantly…

Leaving her seat, she went to kneel on the floor at Dax's feet, as per Bruno's instructions. Having his leg so close was a temptation. Maybe if she sunk her teeth into his knee, she'd get a reaction then.

Obviously, Dax didn't get what she was doing. Rather than ask her for an explanation, he looked to Bruno.

"She's waiting for your instructions," Bruno said. "You have to tell her that it's okay to carry on with what she was doing. You're the owner, remember?"

"Right," Dax mumbled. "Carry on."

Climbing to her feet, she went back to sit beside Bruno wondering why Dax wasn't as adept with the enslaving thing.

"Want our little slave to cook you something?" Bruno asked, then opened his mouth toward her in expectation of another bite.

It was so demeaning. That was the point. To belittle her. But it took every ounce of her willpower not to shove the toasted lump down the letch's throat.

"No," Dax said, spreading open the newspaper.

"You made your mark on her last night," Bruno grinned, fondling her breasts while watching Dax read his paper.

Was he expecting a reaction? If he was, disappointment lay in his future.

Ivy wouldn't give Bruno the satisfaction of recoiling and didn't want to end up back in the basement. Undoing her progress would be foolish. What was Dax's reasoning? What made him tick? He had said he wouldn't touch her sexually on the same day as another man.

"They taste as good as they feel?" Bruno asked Dax, slipping his hand into her cleavage.

"Not really," Dax said.

The indifferent insult was preceded by him turning the page.

"That sweet ass is red raw," Bruno said.

"She deserved it," Dax muttered.

"No argument here. You know how to do your job."

Still, no reaction. What was this guy's deal? She'd never felt so invisible, his insulting indifference boiled her blood. She wanted to start launching condiments at him over the table, he wouldn't be able to ignore her then.

"Brad says he might need you next week," Bruno said, changing the subject.

"For what?" Dax asked, still reading his paper, completely uninterested.

"Didn't say, you know how these things can change last minute. Just thought I'd give you the heads up," Bruno said, taking another bite of toast from the piece she held. "I ordered a bunch of toys." Bruno squeezed her breast. Keeping the tension from her jaw was difficult. "I can keep taking care of business if you've gotta split."

"Cool," Dax said and closed the paper then left the table. "I'm going downstairs."

"No worries," Bruno said. "I'll take care of things up here."

Dax wasn't listening, he was already gone. Bruno was nonplussed and opened for her to guide another bite of his breakfast between his teeth. With a deep breath, she fought to maintain her restraint.

BRUNO'S IDEA of *"taking care of things"* meant giving her task after task to do while he supervised. If he thought expecting her to graft was a hardship, he clearly didn't know much about her background. Scrubbing the kitchen was nothing new. She'd done her share of waitressing in various restaurants, which meant being part of the monthly deep clean in the kitchen. No one had seen grease until they'd pulled out the in-built fryer at a fast-food joint.

Either he wasn't satisfied by her willingness to simply do as told or he really wanted this beach house to be spotless. Each duty built on the last. She skimmed the pool, then did the yard work as instructed before polishing the living room and doing laundry, stripping all the beds to really maximize the workload.

The day was almost over when he left her alone in Dax's bathroom. This bathroom and the basement were the only two places she had any peace. That didn't mean it would last.

Bruno told her not to leave and gave her another scrubbing brush to clean. As soon as he closed the door, she tossed the brush aside and kicked off the heels. Running the cold water, she rinsed her face and upper chest, closing her eyes against the cool relief offered by the refreshing water. Moments to herself were rare; she wouldn't pass up this fortuitous one.

The door opened, shattering her seclusion. When she opened her eyes to her reflection in the mirror, she saw Dax come into the room, shirtless and sweaty in a pair of workout shorts.

"Get out of here, I need a shower," he said, though he'd already closed the door.

"No," she said, turning on the faucet to wash her hands again. "I've been directed to stay in here."

"Fine, you can soap my back," he said.

The harsh, unexpected smack on her ass made her

grunt.

"Would you please stop spanking me," she said in no way concerned that he would demand she return to the basement for her insolence.

He kept on coming toward her until his body pressed hers into the vanity. Pulling the ties from her hair, he dropped them and shook his spread fingers through her locks to loosen them.

"That's what you get when you're a naughty girl," he said, tipping her head aside to kiss the side of her neck through her hair.

"I did nothing wrong," she said, watching his hands in the mirror as they tugged up her bikini and closed around her naked breasts.

"You said the word no to me," he whispered in her ear then kissed his way to her shoulder.

That she had to concede. "Who is Brad?" she asked, arching her back to squash her tingling ass against the throbbing bulge of his groin.

"None of your business," he said. "You do what you're told, don't ask questions."

"I wanted to ask Bruno where you were this morning. It's not nice for a girl to wake up with a different man than the one she went to bed with."

"You better get used to it. If Brad sends the boys up here, you'll have a lot of cocks to keep happy."

She didn't like the sound of that. "You're going to share me with your friends? I'm a free agent?"

Standing straight, he drew his hips away from her as though the mood had left him. "More like free for all."

Running her fingers through her hair, she arranged it to cover her breasts. "You didn't mind when Bruno had his hands all over me this morning. I shouldn't be surprised you'd be happy if others did it too."

"You thought because I fucked your cunt last night, I'd start giving a fuck about the rest of you?" He slid open the shower stall and turned on the harsh spray before closing it to trap the steam. "Sorry, Minx, I'm not wired that way."

"What way is that?" she asked his reflection. "Like a

decent human being?"

Lunging at her, he thrust her forward, bending her over the vanity, causing her hands to land on either side of the mirror. She wanted her reflection to burn her anger into him, but he was fixated on her butt. With two fingers he tugged her bikini briefs halfway down her thighs and parted her ass cheeks. With his erection in hand, he leaned closer, but she shot upright.

"I don't think so, big boy," she said.

Her attempt to push him away only gave him the opportunity to take her hand to his erection. Drawing his hips back and forth, he fucked her closed fist.

"You get wound tight when you're angry, Minx," he said, lowering his head to lick her earlobe.

"That gets you horny? When I'm angry?"

His hands took her breasts again. The way he massaged her with those large, rough digits made her groan.

"Suck me off," he murmured in her ear.

"No!" she exclaimed.

"You know you want to. You object on principle, but you know wrapping that smart mouth around my hard dick is exactly what you're thinking about right now."

"What I'm thinking about is cracking that hard skull of yours," she said and tried to butt him back out of the way, but she failed.

He took his erection from her and prodded it between her cheeks. "You get down there and suck my balls empty, or I fuck your tight virgin asshole raw. Your pick."

"And if I refuse, you're going to turn me over your knee again?"

"I'm probably gonna do that anyway."

"Empty balls it is then," she said with a false smile as though it had been her intention all along to comply.

He gave her enough space to turn and fall to her knees but didn't give her enough time to blink before he squeezed his dick through her lips, forcing the bulbous head to smack the back of her throat. She swallowed to relax her throat to prevent a gag reflex, but her actions made him groan.

Sighing, she pushed his hips back, pressuring him to

withdraw. "Don't get over excited, I've said I'll do it," she said, moistening her lips, lathering her saliva.

When she was ready, she took him in hand and set to work. Though his hand remained on her head throughout he wasn't too forceful. He let her vary the pace and use her own experience. She sucked, licked and fondled until the pulse in his shaft throbbed and he swore out loud.

Instead of shooting his load in her mouth, as she had expected him to, he came out of her mouth and showered her breasts with the milky liquid. The heat of it slithered down her body. He tucked himself back into his shorts while she hung there in mid-air still agape.

"What did you do that for," she asked when over the surprise. "I would have swallowed."

"Next time you will," he said. "Bruno wants you by the pool."

"And you didn't tell me that when you came in?"

"I wanted you first," he said, opening the shower door again and testing the temperature of the water with his hand. "I'm your owner. I make the rules about where you go and what you do. Getting your face fucked was more important than running his errands."

"I can't go down there looking like this," she said, getting to her feet. "He'll see that you're… all over me."

"That was the point."

"I need to shower."

When she tried to pass him to enter the cubicle, he grabbed her and pulled her back before she could step inside.

"No! You go down there, exactly like that!"

"But I—"

"He'll think twice about touching you now, won't he?"

Her indignation waned and for the first time when their eyes locked, neither gaze contained anger.

"You do what you need to do, to get the job done," she muttered.

"Yeah. Which includes letting any of the rest of them touch you in any way they want to."

"Even if you don't want them to," she said. "You're

numb. You just go through the motions, don't you? Do you feel anything? Do you even know what you want?"

Lifting her hand to reach for his jaw, he ducked away to avoid her caress. "What I want doesn't matter," he snapped.

"It does to me."

"Why?"

"Because we're both the same. Trapped," she said, easing her arm from his grip to take his hand. "Doing what we have to even though we don't want to."

"Don't start thinking that I care about you. I don't."

"God forbid you let yourself care about anything that they might take away."

"You don't know who they are. You do what you're told and let the men worry about the serious shit."

"Just like you do," she said. He had meant to insult her. What he didn't get was the same people trying to brainwash her, had already done the job on him. Bruno knew what he was doing because he'd obviously been party to this kind of manipulation before. Dax, on the other hand, did what he was told and failed to see he'd been manipulated into it. "They have your free will. Is that why you think you can take mine? I won't let you."

"I'll take whatever the fuck I want from you," he said.

Peering into him, she read his attempt at anger. The show was believable… sort of. The rage wasn't there. His fury didn't burn from his guts like hers did.

"You haven't forced me into anything. They have, but not you."

"You think I'm here to look out for you?"

"I don't think you even know how to look out for yourself, street rat."

"You don't have the first fucking clue about me," he said, but she wasn't insulted by his attempt to belittle her.

"How could I?" she asked. "You don't know anything about yourself either. You keep giving me advice like some subconscious part of you is trying to save me from what you failed to escape from."

"Your dad a shrink or something?"

"Ex-boyfriend," she said. "He did try to save me.

Turned out he was more screwed up than I was."

"Get around did you, Minx?"

"I don't consider my life in the past tense."

"Maybe you should," he said. "You can't fight fate, right?"

"You can't know its plan either. Maybe we're supposed to fight against being forced into something we don't want. Life doesn't always turn out the way we think it's supposed to."

"No, it doesn't," he said.

"If you don't want him to touch me, tell him."

Dax shook his head. "I can't save you. If it's your game to get in my head 'cause you think I'll get you out of here… you've got the wrong guy. You're too important to them."

"And what am I to you?" she asked. "Am I important to you?"

Snatching his hand away from hers, he backed off. "You're manipulating me. You think you can use sex to soften me up? That I'll believe you give a shit about me and fall for your wounded vulnerability thing? I'm not gonna set you free."

"I haven't asked you to set me free today, Dax, have I? All I want from you right now is one thing," she said, rising to her tiptoes.

Capturing his face in her hands, she joined their lips. Their conversation was abandoned to the oblivion of the hormones that drowned them. When Dax picked her up, she twined her legs around him as he carried her into the shower.

Maybe talk would give her a better handle on the man she shared her body with. Maybe. She wasn't so sure he was enlightened about his situation. Dax was a prisoner in his own life. How did he find himself there? Why was he okay with being their lackey when it was clear he was capable of so much more?

As he pressed her into the slippery tile next to the scalding shower spray and loosened the ties on her briefs, she vowed to find out why he was so detached from his own existence. She was a prisoner. Herself and her freedom were still her priorities. But if she had the ability to hold a mirror up to Dax before slipping out of his life, she would. Maybe they would both be able to free themselves.

TWELVE

AFTER SCREWING HER IN THE SHOWER, Dax told her to wash and go outside to Bruno. That was the last of Dax she saw that day. He was avoiding her and didn't even appear for dinner.

Spraying her with his seed was intended to show Bruno they'd been intimate. That was one visual a guy couldn't miss. Rather than some kind of primal marking, she guessed it was more about grossing the older man out. Bruno would think twice about touching her breasts if there was a chance another guy's spunk was all over them.

Unfortunately, the shower washed away the evidence, with it went her chance of reprieve.

Bruno didn't seem to notice or care that Dax wasn't around. Not while he had her to jeer and leer at. The sad truth was she was getting used to the middle-aged man's innuendo and advances. That didn't mean she liked them, not for one second. Bruno instructed her in every task then watched as she completed it, salivating and goading her every minute.

The fondling was lessening. Maybe because she didn't give him the reaction he wanted, or because the novelty had worn off. His biggest thrill was exercising authority in other ways, demeaning her with words and actions. Such as spilling food on the floor and demanding that she clean it up after driving it into the tile with his Croc covered feet.

Her *"owner"* appeared when it was dark outside and told her to go to bed. He proceeded to sit with Bruno and drink beer into the night instead of joining her. Anyone who chose TV and beer over sex like he had, couldn't deny avoidance was their motive.

Whatever. The reprieve gave her a chance to rest. Massaging Bruno's feet was giving her blisters. Just when she started to think maybe they were building trust Dax appeared for just long enough to zip tie her to the bed while grumbling something about not being bothered with her anymore.

When he eventually joined her in bed, he went to sleep without gratification.

The next day, when she woke up, Dax was gone from the bed. Trusty old Bruno was there with a long list of tasks. That day played out much as the previous one.

The sun was high in the sky, the blazing heat made her sweat, so when Bruno drifted off to sleep in his lounge chair by the pool, she went back into the house. With a quick check around, she found no sign of a key for the front door, or one for the drawer of knives.

That moment could be her only chance to escape. Her strength wasn't back full force, but could she ignore the opportunity? Upstairs, all the doors were locked except Dax's bedroom. His room held no tools for escape; even the walk-in closet was locked. One of the men had to be carrying the key on them or they were hidden somewhere.

Getting out of the house was sort of important. She needed to get out and into the car in the driveway... keys would be needed for that too. Without transport, her captors would catch up to her quickly. In her time undressing Dax and tidying up, she had never seen keys. Finding out where they were kept became her next goal. For that, she'd have to get closer to the man who shared her bed.

Finding Dax was a piece of cake, he was where he always was: downstairs. Going back into that basement voluntarily turned her stomach, she bolstered her gumption and headed for the door. Winning Dax's sympathy or assistance would be impossible if she let him maintain distance. Stepping into his world, into his personal space, would take him out of his comfort zone.

Showing him she was human, and in need of a connection, there was a chance he'd care enough to set her free or help her escape. It didn't take a rocket scientist to figure out that Bruno wouldn't ever consider doing that for her.

Descending into the basement, she could hear the thump of fists hitting leather and the occasional masculine sniff or breath. When she went lower, she paused at the vision he made. Wearing nothing but black shorts and black straps on his hands, Dax threw one punch and then another, staying loose, keeping his hands near his face and his elbows in close to his body. The sheen of sweat across his back and arms reminded her of their shower. Of the texture of his skin under her fingertips when water cascaded over both of their naked bodies.

His fist flew out to hit the black punching bag at the head of the basement gym. He slid back in an expert maneuver and threw another two punches, one with each hand in quick succession. The rough callouses and intersecting scars on his knuckles and hands made sense now. She'd noticed them in bed, but hadn't asked about them, now she didn't need to.

He must have sensed her because he paused and straightened up. Tensing to turn, he glared over his shoulder at her figure on the darkened stairway. Still, the blue of those eyes shot agony at her. Such a pure color wasn't meant to be so impersonal, yet in him it was. Like icebergs on the sea, powerful and formidable, but also lonely, isolated. Out on the ocean without a connection or a place to call home.

Drifting out on the open water epitomized Dax. Her own life had been much the same way, out there and alone. Was she as hard as him? If she wasn't, what had he been through to disconnect him from humanity?

"Where's Bruno?"

"Sleeping," she replied, continuing down the stairs toward him.

He unwound the hand straps from his hands. "And

you're still here?"

"I couldn't get out. The door is locked."

"No one ever taught you how to pick a lock?"

She shook her head. "But I'm ready for a lesson if you want to give me one."

"I don't have the patience to be a teacher," he said, tossing the straps to the bench beside him, stretching out his fingers as he did.

"Did you used to be a boxer?" she asked, taking one of his hands.

Holding it open, she massaged his knuckles.

"Boxing is too disciplined," he mumbled, watching her fingers work on his. "My sport is less regimented."

"What is your sport?"

"I'm an underground fighter," he said, fascinated, or perhaps perplexed, by what she was doing.

"Like in basements and cellars?" she teased.

"Like on the underground circuit," he said, withdrawing his hand. "Since I was eight. I don't need to be pampered."

"Maybe I want to pamper," she said, taking his other hand to give it equal treatment. "How does it work? Underground fighting?"

"Two guys in the ring and no weapons," he said.

"There's a ring?"

"Sometimes," he said on a semi shrug. "Depends on the venue. Some places treat it as a business, sometimes it's a barn with a wooden fence, or just a line drawn in the sand."

"Fitting," she said. "What are the rules?"

"I told you. Two guys, no weapons, and you don't hit a guy when he's down."

"That's it?" Her massaging stalled. "Anything goes?"

He nodded. "Anything at all."

"So they could gouge out your eyes or bite off an ear or something?"

Leaving her side, he retrieved his hand wraps to tuck them into the back of his shorts. "If they ever got close enough to do that then yeah," he said, flashing a flippant, yet smug, smile.

"Since you were eight, huh?" she asked.

"Yep."

Crossing to the punching bag, she smoothed her hands over the leather. "Is this how you stay so calm?" she asked. "You express your emotions to the punching bag?"

When he didn't respond, she twisted around to rest on the bag, pushing her shoulders back to slide her hands onto its sides as her arms curled against it.

"I guess," he said, and took one step toward her.

"Is that why my anger turns you on? Because you don't know how to be open like that, to experience that kind of emotion?"

"I know anger," he said, coming closer still. "I know hurt and isolation. I know revenge and retribution." He came so close that his body made contact with hers. "I know fear and misery. I know respect and I know loyalty."

"What about compassion?"

He shook his head. "Weakness."

"And forgiveness? Do you know that?" He shook his head, taking the ties from her hair, tugging on her locks, sending a hiss through her teeth. "Do you know leniency or pity?"

"No. But I know shame and rage."

"What about love? Do you know that?"

"Never heard of it," he said, taking a fistful of hair to yank her head back and plant his mouth on hers.

The squeal of her refusal was lost in the grip of her hands on his neck. If this bag had been able to support them, she'd have leaped into his arms right there. As it was, her fingertips skimmed down the bulge of his shoulders to his elbows. When she tried to urge him away, he took her waist and lifted her off the floor, holding her body to his.

"Dax," she whispered. His mouth trailed to her neck. The press of his lips to the artery pulsing beneath them made her weak legs wobble. For stability, she locked her ankles at the small of his back. "I came down here to talk."

"Talk isn't what I need from you."

The word "*need*" sent a sluice of ice through her torso. Just a slip of the tongue? In the second he said it, she wanted him to mean it. That scared her. No man had ever needed her, and she'd never needed them. Her role in seducing Dax was meant to be manipulation, to make friends, to make him want her freedom. Bringing need into the equation was a totally different thing.

In a show of strength, he locked one arm around her waist, holding her up so his other was free to loosen her bikini. "Get my cock out my shorts," he said.

"I am not a part of your work out, stranger."

"You are today, or I'm a part of yours."

Seating himself on the inclined weight bench, he leaned back and nodded downwards. "If you make me do it, you'll get a spanking when we're through. I've got weapons down here."

Coiling her arms around his neck, she pulled herself close enough to press her face to his. "I thought weapons were against the rules."

"You wouldn't stand a chance in the ring with me, Minx."

"Throw in some jello, take away the clothes and the audience… I think I might be able to pin you down."

His smile creased his cheeks. The reverberation of his laugh was alarming in its novelty, it was the first time she'd heard it.

"You've got me pinned now."

That wasn't really true, his arms were still around her waist. Although she was on top, he was definitely in control. Her parted thighs gave her premium position to undulate against the thick organ protruding from his shorts.

"You didn't fuck me last night."

"I'm not gonna fuck you now," he said. "You're gonna do it all by yourself."

"How do you manage to stay in control even when you're underneath me?"

"You want to please me, don't you?"

And she nodded, realizing that his pleasure was important. Seeing how she could control and influence this monolith of a man made her feel powerful in a circumstance where she was otherwise powerless. God, she got a kick out of that.

"I do, Dax… Master."

"I hate that word," he admitted, much to her surprise.

Honesty was a turn on. Who knew?

"Okay. What would you rather I called you?" she asked, spreading her hands on his bare chest, moving her hips against him. "Chief? Major? Guru?"

"Stranger will do just fine." Taking a breast in hand, he squeezed then tensed his arm to arch her back giving him leave to suck her nipple into his mouth. "They do taste good, damn good."

That was something close to an apology for what he'd said in front of Bruno. At least, that was how she chose to take it. Every day more of her jailors' dynamic was revealed; every day it perplexed her more. In front of Bruno, Dax acted like she was nothing. He tried to maintain that indifference when they were alone.

Yet, he was far more honest than she'd have believed possible and thought nothing of revealing the truth in these rare moments of intimacy. Had he ever lied to her? Would she be able to tell? When they were alone, he battled to maintain his disinterest but often failed. Sex made him honest, and he seemed to demand that same honesty in return.

Maybe he only wanted to have sex with her if he could be himself while he did it. Could be he only wanted to have sex with the true her. He didn't want her scared and pitiful, he wanted her fire, the truth of her personality in his bed. Outside the bedroom, and in company, he didn't care who she was, but he didn't play games in bed, not of the emotional sort. Maybe he was supposed to, and he just sucked at the game, or maybe lulling her into his confidence was a game in itself.

She could only judge the situation on what she witnessed; Dax didn't get off on demeaning her like Bruno did. In fact, Dax seemed happier to leave the room when Bruno was exerting control over her. As long as Bruno did his work in a place where Dax didn't have to see it, he could ignore it.

Whatever Bruno's game, Dax felt the need to play

along with it when they were all together. He never corrected or questioned the older man. However, when Bruno wasn't around Dax let the shield fall. It could mean he cared, or it could just mean he didn't care about Bruno when Bruno wasn't around.

Except one thing kept nipping on the periphery of her mind, she was keeping a secret for Dax. He let her question and talk to him as an equal in private. If she did that with Bruno, he'd send her to the basement.

By not revealing Dax's indifference to Bruno's rules, she was keeping his secret. She played along with the rules in front of Bruno and Dax didn't get her into trouble for what she said to him, so he was keeping her secret too. In each other, they already had an ally.

"If I call you stranger it's like we're not connected," she said, reluctantly stealing her breast away from his kiss. "It's like we're still in that alley."

Kissing his way to her throat, he completed the triangle by tracking his mouth to her other breast. "I wanted to fuck you then," he said.

His arm shifted to whip the lower half of her suit away. Casting it aside, he ran a finger between the cheeks of her ass.

"You said that you didn't."

"I lied," he admitted. So, question answered, he hadn't always been honest with her. "Your body is hot. You've got those fuck me eyes, like the only way a guy will ever get your respect is to fill that smart mouth with cock every time you step out of line."

"I'm entitled to my opinions, why should I shy from voicing them?" she whispered, aroused by the idea that he'd even considered earning her respect.

The speed of her heart quickened her breath. Her lungs weren't taking in enough air and there was only one remedy.

"You should know your place," he muttered.

"Beneath you."

"That's right."

Her fingers found their way into his shorts to coil

around his solid cock. Sighing out her bliss wrought a reaction. The heat of her breath; that's what it was. Opening his mouth on her, his teeth dug into her bosom until she squeaked.

"Sex is all you ever want from me," she said. Squeezing his member in her clenched hand, she removed it from his shorts and elevated her hips to prod his dribbling head onto her clit. Undulating, she merged their juices, stimulating herself with him. Her wetness lapped and licked the bulb eager to conquer her. "Is Bruno your boss?"

"We work for the same man," he said, licking her breast and rolling the peak between his warm fingers.

The bench was narrow. Her feet were hooked up behind her over his thighs. The position gave interesting leverage, but the chance of cramp was high.

"I need..." she inhaled, not sure how to make the best of the position.

"What?" he asked, stroking up to her shoulders and down her spine with the very tips of his fingers, making her quiver. "What does my babygirl need?"

The pet name turned her to liquid. Relaxing her torso to drape herself against him, her breasts squashed on his damp chest as he swept her hair out of the way to suck and nibble on her ear and neck. Words were gone from her brain. All she could do was take hold of his wrists and guide his hands down to her ass, giving him some of her weight.

"Like that?" he grumbled. She nodded, nuzzling his throat. Pushing her weight to her shins, she rose and lined him up. When she released the tension in her legs, she sank down onto him. "Oh yeah, like that."

Moving up and down, her pace didn't languish, she didn't want to take her time. He'd ignited something that got her so wet their bodies wouldn't rest or relax until they got completion with each other.

"You feel amazing inside me," she breathed into his mouth on another kiss. "Dax, this, your dick..."

"Yeah?" he asked, gripping her ass, using his own strength to raise her body faster until it became a fight.

He pulled up and she pushed down at the same time his body fought to remain in her.

"I've never…"

Maybe it was the position, her legs were stretched so far apart that her thighs burned. She was entirely at his mercy; his body was the only thing supporting her on the narrow bench.

"Say it," he demanded.

"Don't ever take it away from me," she screamed out at the first ember of orgasm.

His roar wasn't one of climax, but his arms clamped around her. She yelped when he stood up and slammed her down on the bench to pump into her with such fierce single-mindedness she couldn't see man, only animal.

"Look at me!"

Grabbing a handful of her hair, he wrenched her head around to marry their eyes. Like a missile aimed for her weakest spot, the cool iceberg in his gaze was aflame with determined possession.

Shrieking out his name, she didn't care about volume or Bruno. Dax couldn't either because at the same time she arched up, her body locked in spasm around his. The boom of his orgasm shook through her. They growled together, their eyes matched in epiphany.

One huff followed another. They stayed right there, him above her, inside her, staring down into her eyes.

"Shit," he whispered.

His mouth came to hers in a slow, punishing kiss that pinned her skull, allowing him to pour the truth into her. He did care. Her admission amid their passion that she wanted this, wanted him, was enough for him to release that truth to himself.

Jerking his mouth away, he dismounted the bench and pulled his shorts back up. "No more bikinis," he said, picking up his hand wraps from the floor to begin wrapping his hands again.

"Okay," she said, retrieving her bikini from the floor because it was all she had to wear right then.

"I can't stop him touching you. If I tried it would… raise too many questions."

"What kind of questions?"

He paused to show her anger; that emotion she definitely recognized. "You don't understand what's going on and how we all fit into the bigger picture."

She tied her bikini back on. "What is the bigger picture?"

"I can't tell you that," he said. "It's not my decision when you're told your purpose. You don't belong to me."

Finishing the knot behind her neck, she crossed to him, resting her hands on his hips. "I... I think I want to."

"That's what they want," he said, his timbre low and quiet. "They want you to think that."

"What do you want me to think? You don't want to own me?"

Grinding his teeth, emotions washed over his face. "I want you to go upstairs, get showered and changed, then get back to work."

"That's it?" she asked. "You tell me not to wear bikinis anymore, that I don't belong to you, then you just dismiss me?"

"Yeah," he said. "That's it. Get to it, or you'll get more than a spanking."

Lowering her chin, she slid her arms around him. "Now I'm curious."

"This time not from me," he said, unlocking her arms from around him. "If Bruno catches you not where he left you, you'll be going back in there."

His eyes moved behind her and she turned to see the door to the cage room. "You'd let him put me back in there?"

"Yeah, I would," he said, without hesitating. "Though I'm not sure I'd be able to leave you alone at night."

The idea of being back in that hovel was nauseating. Knowing that Dax might come down because he was compelled beyond logic or reason to join her, was enlivening.

"I'll do what you say."

"I know that you will," he said. "You were told that's the only thing you have to do, what you're told."

"I'm not doing it because it's Bruno's rule. I'm doing it because..." Time for a leap of faith. "Because I want you to trust me. I'll have your back, Dax, if anything goes down. I'll be on your side."

"Talking like that could get you hurt," he said with a frown. "You worry about yourself, Minx. Nobody else."

"Are you doing the same thing?"

Leaving him to consider that, she headed for the stairs. Pushing for an answer could lead him to say something neither of them wanted to hear. If he admitted caring for her, he would be in trouble. But if he denied it, he'd be lying.

Keeping up appearances for Bruno was important to show Dax he could trust her. When they were alone, however, she'd keep pushing his buttons. Why? Was she manipulating him to ensure her safety and escape or were her buttons on show as well? Protecting her heart from the street fighter with the sinister eyes and the rock-hard body was paramount. Messy feelings would make her weak and that wouldn't help either of them.

THIRTEEN

A FEW NIGHTS LATER, lying in their bed in the dark, she decided to push for more. He had connected her ankle to the bedpost, as he always did, while he went into the bathroom. A burst of light signaled his return. The light went off, the door closed, and then the bed moved.

In the darkness, there was no way for him to know she was still awake. Snatching her hand, he hauled her body to his as he turned onto his side, coiling her arm over his waist to flatten her hand on his torso.

"Why do you let me do it?" she whispered against the smooth skin at her lips.

"Do what?" he grumbled.

Dax enjoyed his sleep and when he decided it was time to rest, he didn't like delays.

"You let me be me here, in this room, when we're alone. Why don't you tell Bruno I'm playing him?"

"You're not," he said. "He wants you to do what you're told, and you do. You let him do whatever he wants with you."

"You think if I keep taking his orders, it will eventually become automatic?"

"What do you want from me, Minx?" he asked. "Do

you want me to beat you and lock you up?"

"No."

"Bruno is here to teach you to take orders and I'm here to fuck you into line."

For the most part, she was compliant in his bed. So, he was right, in a way, he did his job just by sharing a bed with her. That didn't explain why he let her sass him in a way Bruno would never tolerate.

"Do you have family?"

"No blood," he said.

"I haven't seen my mother in years," she said. "My sister stays with my aunt, least she did the last I heard—"

"I don't need your life story, just access to your pussy."

"What about your parents?" she asked, bending her elbow to curl a hand under her pillow, the other was still confined in his.

On nights like this, after she was tied to the footpost, they often slept further down the bed, but her face was still buried in his back.

"Never knew my mom, dad started me fighting at eight to make us some money. He sold me to the circuit when I was about ten. I ran away a few times, got picked up by the cops a few times, then I met Mauri."

"That's so sad," she said, kissing his spine.

"No sadder than your step-dad molesting you."

"He didn't actually... you know... he just tried it one too many times. I knew I could only fight him off for so long. My mother didn't give a damn and so I left. I stayed with my aunt sometimes, then she moved to Florida and—"

"Minx," he mumbled. "I don't care. Unless your mouth is filled with cock, it should stay shut."

She wasn't deterred, she was getting through. As much as he didn't want her to believe it, he liked her. She'd noticed how he tensed when Bruno touched her. Dax's touch had changed too. Not all the time, most of the time he still treated her like a piece of meat. But sometimes, he'd brush a lock of hair from her face, or slip his fingertips down her spine. Something different passed between them in those moments. Something that was never said.

"Sex is better when you know who you're doing it with," she said.

"Not in my experience. Now shut up or I'll gag you too."

That wasn't completely beyond him. Sleeping with her leg connected to the bed was difficult enough. Another tether may be more than she could handle.

FOURTEEN

FOR THE NEXT MONTH, things continued in the same way. Bruno ordered her around all day, she cooked and cleaned and did everything as told. At night, and in daylight when his libido itched, she became Dax's.

During the day, Dax came and went. She'd heard talk of Brad and Mauri, and murmurs of some other names. One name she never heard was Trystan, the man responsible for her current predicament.

That morning, Bruno had come into their bedroom early to speak to Dax. Once the older guy was gone, she'd tried to ask what was going on. Instead of answering her, he goaded her into fucking him. Morning sex was unusual, as was the nap that followed.

He still tagged her ankle to the bedpost, but their spoon arrangement, with her behind him, was their normal sleep position these days. He'd hold her arm around his waist and over his abs, shielding her, providing a barrier to separate her from the rest of the world. Maybe it was just his way of ensuring she stayed put, she preferred her thinking.

The words he used when addressing her were no less harsh. In front of Bruno, he spent most of his time ignoring her. Yet, when alone, there was a subtle shift. Her contempt raised its head, and he, of course, belittled and objectified her, but that glimmer of respect they'd garnered for each other hung on, only revealing itself in private.

Unsure if he was sleeping or not, she rubbed her lips on his back. Sealing them in a puckered O, she traced a vertical line of kisses on his shoulder blade. She was about to move onto the V of her name, when he spoke.

"I've got plans, Minx," he grumbled. "You're not getting any more of me now."

Sex hadn't been on her mind—though it was because it always seemed to be around him—but the kisses weren't a prelude to it.

"Do you miss the east coast?" she asked him, now aware he'd done his growing up in New York.

"Nope," he said, releasing her hand to stretch out his muscles.

She stayed against him just to experience the tactile motion. "You never ask about me."

He nudged her onto her back and rolled off the bed. "Why would I?"

"We've been having sex for a while, Dax. A month. You're not curious about the woman in your bed every night?"

"What is there to know?" he asked, going into the bathroom to turn on the shower, then returning to the bedroom. "You grew up somewhere, had parents, maybe siblings. I don't give a fuck."

She sat up and wrapped herself in the sheet that had been kicked to the end of the bed. "I was born in Chicago. We only lived there for a few years, and then we kicked around Ohio where my grandfather lived. That's where my mom met Ted, in Cleveland. He took us to Detroit; we lived in a shitty trailer park—"

"I don't care," he said, standing in full naked glory beside the bed.

"You cared enough to make sure your accomplices took blood from me before we left LA," she said.

"To check you weren't diseased."

"So you could get your groove on without wearing a raincoat, I know. We had that conversation two weeks ago."

"I know, but you're still bitching about it."

She bitched to remind him of everything they had gone through to get them there. Sometimes when they were alone in this bedroom it was easy to forget that they weren't a "*normal*" couple.

"I hate needles," she said.

"You've told me that too, babygirl. Maybe I don't need to ask questions because you volunteer every damn thing."

Getting under his skin was easy. "Are you going to free me today?" she asked, bending her knee to flash her thigh through the sheet.

After retrieving his flick knife from the drawer, he came around the bed to cut her loose. She grabbed his arms and tugged him forward, bringing him down onto the bed on top of her. Latching onto him, she hooked her arms and legs around his body.

"I said no more sex," he said.

"Why is getting to know me so dangerous? You answer eighty percent of my questions, I know you're an only child from New York. You grew up with your dad until he left you with the circus and took off." His father left him with a group of fight organizers. Calling it the circus irked him, which was becoming her favorite hobby. She needed some way to amuse herself after all. "You ran away from every foster or group home they put you in, and you've been on the street since you were ten. You answer all of my questions about the past and none about the present."

Getting information from Dax required asking the right question at the right second. He didn't get steeped in conversation. He gave her pieces of information here and there as she seized the appropriate moments. Didn't always work, progress was slow. Still, it was progress.

"I don't have to answer your questions at all," he said.

Slanting his mouth on hers, he parted her lips with his tongue and began to grind his hardening dick against her sensitive inner thigh.

"No sex," she said, taking hold of his arms again. "Why is it so wrong for you to talk to me?"

"Why do you need answers? Why do you need me to care?"

"Why won't you admit how you feel? You hate it when Bruno touches me." He tensed, sort of proving her point. "All the rules from out there go out the window in here."

"In here you open your legs for me on command and that's all I care about."

"And you let me play with your cock anytime I want."

"Do I?"

"Case and point," she said, squeezing her hands between them to take hold of him with both.

"You can play with it later, Minx," he said, rolling off her and stretching again. "I have stuff to do today."

"Stuff like what?" she asked but he was already on his way to the shower.

Joining him in the bathroom might allow her to goad him into sex, but she wasn't in the mood to speed her journey down the stairs to join Bruno. The only time she got to shower without a witness was when she was doing it with Dax… his eyes didn't count.

So she left the bed to join him, but by the time she got there he was already rinsing off. He handed her the loofah and tried to squeeze past her in the narrow doorway, but she crowded him, being sure her naked breasts made complete contact.

"Where are you going in such a hurry, stranger?"

"The clingy thing isn't attractive."

"Neither is the distant brooder."

"Who are you kidding? Every time I snap my fingers your panties melt."

And with that statement her arousal cooled. "Jerk," she said, shoving her way past him to get under the spray.

The draft told her he hadn't closed the sliding door. Opening her eyes, she deciphered the outline of his figure just standing there. Stepping out of the engulfing water, instinct drew her eye down to his intimidating erection. The idea of using it faded when she noticed the aloof expression on his face. It reminded her of the night they met.

"There's a guy that owes Mauri money," he said, all cool like. "A lot of money, Mauri trusted him with some product and didn't get his return."

"So?"

"So I'm going to get that money back for him today."

"If you're just a thug for hire then what am I?" she asked.

"A massive pain in my ass. You'll be alone with Bruno today, wear the denim cut-offs."

She'd found them on her side of the closet and worn them two days ago. He'd been unable to keep his eyes, or his hands off her ass. Since their union in the gym when he'd told her to stop wearing bikinis, wardrobe choices were made by him every day. Bruno didn't question or refute Dax's authority… not in front of her anyway.

"Okay."

"Are you comfortable here at the beach house?" he asked.

"I'm comfortable with you."

"What would you do for me?" His question came quietly, but determination bled through him. "Would you do anything I asked?"

"I'd give you shit for it first but, yeah, I'd probably agree to try most things. I'm not ready for the ass thing yet though, so don't even go there."

"How did they get you?" he asked as though carrying on a conversation there, naked, like this, was a normal occurrence. "How did you end up at the Stark mansion?"

"I answered an advert for a live-in housekeeper in Vegas," she said. "Three days after getting the job I couldn't get out of the house. From there they took me to LA. I had no idea what was going on or who they were until I saw you, downstairs in the living room." The story was entirely true, but he didn't respond. "What is it?"

"Have your shower. I'll be back this afternoon."

He slid the door shut and the confined space quickly filled with steam. The scent of his shower gel lingered, bringing back her arousal with the subtlety of a freight train. If he was dressing and leaving, all she had waiting for her was

Bruno.

Letting her fingers glide down her abdomen she shifted back under the spray and began to imagine that Dax was still with her. He'd asked her a question, of his own accord, whether he liked it or not their intimacy was growing deeper.

FIFTEEN

MAURI'S BIDDING was what he did best. Dax needed to clear his head. Going through the motions, expelling some tension, was overdue.

Running errands for Mauri was his life. Doing for the old man what he couldn't do for himself was his duty. Being relied upon gave him importance, he'd always believed himself valuable to the Stark organization.

While Trystan sunned himself and fucked his way through Europe, Brad handed out orders, dealing with business in preparation for one day taking over from Mauri. Everyone had their role. His was beating up lowlifes, threatening them until they paid their debts, as they always did after a visit from him.

The truth was cold. Although Mauri valued him, the Stark sons didn't care about his loyalty. They made no secret that he wasn't special to them. His future was uncertain. The confusing thing was he'd never cared about the future before. Why did he suddenly care about it now?

Bruno would expect him back at the beach house and he didn't want to leave the pervert alone with the Minx for longer than necessary. Maybe that explained his lead foot. The shipment of sex toys Bruno ordered online had arrived a while ago. They were in the bedroom closet, but he refused to look through the package. His indifference was a shield for the fury that built when he thought about any man penetrating his property. Didn't matter what it was, a cock, a dildo, a whatever, the idea got him so lost in a red mist he usually had to walk out.

The Minx drove him crazy. The way she strutted around in those too high heels and pushed out that tight butt, presenting it to him. Even when it was red raw, still glowing from his handprint, she teased him with it as though daring him to spank her again. In private, she fought with him, questioned him, but she never stepped out of line in public. He didn't get it.

As far as Bruno knew, he was doing his job. The Minx was obedient when it counted. Always. Though it was tough to admit, he wasn't doing his job with her, not the one Mauri expected.

She didn't fear him, she respected him. She didn't submit to his sexual will, she enhanced it with her own craving for his domination. Unconventional as it was, they'd forged a sort of private relationship. An understanding. Her actions proved he could trust her. But he could never confide in her, could never tell her the truth.

One day, soon, he'd have to hand her over to Trystan. Either she would fight and get herself killed, or she would comply with his depraved requests and marry him to save her life.

Both options sucked. He couldn't claim her. Even if she did stand beside him, not that she definitely would, it would mean nothing. If Trystan found out he'd even considered keeping the girl for himself, it would only increase the spoilt little prick's want for her. He was a man who wouldn't be beaten, and their fates would be sealed.

The trap set up to snare her was the type he'd usually oversee. He wouldn't have been able to join the plot because they'd met, he didn't need to ask Mauri for his reasoning on that. No doubt the Starks had paid off one of the Minx's friends to recommend the position. After losing her job at GoldSpring, she'd need a new source of income, fast. Living that kind of breadline existence wasn't easy.

Despite being from the bottom of society, she carried herself with grace and class. Even when she was being demeaned by Bruno. Class that went as far as the bedroom threshold at least.

That morning, despite already being late when she'd pulled him back into bed, he'd been tempted to screw her anyway, hard and fast, then punish her with a thorough spanking for delaying him. Refusing her was getting harder, resisting her a chore. And when he'd heard her moaning in the shower, that breathy desperate sound usually followed by a curse, he'd been tempted to join her or wrap his fist around himself.

Being with her had taught him about himself. The most dangerous thing he'd learned? He liked mouthy brunettes who weren't shy about their bodies.

Stopping in the beach house driveway, he killed the engine and slammed out of the car, letting those inside know he was back. Except when he got through the front door, the living room was empty. Bruno would never be downstairs in the gym, and the letch couldn't do anything with the Minx in bed. The kitchen or back deck were his best bets.

And he was right. Bruno sat at the kitchen table with a thick smoothie and a nine-millimeter flat on the tabletop under his palm. Their captive was at the center isle brushing spices onto skewers of chicken, onions, and peppers. When she saw him, she fell to her knees as Bruno expected. The instant submission was kinda neat, maybe for its novelty, she never acted that way when they were alone.

"Up," he said to her. "Carry on."

She went back to what she'd been doing.

The gun drew his attention. What was it doing there? Had there been trouble? The Minx could drive the sanest of men to murder, he got that, and Bruno was far from sane.

"We're having company tonight," Bruno said.

"Company?" he asked, crossing to stand behind his girl.

"The guys are coming over. We're gonna barbeque and have ourselves a party."

"Brad coming?"

"No, he's got business. I talked to him about today. You did good."

"I got the job done. Brad should have sent me in two weeks ago."

"You were busy. We'll celebrate today's success tonight."

"I don't need praise for doing my job."

His fingers crawled onto her hips, creeping under the top of the cut offs he'd instructed her to wear. After telling her not to wear the bikinis, he'd had a conversation with Bruno, making up a cock and bull story about how dressing her every morning took away more of her free will. The truth was, he wanted her in clothes that didn't give Bruno such easy access to flesh. Bruno didn't argue, thank God, because debate would be a waste of energy.

Not like when the Minx contradicted him; fighting with her turned his blood to lava. Then she'd throw him for a loop by complying with the simplest requests. Damn, she intoxicated him. This broad was as stubborn as him but had a smart head on her shoulders. She used that savvy to her advantage as much as she did that explosive body.

Possessing one another was impossible. Why did he keep thinking like that? Their paths would cross from then on. In time, she'd become entrenched in the Stark family, in the position of Trystan's wife. Eventually, the memory of their brief time together would fade. No one would know what went down in their bedroom... no one except them.

If there was a woman in the world for him, one he could trust, she was as close as he would ever get. But being together wasn't an option. No matter what, he'd be giving her up, and that meant closing off as much of himself as possible. If he even hinted at wanting her longer term, it would screw everything up. And if he told her the truth... she'd go fucking nuclear. Why should he deal with the aggravation when there was nothing he could do to change the facts?

"Did this one behave?" he asked, bumping his chin on his Minx's head.

The answer was important. If Bruno punished her, he

might be tempted to do some punishing of his own… but not of her.

"Just. Place is in great shape for the guys and she's prepping for the grill. She's going to have the time of her life tonight. Meeting the crew is a big step, she'll be kept busy."

Her ass shifted back slightly, enough to rub that rump on his dick. As though she'd cast a spell on his blood, it did as she requested and began to fill his now distracted organ.

"How long we got until they show?" Dax asked Bruno.

"About an hour."

He spanked her right ass cheek, jolting her body. "Then you're done here," he said to her. "I need something to wear, get upstairs and iron my shirt."

"Which—"

"I don't know yet," he said, "start at one side of my closet and work your way across."

He'd never get away with a comment like that upstairs. Down there, she bumped him with her ass again and toddled away upstairs.

When the door swung shut behind her, he switched to Bruno again. "Who's coming?"

"Don't know, whoever shows up… they're gonna love her."

The light in Bruno's eyes was wicked, betraying exactly what would be expected of the Minx. He'd been to these kinds of parties before, plenty of times, with Trystan, since they were kids.

"If they want female company, tell them to bring it with them."

Bruno's grin twitched, then vanished. "What?"

"No one touches her."

"Wait a minute, Dax. She's not your woman, our job here—"

"Is to get her ready for Trystan. It's all fun now, but Trystan won't marry a woman every other guy has got his hands on first." Bruno's eyes drifted as he considered this. "He'll want every guy to want her, and he'll want to share her around on his terms. His choice. If she's already done the rounds—"

"How do you think he'll feel about what you've done with her?"

Dax shrugged. "I've fucked Trystan's women before. I can be discreet… Tonight, we need to change up the game."

"How?"

"She's obedient, right? We know she'll open her legs when Tryst wants it."

"Okay."

"Now we teach her to keep her mouth shut. To be a proper wife. To restraint herself. The last thing Tryst wants is a cheap ho," he said, using Trystan's own words.

"So we dress her up pretty tonight, let her know it's her job to play the hostess who turns a blind eye?"

"That's it."

"We better get you some company," Bruno said, taking his hand from the gun to retrieve his cellphone from the back pocket of his shorts.

"The guys will bring women. There will be plenty to go around."

"Mauri wants her to spend some time at the mansion before Trystan gets back, he wants to check her out… see she fits into the dress."

Bruno's grin returned. Forcing himself to try and return it, his expression came out as more of a grimace than a smile.

He went to the fridge to get a beer. "I'm going to check on her," he said, twisting off the cap and tossing it away before he left the room.

SIXTEEN

TAKING A LONG DRINK from the ice-cold bottle, Dax went upstairs to the bedroom. And what a sight waited for him there. The Minx lay on the middle of their bed, naked, her knees pulled up and far apart, giving him a sweet view of the snatch she was juicing up for him.

Lowering the bottle from his lips, his surprise must have registered, but the Minx didn't acknowledge it. She just kept on toying with her clit, then moved south to circle her opening and probe herself with the tip of an index finger.

"Don't be shy," she purred. Sliding her finger out, she brought it to her lips to lick the length of it. "Come over here."

If he'd needed evidence of his failure, he was looking at it. She wasn't supposed to be seducing him without fear, he was meant to be intimidating her into submission. With most women, his act worked. Not with this one. She'd seen through him and embraced what he was.

"Not a chance," he said, without even trying to hide his smile.

Unfortunately, the scorch of blood flooding his cock wasn't comfortable, he needed to loosen his jeans to alleviate the pressure. But with her there, like that, he couldn't do it, or she'd think he'd surrendered. Man, everything was back to front.

The real torture came in those fluttering eyelashes, tempting him, and the mountains of her gorgeous tits calling for his hands, and that cunt… Already it was swollen and wet enough to slide in; no prep required. He could see the glisten of her delicious nectar coating the ripe, pink flesh begging him to sink his cock into it.

"You said I'd come to crave you, that I'd be addicted to your spunk. Here it is, Dax, that day has come. I want you. I need it. I need you to fuck me now. I need your dick—"

"What is going on here?" he asked, putting the beer on the dresser and crossing to stand at the end of the bed.

She rose onto her knees and walked on them to the foot of the bed to drape her arms around his neck. "Come to bed," she murmured, pouting those lips. "Get rid of your clothes and come to bed with me. Please, tough guy."

Her husky whispers did nothing to improve his cock situation, but this was too suspicious to just give in. She'd never been this easy. Even when she was horny as fuck… Those times he loved to take advantage of, this was different.

"You're supposed to fight with me, Minx. You're supposed to be here against your will."

Unbuttoning his jeans, she slid her hand in to coil her fingers around him. "Is that what you need?" she asked, using her whole arm to massage his shaft. Her shoulder pressed into his chest as it moved up and down, the rhythmic motion vibrated through his whole form. "Do you need me to beg for release? Please let me go, Master, please, please."

"Okay," he said, snatching her shoulders to shove her onto the mattress so hard she bounced. "What's going on? You think you can keep me here all night? That if we fall into bed, we won't get out 'til morning, and you'll miss the party?"

She shook her head and got back onto her knees, but the act was gone. "No."

"You're supposed to be ironing shirts."

Pointing behind him, he turned to see that there was a black shirt hanging on the closet door. "Wear that one, you look hot and dangerous; it makes the color of your eyes more intense."

Usually he picked out her wardrobe, and now she was doing it for him. The funny thing was, he didn't care. Clothes meant nothing to him. They were clothes. That was it. Her picking something out gave him a break on making the decision himself. He told her what to wear, what to eat and when, he told her when to sleep and when to open her legs, giving her a tiny bit of control was insignificant.

"And the act?" he asked.

Her eyes dropped to the bed. "How many men are coming over tonight?"

"I don't know. Could be five, could be ten, could be fifty. I really don't know."

"Okay, we don't have much time," she said. When her eyes came up to his, he read fear for the first time. "Do you have lube?"

Scratching the side of his neck, he tried not to be influenced by her rare moment of vulnerability. "You looked pretty lubed up there already, babygirl. I don't think you need—"

"It's not for that."

"I don't follow."

"You said… you told me once that when the guys came over, I'd have a lot of cocks to keep happy. It's my guess that the men who are coming over tonight won't be as understanding about my reluctance as you have been."

"Reluctance," he said.

He'd fucked her every way invented. Never shy of being the aggressor in their bed, she'd kissed him first and never been reluctant about anything. No, she had… one thing…

She got up and went to pick up his beer from the dresser, downing the liquid, one long gulp at a time until it was all gone.

"Do you have anything stronger?" she asked, putting the bottle down. "Or maybe some Valium? If you have a mickey—"

"You want me to drug you before I have sex with you?" he asked. "Isn't it too late for that?"

The fear was gone and replaced instead with a

pleading determination. "I want you to drug me before *they* have sex with me. I'll drink anything you give me, Dax, take anything. I trust that you'll—"

"You're getting ahead of yourself, babygirl," he said, taking her hand and leading her back to seat her on his side of the bed. "No one will have sex with you."

"No one?"

Her shock pissed him off for some reason he couldn't figure out.

" 'Cept me. I still expect you to put out when I bring you to bed. But I'm the only guy who'll touch you. If anyone else tries it, you come to me, I'll deal with him."

"Oh, Dax!" Her exuberance almost knocked him sideways when she leaped forward and wound her naked form all around him, burying her face in his shoulder. "I was so worried! I really thought they'd all take a piece of me, and if there were a few of them who wanted me at once… I've never done the anal thing and… I thought I was… I was going to ask you to take me that way now, to ease me into it, you know, maybe to make it easier tonight when I had them all inside me at once."

"I opened my mouth too soon," he said. "I just did myself out of a chance to fuck your asshole."

Much to his surprise, she laughed and tightened the circle of her arms around his neck. The maneuver felt too intimate, to be holding her like this, without expectation of sex. For no purpose other than to make her feel better, or rather for her to show gratitude.

Gripping her elbows, he tugged her away, but she remained in his lap, not catching on to his discomfort. Touching his forearms, her hands ascended until her fingers disappeared into the sleeves of his tee-shirt. More intimacy, this touching and holding each other was a head fuck. But he had no time to get away, she frowned, and his anxiety gave way to curiosity.

One of her hands dropped. The other slid down until she was tracing the shape of his tattoo, examining the dragon he'd had inked more than a decade ago. Except the dragon wasn't what fascinated her. No, her attention was fixed on the plant coiling itself around the dragon's feet. The nest of vines the dragon emerged from to hunt for sustenance; it's sanctuary.

"What?" he asked.

"Is this where the dragon lives?"

"Yeah."

"When I first saw it, I thought it was pulling the dragon down, that it was trying to hold him back."

"No," he said, bringing his arm around. To show her the full picture, he pulled up the short sleeve of his tee-shirt. "That's the dragon's lair, where it hides so predators can't find it. He can peek out of the plant to check what's going on without being seen. It's his refuge."

Her smile became a whisper of a laugh, and she continued to trace the shape of the leaves. "That's funny."

"Why is that funny?" he asked.

His tattoos had been called a lot of things; funny was not one of them.

Her amused expression brought those long lashes back to him. "It's ivy," she murmured.

"So?"

The smile became wider, and she shook her head. "Nothing."

"It's something."

"Nothing you have to worry about," she said.

The promise of more came when she coiled her arms around him, seeking his mouth with hers. He didn't shy from her kiss. Despite being slower and way less urgent than their usual kisses, it was just as stimulating.

Already his jeans were open, so when she climbed up and coiled her legs around him, she had complete access to slide herself onto his dick. Yet, it surprised him, he had been more focused on the new sensation of such a tender, mellow kiss.

Trust. For the first time, when he splayed his hands on her back, she felt small… fragile.

This woman acted like a formidable force. Like she was equal, or superior, to any enemy. He could identify with her bull-headed stubbornness and refusal to show vulnerability. Being a man capable of handling himself, he could get away with being arrogant. Few people would have the balls to call him on it. Weakness was something he avoided. Usually at all costs. In this kiss, he learned his girl was fast falling into that category.

What he'd said to Bruno was true, every word. But he hadn't said it with Trystan's best interests at heart. He wasn't sure he'd said it with his girl's interest at heart either. The idea of watching other men paw her, or make love to her…

Breaking their kiss stopped the rhythmic motion of her hips. Her lazy tempo had matched the kiss, drawing more intimacy into the moment as her pussy swallowed and released him with each undulation.

"What?" she asked. The rasp of stubble burn on her chin and swollen lips heightened their rosy color. Her eyes were glossy, swimming in a dream. "I don't feel good?"

Elevating her ass, she relaxed, enveloping him again. He hissed when she squeezed and caressed him from within her tight passage.

"No," he said, though she felt better than incredible.

"Okay," she said, undeterred.

The hitch of her breath when she expelled him from her slick channel rustled every hair on his body. But when she slithered off the bed and onto her knees on the floor, he tensed.

Her complete focus was on the engorged head of his cock, she licked him like a lollipop then sucked him deep and slurped her way back. Stroking the length of him with one hand and tickling his balls with the other, she smiled and kissed the tip of him.

"I taste so much better on you," she said and opened her mouth.

He pushed her away. "Fucking stop it."

Bounding off the bed, he had no chance of getting his jeans done up again, so he tugged his tee-shirt down over his groin.

"It's okay," she said.

A woman fucking a guy and being told she didn't feel good, shouldn't be understanding. Neither should one just shoved away while sucking a guy off.

Spinning around, he couldn't believe he was the guy pushing away such a hot naked woman. Everything was messed up.

"What the fuck?" he asked.

"Performance anxiety is probably normal in a guy who's spent his life taking drugs and partying. You're already hard," she said, walking on her knees across the floor. "If you relax and let me—"

"I don't fucking think so," he said, marching over to grab her hair and haul her back to the bed.

Sitting down to turn her over his knee, spanking her was about the only thing that made sense. She yelped and whimpered, clutching his calf, trying to lift her head. He kept her pinned, raining down blow after blow on that tight ass watching it grow pinker and redden.

He'd never thought of making love with a woman or consoled one. He'd sure never passed up a chance to do something as sweet as she'd been offering. The Minx had taken him into her body with entitlement like she had some claim on him. He was supposed to have claimed her.

The hot body that mesmerized him, the sassy mouth that tormented him… they shouldn't belong to a man like Trystan Stark. Trystan wouldn't appreciate her; he'd want to change her. No one should be allowed to alter this sexy, dynamic woman.

No better woman existed. No flawed woman more perfect. She couldn't change. Except she would. Because everything changed.

Thinking like that… wanting to… She wasn't his. He had to push her away. Had to maintain distance. Detach himself. Close down. Shut off.

Rolling her off his lap to the floor, he stared at the glow on her crimson flesh. "What was that for?" she panted, remaining face down at his feet.

"Making me want you," he confessed. When she tried to move, he put a boot on her ass and pushed down. "Don't move."

Rocking her body with his foot, he ignored her wince

of pain and kept going. "You wanna get me off? Maybe this is what it takes," he said. "Maybe I wanna roll you over and piss all over you until you stink of me? Then I'll whip those hefty tits 'til they're cherry red, would you let me do that?"

"Is this a test?" she asked. "Like you said earlier, to find out what I'll do for you?"

Dragging his boot off, he rolled her onto her back and squatted down over her. "You'll do anything you're damn well told. If I tell you to spend all-night buck-naked serving beer to me and my friends, you'll do it. If I deny you the right to use the bathroom until you piss all over yourself, you'll do it."

"What's with the sudden obsession with peeing?"

"Still don't know when to quit, Minx."

Despite blanching with discomfort, she pushed up onto her elbows. "And you worry too much."

"It's in the job description."

"Of thug for hire?" she asked. "I'd think it's just your job to show up and kick the shit out of whoever your boss points at."

"In my line of work, you can never trust anyone to watch your back. Always assume everything will go to shit."

"If life has taught me anything, it's that you never know what's around the corner. I didn't choose to be here… I don't think you did either."

Extending his legs, he rose to full height and offered her a hand. "I didn't plan it or decide what to do with you."

She blinked but took his offer and he hauled her onto her feet. "I know," she said. "But I'm happy you're sharing my bed instead of him."

"Bruno? He can't get it up," Dax revealed. "He's Mauri's right-hand man, he trusts him with everything."

"Mauri doesn't trust you?"

"He trusts me. Brad and Trystan are another story."

"You said something, that night in Vegas, about teaching me a lesson about my attitude."

"I think I just did," Dax said, taking her hand and lifting it above her head to turn her one-eighty. "I love punishing that ass."

"Do you spank me so hard because I won't let you fuck it?"

"I could fuck it if I wanted to," he said, stroking the cheeks.

"Are you Trystan's bodyguard?"

"Sorta, I guess, more like his mess fixer and problem solver. As you know, he pisses people off when he's high… which is pretty much all the time."

A wash of guilt prickled him when she flinched from his stroking. Crouching to his haunches again, he began to cover the red handprints with kisses.

She laughed and twisted to rest a hand on his head. "What are you doing?"

"Would you ever tell me to stop? When I hurt you—"

"You don't hurt me," she said, turning in a crouch to face him and take his hands. "I'm… trouble. I know I'm difficult, but… I've never met a man who rises to it, embraces it… not like you do. I didn't know I wanted a man who would challenge me… until you found me."

"Don't," he said, shaking his head, bringing them both up to full height. "Don't think this is more than it is. You're my prisoner, here against your will and—"

"Where would I go?" she asked. "We won't be here forever. I know there's a deadline. Bruno is a pig, but… I'll put up with that if it means being close to you."

Every curse word known to man ran through his mind in new combinations until he'd exhausted them all. In coming to terms with his own attachment to this woman, he hadn't figured she might feel something for him. Women were attracted to his body and the glamour of Stark money; he'd had his share of the Stark groupies. But feelings…?

For someone to care about him, for *her* to feel something… it was so unimaginable, it hadn't occurred to him. Maybe he thought this girl would be happy rolling around in the sack with him for a while, he hadn't figured she'd link him to any kind of emotion. Most women had ulterior motives of the practical, or material, variety. That kind he kicked to the curb long before they could latch on.

"I'm using you for sex," he stated.

"I know. I'm using you too. What woman wouldn't want to use that body?" Locking her fingers between his, she altered the angle of her hands so that her palms pressed down on his. "Lift me up." She locked her elbows.

"Why?" he asked at the same time he bent his knees then straightened, taking her off the floor, balancing her miniscule weight using his upper body strength.

She dipped her head to kiss him. With the taste of her tongue, he forgot about tomorrow's worries and took her to bed.

"When we get back to the city, can I come see you fight?"

"Not a chance," he said, laying her down on the bed.

He kneeled astride her to grab the neck of his tee-shirt and dragged it off.

"Why not?" she asked, sitting up to stroke his chest with an appreciation that drove him to puff himself up. "Women aren't allowed?"

"They're allowed, though most of them are in bikinis or hooker boots."

"I can handle that."

He stood up to shirk his jeans. "I'm still not taking you."

"Why not?"

"You're too much of a distraction," he said. "I wouldn't be focused on the fight if I was more concerned about you being hit on out in the crowd."

"I can take care of myself."

"So you keep saying," he said, snatching her foot when it moved towards his cock. "But there's no fighting allowed outside the ring. It will get you barred, or worse."

"That means even if you were with me in the crowd while I got hit on, you couldn't do anything about it."

"Oh, there's plenty I could do, babygirl," he said, imagining the ways he would make a man pay for ogling, or upsetting, his girl.

"Can I ask you a question?" she asked, opening her arms to him when he came down on top of her.

"I wish I knew a way to make you stop asking them." One method had been successful in the past. Tracing his lips on her jaw, over the tiny scar, and down her creamy neck, he tried to change the subject. "What's the question?"

"What would you do for me?"

This made him falter. "What?"

"You asked me earlier, in the shower, and I've been thinking about it ever since. So I'm asking, what would you do for me?"

"Win," he said and going for the most effective silencer, he kissed her.

SEVENTEEN

THEY'D SPENT FAR LONGER naked than they should have. Not by her standard, but probably by Bruno's. Good thing Dax overruled Bruno. There at the beach house anyway, she didn't know about their day jobs.

Being with Dax felt real. She wanted to stay in their private shelter for as long as possible. After sex, they'd showered—and had more sex—then he'd carried her to their bed, laid her down, and told her to wait while he went into the closet.

"If you hate the shirt I picked out, I will iron another for you," she called out, wondering why he'd left her there.

A few seconds later, he came out and tossed a ball of material at her. "Put that on."

Unwinding the blue fabric that was almost the color of his eyes, she discovered it was a short, backless, cowl neck dress that would show off plenty of bosom without attaining slutty levels.

"I'm grateful I won't be naked," she said. "Do I get underwear?"

"No," he said, yanking on a fresh pair of jeans and donning the shirt she'd picked out for him.

Music was already blaring from downstairs; the party

had started without them. She quickly dried her hair, knowing it would settle in waves, and Dax was kind enough to reveal a makeup kit in one of the dresser drawers.

For the first time in a month, she felt like a real, ordinary woman again. Slathering on the gloss, she finished then spun to face him where he waited by the door.

"What do you think?"

"Great, whatever, can we get out of this room?"

He could've left at any time but waited. She wouldn't have to enter the party alone, although he didn't explicitly say that, it was appreciated.

"One second," she said, approaching him to loosen a few buttons of his shirt.

"What are you doing?" he asked. The obvious tent in his jeans betrayed his lack of offense. "I'll give you more sex later. We have to make an appearance."

She spread her palms on his chest, opening his shirt as much as possible. "It's going to be hot down there."

"It's dark out."

"Things might get intense. I could get anxious and need a distraction." She kissed the width of his chest. "And this is it."

He took her hands out of his shirt but didn't button it. Obviously, he didn't mind providing a distraction. "If I get anxious, will you flash your tits and let me kiss them?"

"Yeah," she said, much to his surprise. "If you bring me up here first."

"Whatever, let's go."

"Wait. What should I expect down there?"

He exhaled. "You're not expected to fuck any guy or suck any cock, except mine," he said, taking a front length of her hair between his first two fingers.

"That's it? That's the only information you can give me?"

"Expect everything else to go wrong," he said and shrugged. "Do as you're told. Don't contradict anyone, and make every guy down there want you."

Trust Dax to drop a bomb like that at the last second. "What? How am I supposed to do that?"

"Just walk in the room, babygirl. Every guy will have a hard-on."

"That I'm not supposed to attend to, right?"

"Be sexy, be flirty, but don't cross the line into slutty. You'll have them all drooling, that's what we want. But make sure they know you're my girl and you love it. Adore me, let them think you're obsessed."

"Addicted to your dick?" she asked, not fooled.

"Right on."

"Oh, you're going to pay for this later," she mumbled, but followed him out of the bedroom and down to the party.

SHE DIDN'T STAY LONG in Dax's wake, or even in his company. As soon as they reached the bottom of the stairs, Bruno commandeered her. Instructing her to keep the guests happy, he explained it was her job to play hostess.

Topping off glasses and cooking at the grill were her main duties. Also her purview? Stocking the fridge, making cocktails, and cleaning up messes. Her work experience to date came in handy.

The music was constant, the alcohol flowing, and lines of coke were available on the bar at the outer deck. Twenty guys had shown up with a posse of women happy to show off their figures around the pool. Some guy suggested skinny-dipping… a lot.

Outside, Dax was on a lounger, flanked by women and surrounded by men. Though she didn't see him say much, most of the partygoers were happy just to be in his presence. Bruno took up another corner of the back patio, more women than men adored him, but she figured that was by his request.

The party guests were getting louder, being in the middle of nowhere meant no neighbors to bother. Well after midnight, the party was still going strong and didn't appear to be letting up any time soon.

For the first time all night, the kitchen was empty. She was alone. Halfway through her task of filling the canapé trays, she glanced at the kitchen door. Would anyone notice her making a break for it? If the front door was unlocked, she could get a head start. Would it be unlocked? It never had been before.

Just then, someone came in from the back deck, annihilating her escape fantasy. "Do you need any help?"

She hadn't expected the tall stranger to ask that, or for him to come around to her side of the island.

"No," she said, happier to be occupied than mingling. "I'm almost finished."

"I've seen you running around tonight. You haven't had a chance to sit still. Let someone help you and you might actually enjoy yourself."

His hand covered hers when she reached for the box of crackers. "I'm happy to stay busy."

"You're quite the pick," he said.

All night people had been making comments like, "*I see why you were chosen*," and, "*he's a lucky guy*."

"Dax knows what he wants," she said, finishing her task.

Mixing daiquiris and margaritas was next on her agenda.

The stranger discarded his drink and rested back on the counter, getting in her way. "Dax does what he's told. He didn't pick you."

"I don't know what—"

"I know what's going on. Everyone here does. You won't catch a break like this again."

Meeting his green eyes, she forgot about the task ahead. "Who are you?"

"Your chance to get out," he said. "I'm your chance at freedom, probably your last one."

"Maybe you're not as clued in as you think," she said, figuring no one told him about the deadline.

"If you want to get out of here, you have to come with me. Now."

"You expect us just to turn around and walk out?"

"Yes," he said, twining his fingers between hers. "This time tomorrow you could be far away from here and never have to see Bruno or Dax again."

Except she wanted Dax in her life. "Is this a test? To

see if escape is in my mind."

"No test and no time to waste. Do you want to be free?"

Freedom sounded like bliss, with Dax, not with this person. "I can't just walk away from him."

"Dax doesn't want you. Don't make the mistake of falling for him. He's here to fuck you into shape, to win your trust and obedience. And by the sound of it, he's doing a damn good job. Being with you, here, wasn't his choice. If he succeeds in this mission and breaks you, he moves up in the organization."

"What?"

"Those guys out there worship him because he used to be one of them. Hell is where Dax came from. He's done everything Mauri ever asked of him to make sure he never ends up back there. To him, you're a stepping stone, nothing more."

"And you're here to save me? Yeah, right," she said and tried to take her hand from his.

His grip tightened and he tugged her body to his, smoothing fingers down her cheek. "I don't want you to forget this conversation, Ivy," he murmured. "Now there's no hope for you. You've passed the point of no return."

"What's going on?"

She whipped around to see Dax enter the kitchen, a suspicious scowl spread on his face.

"Nothing," she said, returning to her canapé job only to be reminded too late that the tray was full.

"I was just getting to know Ivy. She's some woman."

The stranger was using her name. No one ever did that.

"Ivy," Dax said, locking his eyes on hers, probably thinking of their earlier tattoo conversation.

"Geez, Dax, you've been fucking the woman for how long and you never asked her name?" The stranger laughed and rounded the isle to pat Dax's shoulder. "That's what I love about you, man, you could never be confused for a guy who cares. Dax takes not giving a shit about anything except himself to a new level, Ivy, wouldn't you agree?"

"Thanks for the input," Dax said.

Before she could question him, the stranger headed for the deck. "You've got that thing to do," he said to Dax, taking on a sterner air.

"I'm on it." Dax nodded then the stranger was gone. "You just can't behave yourself, can you?"

"What?" she asked, surprised by his anger.

Storming over, he swept an arm across the counter, sending all her neatly trayed snacks cascading across the floor.

"I just—" Jolting her in front of him, he crouched to slide his palms up the backs of her thighs under her dress. "What are you doing?"

Bringing his lips to the shell of her ear, he whispered, "What do you get when you're a naughty girl?"

"You're not going to—" The buzz of his hand smacking her ass shut her up.

"You know I like to hear the answer. What do you get, Minx?"

"A spanking."

"That's right," he said. "Bend over the counter like a good girl."

"No, Dax, not here. Please don't—"

Shoving her down over the counter to gather up her skirt, he exposed her ass. The door to the back deck was wide open, anyone could walk in any minute.

"Still tender," he said, smoothing his hand on her butt with increasing pressure.

His hushed, throaty timbre didn't give her confidence in them not being discovered. "That's because you already gave me a hiding earlier. I haven't sat down all night." His hand left her and came back with a harsh thwack sending a spear of pleasure to her gut. "Oh, Dax, not here," she whispered but he hit her again.

"Worried you might get overexcited?" he asked. "Spread your legs. Get them further apart."

"Dax—"

"Do it."

His volume increased and she got another smack. Refusing him again would be too risky. His hand skimmed down until his finger dipped between her folds.

"Fuck, you're wet…" The strangled groan that accompanied the words confused and stimulated her. As opposed to angry, he sounded juiced up and agonized all at once.

"Do you want me to apologize for that too?"

"Just tell me Brad wasn't the one who—"

"Who? Your creepy friend? He didn't turn me on, he freaked me out… and I don't think he likes you very much."

"No, but he trusts me; that's all I need from him."

"I thought he wasn't coming."

"Change of plans, and you need to stop listening in to conversations that don't concern you."

"There's not much else to do around here," she said, and he spanked her.

Their casual conversation had made her forget she was half-naked, presenting for him.

"Watch your mouth, Minx."

"We could slip away. Go upstairs, you could let me apologize—"

"I have something to do," he said, moving in close. "And I don't know why this matters to me but… I need to hear you say that you trust me."

"You need my trust before you fuck me? Since when?"

"That's the thing, babygirl… you're not the one I'll be fucking."

A blonde wearing a green satin dress came in. "Ready?"

Dax tugged down Ivy's skirt. "Didn't I tell you to wait out there?" he asked the blonde.

"I'm impatient," the green dress girl pouted. "You promised me an intimate tour. Not many girls get that offer from the great Dax Harrow."

"Wait here, for real this time," he said. "I have to get this out of our way first."

Attraction and awe glittered from the size two blonde, and that tone, in Dax, yeah, she knew that tone of promise. He was going to have sex with that woman and the "*this*" he had to get out of the way was her.

Having been so preoccupied with the virtue of her own chastity, she hadn't considered Dax's fidelity… or his lack of it. He pulled her out of the kitchen and through the living room. She staggered along in a daze, knowing that she had no right or ability to ask for his loyalty. How did she feel about…? Maybe Brad had been right. Maybe Dax didn't care about her at all.

Reality jarred back into focus when Dax bypassed the route up to open the basement door and yank her down the stairs.

"No," she said, dropping all her weight toward the floor, fighting to pull him back. Dax swung her up into his arms and tossed her over his shoulder like she weighed no more than a bag of sugar. "No, Dax, please! I'm sorry!"

What had she done to be relegated down there again? After such a long reprieve, being back down there… the burn of acid fired up her esophagus.

"It's just for tonight," he said.

"Please! I'm sorry! I shouldn't have spoken to him!"

Talking to Brad. That had to be it. How was she to know Dax was the jealous type? He'd never cared about Bruno pawing her.

"It's not about him," he said, carrying her through the gym then opening the outer door to her previous prison. "I need the bedroom and while I'm busy in there I can't keep an eye on you."

"You think I'll run? I won't!"

He opened the door to the cage and tossed her inside, slamming the door before she could get to her feet.

"Or that one of them will take what isn't theirs," he said, locking the door.

Remaining on his side of the bars, he reached for her.

She leaped away. "You're going to have sex with her? In the bed you shared with me? Our bed?"

Curling his scarred fists around the cold metal bars, he scowled with Vegas intensity. "Nothing is ours, it's you and me," he spat. "I told you I'd get bored of you eventually."

"You fucking bastard."

"Yeah," he said. "But have you seen the sweet buns on that slut? She'll let me ride that tight ass all night long… I'll let you suck me off in the morning, if you're still hungry for it."

"Not a chance," she said, wishing for the ability to lash out.

The inability was just another example of how her freewill was being strangled.

He grumbled under his breath and turned to depart.

Anxiety drove her to hurtle herself at the bars. "Wait," she said on an inhale. He paused. "I'm sorry, okay, baby? I'm sorry. Take me upstairs with you."

Slowly, he turned back, his frown fierce. "What?"

"It might be fun," she said, trying to calm her breathing so her panic would be disguised by the smile meant to be saucy. "You could have both of us."

Reaching through the bars, she beckoned for him.

He came back to her. "You would do that?"

She got hold of the edges of his shirt, hoping to keep him close. "You could have both of us," she said again, pulling her body to the bars. "A fit, strong, healthy guy like you could handle that, and if we tire you out… she and I could always entertain each other."

Covering her hands with his, he watched their fingers mingle. "You want to have a threesome with a woman you've never been introduced to?"

"I trust you."

Those murmured words brought his eyes to hers, the frown gone.

"Good. I need you to remember that, babygirl," he muttered and ducked to kiss her through the bars.

Still hoping he'd consider her request, and let her out of the hole, she accepted his kiss with gusto. All too soon he withdrew his mouth, took her hands from his shirt, and retreated.

"Please don't leave me down here," she mumbled, reading nothing but conviction in him.

He wasn't taking her away from the hell he'd delivered her to.

Dax left.

Distress built to rage. Adrenaline sent a stream of curses flying from her lips. Music, activity, and the building structure would obscure most of her words from his ears, she just wished they'd obscure his actions from her awareness too.

EIGHTEEN

NOT TOO MUCH LATER, although she didn't know the time, the volume of the music dropped. A few vehicles left, but the sun was far from rising and the party kept on going. Three? Maybe Four a.m.? Guessing was a stupid distraction. Lying on the foam pad of a bed, staring up at the ceiling, the time was the last thing she cared about.

In Vegas, her sexual connection to Dax was powerful, even when he was threatening her. After reaching the conclusion she needed an ally, he'd seemed like the safest bet. Certainly the most appealing choice.

Having sex with him was part curiosity, part manipulation, only it hadn't worked. Her curiosity was satisfied. Unfortunately, she hadn't managed to manipulate him into caring. At least not enough to want to ensure her safety, or her happiness.

The latter was a pipe dream. The last-minute desperate dream of a woman who realized too late she'd only gone and fallen for a bad boy. Exactly the opposite of her intention.

"I fucked up."

The words startled her. She hadn't heard him, but there he was, birthed from the shadow beyond her cell. When she identified Dax, rather than a chancing letch from the party, she relaxed again.

Closing her eyes, she implied sleep, like she'd been unaffected this whole time. "I don't need a blow-by-blow."

"Not that," he said, his voice closer. She wouldn't look. "With you."

"Don't worry, I won't let you make any more mistakes with me where being fucked is concerned."

"Every guy in the place wanted you tonight. I told you to make them… only I didn't bargain on being one of them."

"Please," she scoffed. "Spare me the act. Do you think I'm the type of woman who lets her man run around on her? You get one chance with me, and you blew it."

"Watching you up there and watching those guys drool over you… Not one of them would have turned you down. You couldn't care less that they objectified you. You always rise above the bullshit; I don't know how you do it. After everything you've been through and… you're unbreakable, Minx."

"Is that what tonight was about? Breaking me?"

"No," he said. The lock loosened and the door opened, what was he doing? Letting her out of the cell? "Bruno wanted to get you high and let the guys take whatever they wanted. You were supposed to be the only female here and everyone was supposed to take a shot."

"That's not what happened," she said, maintaining her feigned sleep.

"I couldn't let that happen. I told him you were compliant, that we'd broken you and you were ready."

"For what?"

"To put up with anything."

"So you got your chance to screw around and make sure I didn't get ideas above my station? Bravo. Well done."

"You don't get it at all."

His fingers drifted through her hair then his lips met hers. She sputtered away, shoving at him while sitting up to put space between them.

"Stay the hell away from me," she protested, rubbing

off his kiss with the back of her hand.

"That would be smart," he said. "Turns out I'm not capable."

Grabbing her upper arms, he slammed her down on the bed, using his whole body to hold her down. Locking their mouths together, he apparently didn't care or notice that she didn't kiss back, he kept on going. Fondling her chest was a brief interlude on route to her crotch. Her attempts to kick and punch and struggle didn't deter him, he kissed and touched her as though making love to a passionate lover, not an objecting, kicking opponent.

"Stop it," she screeched when she could free her mouth. His strength was too much to fight. Her heart pounded and her body screamed louder when he pulled her legs apart to explore the reluctant moisture seeping from her intimate passage. She wanted to hate him. Did hate him. How could he make her care and break her heart? He was a bastard. A goddamn, motherfucking bastard. Just like all the rest of them. Her hatred stalled when the buzz of his fly crackled in the air. "No, Dax, no!"

"I need to fuck you," he mumbled through his kisses on her neck. "I'm sorry, Ivy, babygirl, I need it. I need to be inside you. It's the place I belong. You need me there."

The bulge of his engorged head probed at her entrance. From the gloss of mania in his eyes, it was obvious he wasn't in his right mind. Invading her body with this Goliath was a forgone conclusion for him. Anger boiled her blood, anger, not fear.

Using all of her might she pounded both fists on his shoulder, hoping to break through. "Hey! I said no, Dax. No!" Halting his advance, he blinked. His attention met hers, clearing some of the haze. "You can't have me, Dax. Your dick has a new place to call home. You moved him in there tonight. That blonde from the kitchen, that's who you belong with."

"No," he said, shaking his head. "I didn't fuck her. I just needed them to think I did."

What the...? Was she supposed to believe that? "What? Why would—"

"They needed me to prove you'd put up with anything, with everything we could throw at you," he said. "Walking away from you, bringing you down here to leave you alone, it… it hit me… Tonight it hit me how bad I'd fucked this up."

Something was going on in him. Her anger faded in the face of his honesty. For the first time, he was opening up, letting her in.

Releasing the tension in her arms, she looped them around his neck. "How did you fuck up?" she asked.

"I was meant to train you to follow every command… Instead, it's me who fell under your spell."

"If that were true, you wouldn't have taken another woman up to our bed."

"Fifi and I go way back," he explained, bracing himself on his elbows to peel down the straps of her dress. "I paid her to lie. She'll tell them I fucked her, that I was the best ride of her life. But I never touched her, not tonight."

"Why should I believe that?"

"Because telling you this, the truth, could get me into a lot of trouble. Tonight, we were supposed to prove you'd let me do whatever I wanted. They wanted to see you so browbeaten that I could fuck another woman and you wouldn't bat an eye." He kissed her. "I was going to let you believe I did it, to put some distance between us, you know? But lying up there in that room while Fifi slept, knowing you were down here by yourself… I couldn't leave you alone."

"You couldn't?"

"I wanted to come down and fight with you. Ream you out for believing I could be interested in that tramp, but I've never given you a reason to believe I give a fuck about you. I do… it just doesn't mean anything."

"It does," she said, combing her fingers through his hair. "It means something to me."

Guiding his mouth down to hers, she was ready to let him fulfil his desire. Never one to shy from doing the work, she took hold of him in a certain fist and elevated her hips to pierce herself with his rigid offering.

That was all the invitation he needed. Without

quitting her mouth, they fell into a slow rhythm far gentler than anything they'd practiced with each other before. Climax came for both of them at the same time.

A new kind of pleasure crept over her when he positioned them in their usual spoon position, taking his place in front of her, pulling her hand over his abs, it felt more like protection than ever.

"You're staying?" she asked, having expected him to abandon her when he was done.

"For as long as I can," he said, kissing her palm then flattening it over his heart. "I'll have to go up in the morning. Kick all those bastards out before I bring you upstairs. But we'll spend the day in our bedroom, all day, no Bruno, I promise."

"That's okay. I'm getting used to him now."

"Hope you're not attached to him feeling you up because it's over. It will never happen again."

Whatever had caused the transformation, she was glad of it. It could have come sooner, but better now than never.

"Does this mean I can come watch you fight?"

"You're determined to watch someone kick the shit out of me?"

A laugh met his spine, she followed it with her lips. "No one stands a chance against my tough guy."

"Thanks for the vote of confidence."

Growing tired, the hard work and lack of sleep were catching up with her. "Just imagine you saw your opponent's hand up my skirt before the fight."

"That wouldn't work."

His contradiction stung a little. Weren't they making headway with their intimacy? "Why not?"

"Too many witnesses when I murder the guy. You've got to be smart about stuff like that, babygirl, think ahead."

Wow. Transformation was an understatement. "Stupid me. What do I know about those kinds of things?"

"All you'll ever have to," he said. "I'll be taking care of business from here on out."

"My business or yours?"

"Both," he said, following it up with a mumble. "I'll just have to figure out how I'm gonna do it."

"Dax," she said and yawned, curling in closer when she shut her eyes.

"Yeah?"

"Does this mean that we're done with the bullshit? That we're being honest with each other now?"

"Yeah, honest, but you've got to trust me. It's not gonna be easy to maneuver our way out of this mess."

Other than being held captive by the man she now held, she didn't know anything about another mess. Dax seemed to have made a choice and for now that choice was her. Whatever was to come, he was smart enough and tough enough to figure it out. Relaxed, reassured, and sated, she let herself sleep behind the safety of his shielding form.

NINETEEN

AFTER THEIR SECOND carnal round, they'd fallen asleep in their usual position again.

With her whole body, she nudged his. "Dax," she said, interrupting his subdued snore.

He kind of snorted and mumbled something, loosening his grip on her hand.

No doubt he thought she wanted to use the restroom, forgetting in his slumber that they were nowhere near their room or internal plumbing.

A guy of his skill probably didn't worry about anyone getting the drop on him. Even if someone got the first punch in, or the first few, Dax would still win a physical fight, with absolute certainty.

The bathroom wasn't her motive, his safety was. Picking up his arm, she read the hands on his heavy watch. Nine eighteen. Shit. The music was off. In fact, she couldn't hear anything except her snoozing lover.

"Baby," she said, returning his arm to his torso.

More nudging and some kissing of his shoulder blades didn't do the trick either.

Slipping her fingers over the corrugation of his abs to the line of dark hair that descended to the invader that so frequently raided her, she took things to a more intimate level in hope of rousing him. In almost the same second she made contact with his flaccid member it sprang to attention with impressive speed.

The cadence of his snore merged to more of a purr. Tightening her grip, she pumped her hold, adjusting the angle of her thumb to swipe the breadth of his head at the summit.

If he came fully awake before he ejaculated, he'd want to fuck her; there wasn't time for that. Climbing over to go down on him, she closed her lips around his cock, inhaling with all her strength while quickening her fist.

"Fucking hell!"

Dax awoke in the same second his salty load drained into her. Her siphoning force emptied him into her throat in a series of delighted, sporadic injections. Tasting him out of his sleep and into consciousness was satisfying. The power flattered. Drinking every drop, she cleaned the drips budding from him before slithering up his body. In passing, she gave the length of him a cleansing wipe in her cleavage to rid him of the remnants of her oral lubrication.

"That was a helluva good morning," he said, still not fully recovered or awake.

"You have to leave," she said, rubbing her jaw on his stimulating stubble.

"Not yet," he said, taking hold of her to insinuate her between him and the mattress.

Though the sensation of his exploring mouth stimulated her into considering what his roaming hands suggested, it was too dangerous to take the risk of further intimacy. The last thing she wanted was Dax in trouble for spending time with her.

"Yes, yet," she said. Extricating his hands from her body by interlinking their fingers, she directed them up to the mattress at either side of her face. "You have to go upstairs. Bruno will be looking for you."

"If he was, he would've found me," he said, straining the muscles in his arms to rise in a push up.

Drawing her lower lip between her teeth, she loved how his taut body could expend energy in such a casual way.

Maybe he recognized her arousal because he did another push up, and another, his fingers still linked in hers against the mattress.

The man wasn't even breaking a sweat, he could probably do this all day. The knowing slant of his amused lips told her how he felt about her reaction to something he considered a mundane action. He was stretching stiff, tired muscles, in his own way. Because she'd had a hold of his hands, he couldn't do it in a conventional way.

He took one pair of their twined fingers around to his back and began to push up with one hand.

"You're showing off," she said, bobbing up to kiss him on his next descent.

"If you open your legs wider and arch your hips…"

He winked and clicked his cheek.

She laughed, giving him points for trying; the man had talent. "You can plank on me later," she said. Bringing their arms around from his back to hold his wrist between their faces, she showed him his watch. "Look at the time."

"Right," he said, clearing his throat then springing up to a crouched stance in such a practiced maneuver, she blinked at the turnaround.

"You have mad skills, tough guy," she said. Getting onto her knees to take his face in both hands, she kissed him, keeping it simple. The thrust of his tongue begged for more, so she separated their lips by an inch. "What would you do if I punched you in the face right now?"

"Try it," he said, attempting to kiss her again.

She resisted. "Are you saying I couldn't hit you or that you'd let me hit you?"

"I'm telling you to try it and see what happens."

Hmm, cocky. Her competitive heckles bristled. "I've punched guys before," she said. "I do have some abilities of my own, you know."

"Show me," he said. Leaping to his feet, he widened his stance and lifted his fists. With four fingers, he beckoned her toward him, moving nothing except those digits. "Come on then, Minx, get up. On your feet, pledge."

"You're naked," she said, sitting up, resting her back

on the wall, her legs lying toward him.

"Not my usual get-up, sure," he said. "You're naked too, we're equal." Stretching across the floor, she snagged his jeans to toss them at him. "You're that worried about protecting my junk?" He pulled them on but didn't buckle the belt. "I guess you're a girl who fights dirty."

"I'm a girl who retreats when their opponent is dazed and confused," she said, crawling across the concrete floor to retrieve her dress, which had somehow ended up near the bars. When she passed, he swooped down to spank her naked behind, earning himself a glare over her shoulder. "I was perfectly behaved last night. You were the naughty one. Should I turn you over my knee?"

His grin burst to a laugh. He bent to snag her arm and lifted her off the ground with such force her feet left the floor for a second.

"Try that any day, Minx. I'd love to punish you for forgetting your place."

Except she didn't feel subordinate when he snatched her against his chest, trapping her arms between their bodies. Something was different this morning. They'd been verbally sparring since their first conversation. Dax had never been sadistic like Bruno. So while the latter issued commands and took pleasure in demeaning her, Dax was happy to receive the same amount of respect he gave. Others may consider the spanking thing disrespectful, before Dax, she might have agreed with them. But damn if she didn't get a thrill when he dominated her.

"Can you take me to the bathroom before you disappear upstairs?"

"I'll come back down," he said, loosening his hold so she could put on her dress. "I just need an hour to get the place back together. I don't want you seeing what went on up there."

"It'll be my job to clean up the mess."

He shook his head. "Not anymore." He kissed her then removed his watch to put it in her hand. "One hour, you can time me."

"I'd still appreciate the chance to pee, baby, please."

"There's a restroom in the gym," he said.

The cell door was still unlocked. It had been all night. He led her through the gym to the door under the stairs, which was apparently a restroom.

He opened it up and switched on the light. She passed him to go to the toilet and lifted her dress while turning to sit. To her surprise, he was still there in the doorway, leaning against the frame, his arms folded across his chest, thumbs resting on his biceps.

"You're going to stand there and watch me?" she asked, unimpressed by his amusement.

Peeing with him in the room was no big deal, she'd done it before. But usually, he was busy with something else, not standing there watching the show.

"Yep. You might try to run away. You are my prisoner, don't forget."

Glancing around, she drew attention to the lack of exits. "There are no windows."

"You're a smart girl, who knows what plans you might have."

He didn't even believe his own accusations. Yanking her chain was growing to be one of his favorite pastimes.

"You want to watch me pee out of the pussy you eat?"

"That's right," he said, not losing that tang of enjoyment.

Relaxing to pee, she wouldn't give him the rise he was looking for. To let him know that, her eyes stayed locked to his, right up until she washed her hands. There was no mirror above the sink, so she didn't see him coming up behind her.

"I don't want to leave you in there," he mumbled onto her crown.

"You said it was important they believe you slept with that girl, and that I believe you did. You have no choice. You have to lock me in there. But you're going to find out what's going on upstairs and then release me, right? Do you want me to be pissed at you up there in front of Bruno?"

"Not pissed," he said, squeezing her waist. "You're supposed to be Little Miss Happy Slave. You should let me do whatever I want and still follow my orders. You have no right to get pissed at me."

Twisting around, she looked up at him. "Do I?"

"Do you what?"

"Do I have the right to get pissed at you if you screw around?"

He sighed and swept her hair from her face. "Babygirl, there's a lot going on that you don't understand. There's a lot of back-room family politics with some betrayal and sabotage mixed in. We're in a fucked-up situation."

"That sounds like the let-down, Dax. You're breaking up with me before we ever got started. I thought you were a fighter. If you want me, why can't you have me?"

"Like I said, it's about family."

"Family?" she said.

"You're not meant to be for me."

"Screw what they want, Dax. I'm here telling you that you can have me. Are you too much of a pussy to claim me, tough guy? Too frightened to step up and take what's yours?"

"Don't," he said, letting her go to retreat. "Don't rile me."

She followed him to the cell, where he finished getting dressed. "Why not?" she asked. "What happens when the great Dax Harrow gets riled? I've never seen it."

"If you start a fight with me, I'll end up fucking you," he said, sticking his feet in his boots. "Do yourself a favor and sit your ass down on the bed."

"I'll never understand enough to help if you don't let me in," she said without following his order.

"Loyalty is important where I come from, Minx. I'm not ready to betray my family and even if I did… You would flip out if you knew the truth and I need you playing along. You're too volatile. If you freak in front of Bruno right now…"

"You don't trust me," she said, stating the obvious, pushing him to confirm it, except he didn't.

He took her arm to pull her inside the cell. "I'll be back in an hour," he said, ignoring her statement.

Kissing her cheek was either a sign he was pissed, or

a sign he didn't want to lead himself into temptation. The door shut with a clang and locked, but she didn't bother to move from her perch leaning on the bars. She assumed he was gone until he spoke.

"I'm trying to hold this together," he said. "What I… feeling anything for you at all is a betrayal of everyone in my life. It could make things worse for both of us. If it comes down to a choice between being with you or saving your life… I'm going to choose the second."

The enormity of that drew her in a semi-circle. Despite him being bathed in the shadow by the door, she could make out the determination on his face.

"What does that mean, Dax?"

"That, if I have to, I will give you up when the time comes. Things could get a whole lot worse for you and I'm not gonna make promises about stepping in to make them easier."

"You'd let them hurt me?"

"They're going to hurt you," he said without an ounce of doubt. "They are, babygirl, and for that I'm sorry. I'll do everything I can to minimize—"

"Don't do me any favors," she snarled. "What's the point in telling me you give a fuck if you're just going to let them follow through with whatever their plan is anyway?"

"I have some pull… I just don't know if it's enough."

"You're going to try, but think you'll fail? Why bother? Is that how you think walking into every fight? Sometimes you have to make a decision, Dax. It's not always the easy choice, but you have to pick what's best for you and the people you care about."

"You're not the only one I care about."

"Do you care about them more?" she asked, filing away his admission without acknowledging or making a big deal of it. "That's the only choice. You pick them or you pick me. Own it and face the consequences."

"Interesting advice, we'll see if your opinion changes when you learn the truth."

"We'll see," she said.

They shared silence for a few seconds before he

turned and left. What else could he do if he wasn't willing to go all in for her?

She was left there, in her old quarters again. For an hour, she'd put up with it while hating every second. Dax portrayed such strength, like he was a man capable of anything he set his mind to. But he answered to others, and those others would ultimately decide their fate.

TWENTY

IVY DIDN'T THINK anything of Dax being a few minutes late. She didn't even think anything of him being an hour late. Movement upstairs along with the rumble of voices gave her a clue. Getting rid of lingering party guests wasn't always easy. It wouldn't be much longer.

Turned out she couldn't be more wrong.

Hour upon hour went by. Night came. The voices stopped, movement ceased, and all she could do was wait. The last car she'd heard was half a day ago. Was anyone still there? Was she completely alone?

Pacing was a useless waste of energy she might need later. Without food or water, there was no way to replace stores. Conserving it, she remained static.

Dax couldn't have forgotten her. Wouldn't have. Except he'd stated if it came down to a choice, he wouldn't choose her. At the time, she hadn't considered that would mean leaving her there, indefinitely. Forever. To die.

Biding her time, she hoped he would be back in the morning.

Except he wasn't. The watch he'd left behind was an ominous purveyor of time. It was the only evidence left of their joining. The only evidence he'd been with her at all. The fact that Dax hadn't come back to her was concerning. The fact Bruno hadn't appeared either was downright disturbing.

By the morning of the second day, the heat was getting to her, despite the running air conditioning. Air was one thing. Food and drink were another. She had to face the reality that something might have happened to Dax. Something that prevented him from coming back.

Had his colleagues figured out he'd spent the night with her instead of Fifi? Had Fifi reneged on their deal and told the others the truth? Maybe Dax had been removed from the equation altogether.

At almost midnight, on her second day alone in the basement cage, she was startled awake by something she didn't see or hear. Fighting the haze of sleep, the noise of footfalls descending the gym stairs filtered through. Those hurried footsteps reminded her where she was and what was going on.

Leaping to her feet, she rushed to the bars, holding them as tight as her sealed breath. The urge to call out for him was almost overwhelming. Thank God she didn't. The door opened to reveal Dax wasn't her rescuer, it was Bruno.

"Don't worry, we didn't forget about you," he said, wearing a jovial smile as he unlocked the cage.

When retrieving her in the past, he'd never been in such a good mood. Even more surprising was him handing her a bottle of water without punishment or command.

"Is everything okay?" she asked, expecting the other shoe to drop.

"Worried about us?" he asked, taking her hand to lead her out of the cell and through the gym.

Following along, she downed the water, replenishing her hydration. He took her upstairs to the living room. All hopes of seeing Dax were dashed. He wasn't there, but she wasn't alone with Bruno either. A blonde woman stood in front of the entertainment center. Short and quite flat-chested. Was the blonde Bruno's pick or Dax's?

"This is Rita," Bruno said, guiding her over to the couch to seat her in the spot usually reserved for Dax.

"Okay," Ivy said. "It's nice to meet you."

The blonde didn't speak.

"Rita is here to look after us. She'll be doing all of the chores from now on."

Looking around, it was clear the remnants of the party had been cleaned up by someone. How long had she been asleep? She hadn't heard anyone moving around. Though Rita was so slight, even stomping around using all her strength, she probably wouldn't draw attention to herself.

"Is she…?" Unsure of her own position in the household, she had no Dax to guide her. Compliant. That was the only guidance she had. Except no one was giving orders. What should she do?

"Ask your question," Bruno said, giving her some much needed direction.

"Is she here against her will?"

Suspicion cast over Bruno. "Would that be a problem?"

"No," she said. "I mean, it's not my business at all, but… well…"

"What?" Bruno snapped.

"If she's here of her own freewill, we know she'll follow your instructions. If not, she'd be a flight risk and will have to be watched at all times. That's all. I wouldn't want to leave her alone, have her run away, and let you down."

Bruno's suspicion morphed to a smile; her answer had pleased him. He believed her to be a dutiful slave, exactly what she wanted him to think.

"Rita won't be going anywhere," Bruno said. "But that was a very good observation. Dax told Mauri you were smart, he was right."

So Dax was still around, or at least still alive? Her relief was interrupted by the door opening and in he walked. Dax. Bruised around the eye. A cut above his brow.

"Master," she said, pouncing to her feet.

The outburst startled him as much as her. The desperate word had just popped out of its own accord. Perhaps some of the training had taken hold. The gesture had been automatic. Right then, it didn't matter, what mattered was her lover's bruises and the reason he'd abandoned her.

"Have you fed her?" Dax asked Bruno, tossing the door closed.

"Not yet."

"Make us food, Rita," Dax ordered, then snapped his fingers and pointed at her. "Minx, you get upstairs now."

Nodding, it was difficult to ignore the tension in her butterfly-filled gut. The fluttering reproduced so fast there was no space for anxiety or anticipation.

Running up the stairs to their room, she tossed off her dress and leaped into the shower to wash the cell from her skin. Spending no more than a few minutes there, she got out fast and took a long drink of water from the faucet.

When she got out, Dax was on the bed, pulling his tee-shirt off over his head.

"What happened?" she asked, hurrying to help him, though he didn't seem like he needed it. Bruises on his ribs made her wince, but he didn't notice them either. When he tossed the tee-shirt onto the floor, she caught sight of the cracked blood on his hands and grabbed one of them. "Oh my God, have you been fighting?"

"Any other girl says that about her man and it's a bad thing," he said. Reaching behind himself, he tugged something out of his back jeans pocket and brought it around to hold it up in front of her face. "Daddy brought home the bacon for you."

The stack of notes was larger than any she'd ever seen in one place.

With wonder and a slack jaw, she took the pile and flickered through it. "You were in the ring? I was down there in that dingy hole, and you were in the ring?"

She hit his shoulder with the bundle of bills, then tossed them into his lap and got up.

"That's ten K, babygirl."

Sinking to sit, her jaw fell again. "Ten thousand dollars?" He nodded. "US dollars?"

He nodded again, this time with a smile.

Taking her hand, he placed the fortune in her palm and curled her fingers around it. "Hide it somewhere," he said.

"Where?"

"I don't want to know," he said, holding up a hand in surrender. "It's yours."

"I'm not taking your money," she said, trying to push it onto him, but he pushed right back.

"I won more than that. I'm not leaving myself broke. It should be enough to get you by… if anything… if you need it for anything… any time."

"Why do I need ten thousand dollars?" she asked, flicking through the bills again.

"I'm telling you, it's an insurance policy, a bailout fund. If you ever want to bolt, take the money and go. No one will ever know about it 'cept you and me."

"Maybe I should invest it in bottled water and a plumbing system for my cell," she said, turning her smile on him.

He didn't see the funny side and cupped her face. "You will never spend the night in that cell again. I promise you, okay?"

She nodded. Disbelieving him was impossible when he was so solemn. "You're giving me ten grand and telling me it's okay to leave. Did you talk to them…? About us?"

Dax shook his head. "I took some of the guys home yesterday 'cause I didn't want them hanging around, asking questions, outstaying their welcome. I got tied up and met Bruno at the mansion; that's when I realized you were still down there alone. Last night."

"So why didn't you—"

"Mauri needed me to do something, then I was challenged. I couldn't… you can't refuse when the gauntlet is down."

"This is going to be some macho, convoluted excuse for leaving me down there, isn't it?"

Leaning back on her hands, she was ready to listen. Turned out, he wasn't ready to give it, her towel-clad body seemed to be distracting him. The temptation proved too much. Without permission, he untucked her towel to reveal her body to his famished eyes. From her shoulder, he stroked down over her breast to her hip.

"Every fighter has a point man, a guy who hooks the

fighter up with a gig. We call him our scout, because he does all the work figuring everything out before we get there. My guy got in touch with me 'cause a rookie wanted to challenge me. I have a rep in that circle and a lot of the younger guys try to take me on. If they win, they'd solidify their place in the arena, and their fee would skyrocket."

"Do they ever win?" she asked, already knowing the answer to her question.

"No," he said, lowering himself to suckle on the nipple he plumped first.

"How do you win? I mean what qualifies as a win?" she asked, caressing his shoulder and bicep. His hand slithered under her thigh to lift and separate it from the other. "You don't kill anyone, right?"

"Either the guy is down for ten, forfeits, or the arbiter calls it."

"Is that like the ref?"

"There isn't a referee," he said, switching to her other breast and sucking harder this time. "No one steps in to keep it fair. There are security guys who come in to break things up if a weapon is introduced, but only the arbiter can give them the nod to enter the ring. If he thinks a guy is near dead, but won't forfeit or stay down, he can call it."

"That's it? Someone has to be near dead before the arbiter calls it?"

"Sometimes a fight goes on all night," he said. Coiling his fingers around her wrists, he took her weight from them and laid her on her back. "If the audience are getting bored and the bookies want it called, the arbiter can declare a winner, but that's rare."

"It is?"

"Sure, he doesn't want to vote against a guy who could beat him to a pulp the next time he goes to his mailbox."

"He's not a fighter?"

"Sometimes," he said. "Most fighters have too many connections to be a fair judge. An arbiter is picked by the fighters' scout before final agreement is made."

Learning about his world fascinated her; seeing him hurt was less enthralling. The more she thought about underground fighting, the more questions came up.

A knock at the door interrupted her thoughts, and her lover.

"Food," he said, leaving the bed to head for the door. "I'm giving you time to eat because you haven't had anything for two days."

"Because you left me down there," she whispered just before he opened the door.

Rita, carrying a tray, tried to come in, but Dax blocked her and took the tray, closing the door in her face.

There were sandwiches and fruits laid out on the tray he brought to the bed. "Eat quickly," he said, hooking her hair away from her neck to nibble on her. "I can't eat until you're finished."

"I thought it was the most dominant in a partnership who ate first," she said, popping a cherry into his mouth.

"What I'm eating isn't on that tray," he said, sliding the tray away from between them, edging in to run a hand up between her thighs. "But if eating first will prove my superiority over you…"

Scooping up her legs, he whirled her around in the bed and lay on his chest, curving her legs over his shoulders. In the cell downstairs, she'd dreamed of food. That came second to this. Closing her eyes, she savored the satisfaction that came from his talented mouth. While he swilled from her core, she fumbled toward the tray to seek out the bowl of berries.

The press of something warm and smooth made her pause and it took her a few seconds to realize he was rolling the cherry she'd put in his mouth up and down, around her clit. Dax was good at improvising. She found herself fantasizing about what else they could do if they took this to other rooms of the house, like the kitchen.

The cherry moved south, and she sighed out her pleasure. She'd be happy for Dax to always be dominant over her, and their relationship, if it meant more of this and more of him. He said that she would never spend another night in that cell, and she believed him. As for the future of their relationship, or even what would happen tomorrow, she didn't know. So all she could do was live in the now, which at that moment was an especially blissful one.

TWENTY-ONE

THE MORNING STARTED out strange… Stranger than usual.

Snoring from the other side of the bed was typical. As were her breasts being squashed into Dax's back, her arm stretched around him. What was unusual? The woman standing at the foot of the bed.

Blinking a few times, she checked to ensure the view wasn't part of a dream. Nope, Rita really was there, in nothing but a leopard print bikini, leaning over, massaging Dax's calf.

Awkward. It sort of felt like she was in the way, intruding. She shifted her own legs away from Dax's, attracting Rita's attention.

The new roommate smiled; Ivy semi-reciprocated.

"Good morning," Rita said, massaging up to the back of his knee.

Dax moaned, but that was it, he just kept on sleeping.

"You… did Bruno send you up here?"

Rita shook her head and leaned closer to massage higher. "No. But after a fight Dax needs to work out the kinks in his muscles."

Did they have history? Dax and Rita? Asking Rita wouldn't guarantee the truth. Her lover was still asleep and useless.

Freeing her limbs, she rolled away, taking the sheet with her, leaving Dax naked. Though the good stuff had already been on show, whether by accident through the night or Rita's design

"I'm going to shower," Ivy said.

Given her supposed dutiful nature, she couldn't issue Rita orders or shoo her away. If Rita said she did this for Dax on other occasions, by the reckoning of everyone else, Ivy had no right to change that or tell Rita otherwise.

"Take your time," Rita said, climbing up to kneel on either side of Dax's feet when he sank onto his front, burrowing the pillow under his chin against his chest.

Almost unable to tear her eyes from the sight, she watched until the last possible second, then went into the bathroom to take a shower.

Although she wasn't wild on the idea of witnessing the potential progression, she also didn't want to walk in on Dax being violated in his sleep. In super quick time, she showered, dried her hair, and returned to the bedroom.

The now topless Rita was straddling Dax's ass. Didn't look like he'd moved.

"Did he wake up?" Ivy asked.

"Dax?" Rita laughed. "No, he sleeps like the dead."

"I've noticed."

The blonde's familiarity stoked a curl of jealousy. That resentment inspired an urge to lash out. Restraining it wasn't easy, it was a necessity. If she lunged for Rita as she wanted to, Bruno would hear of the tantrum. Dax had already implied he didn't trust her to keep going with the act if something happened she didn't like. She wasn't about to prove him right.

"You should get dressed," Rita said. "Bruno is on the back deck if you're looking for company."

No chance she'd leave this woman alone with Dax; not while the naked bed massage was going on. Dax wasn't awake, which meant Rita had lost the bikini top of her own accord. His muscles weren't the only stiff thing Rita wanted to be massaging.

"I'll wait until he's awake."

Rita laughed again. "He probably won't be for a while." Leaning forward, the blonde pressed her naked torso to Dax's back and began to tongue his ear.

Staying at the bathroom door, the wait wasn't too long. Dax's drowsy eyes opened, taking a second to fix on her. Those sleepy lids didn't remain droopy for long after she folded her arms and arched a brow. He must have read her question before he established his own… If she was in his line of sight, far from the bed, who had their tongue in his ear?

To his credit, he flipped over in an instant and pushed his assaulter away without asking any questions. Rita laughed and reached for him, but Dax was already halfway out of the bed.

"What the fuck do you think you're doing?"

"Having fun," Rita said.

Content Dax was awake and able to handle himself, she slipped into the closet, and dumped her towel in the hamper. The cutoffs again? Dax liked those. And hadn't put clothes out for her. Maybe…

Dax came barreling in and slammed the door.

Rage seemed to be where he had settled. "What the fuck was that?" he demanded.

"You tell me. I woke up to find her climbing all over you," she said, forgetting the clothes. "How well do you know each other?"

"Rita's been at the mansion for a while."

"She's a hooker?"

"Sort of," he said and shrugged. "She works for Mauri, does whatever's asked, but she's freelance. She can walk away at any time."

"Why would she walk away with prime specimens like you to mount whenever she's horny?"

"I've never had sex with Rita."

"That's not what she implied."

"You're gonna believe her over me?" he asked. "You could've woken me up, how long did you leave her alone with me?"

"I don't have the authority to say anything."

"You'd be happy if I left you alone with a guy sliming all over you while you were naked in bed?"

"If I'd said anything, she would know I'm not an obedient slave, wouldn't she? You can fuck whoever you want, remember, Master?"

Leaving him with that truth, she grabbed a dress and put it on the chair beside her. His hand slithered onto her hip.

She slapped it away. "No," she said, noticing his plump hard-on pointing at her. "You are not using that on me. Is that for her?"

"No! You're naked," he said, telling her what she already knew.

As he advanced, she backed up. "Uh-uh, no way. You are not bringing that thing near me. You can't get turned on by another woman and—"

"Shut the fuck up," he said, snatching her throat to shove her against the drawers. "You're waving that fucking hot body around in front of me. My cock's doing what it's supposed to."

Dipping down, he scooped up one of her legs to prop her heel on the top of the drawers as he angled himself between her thighs.

"If you wanna keep fighting after your pussy has taken her medicine, we will. Fucking you is the only way I can cleanse myself of that tramp out there."

"You feel violated?" she asked, pleased he had no interest in Rita's blatant offer.

"Yeah, so shut the fuck up and give me and my cock a break."

Sighing, she tilted her head. "Okay, I suppose just this once—"

Surging forward, he slammed into her. In shock, her whole body clenched.

He groaned. "That's right, babygirl," he said on a lazy back slide before plunging in again. "Pull me in deep, all the way."

That ecstasy, his ecstasy, made it impossible to argue with him. He could've had Rita, could've had Fifi. He'd chosen neither. He'd chosen her.

Whatever existed between them was growing, taking on a life of its own. Everything about being with him was instinctual. It felt right. Now as he slid in and out, submerging her in a daze of rapture, she could only wonder where they would end up.

TWENTY-TWO

BEING ALLOWED TO CHOOSE her own clothes was a novelty. Not something she'd ever considered it during normal everyday life.

Since having sex, Dax had become increasingly distant as they got ready. Not being Mr. Chatty Small Talk, he often didn't say much, but there was something different about that morning's frown.

"What's on for me today?" she asked, sliding on a shoe. "If Rita is here to take care of the chores, what is it you want me to—"

"I have to show you the operation."

"How are you gonna do that? Is there a secret meth lab bunker somewhere around here I haven't seen yet?"

"We're going out," he said, fastening the buttons on his jeans and walking out.

The concept of leaving this house stunned her. For a few minutes, she didn't move or speak while the idea processed, while the possibilities processed. Being out meant opportunity to run, to escape.

Except…

Freedom meant forfeiting the prospect of a future with Dax. Unless he came with her. They could leave, that day, without raising suspicion, and just never come back.

Rushing out of the closet, ready to put the possibility to him, the sight of Bruno stopped her dead. Apparently, their bedroom was shared, common space. She couldn't remember either her or Dax authorizing that. Maybe she hadn't been privy to that conversation.

"Morning," Bruno called to her as though they were a hundred feet apart rather than ten. "You're going on an adventure today."

"Yeah, I heard," she said, clasping her hands behind her back and taking her foot off the floor to curl it behind the other. "I'm sort of… nervous."

Calm. Innocent. Compliant.

"Dax will look after you," Bruno said, slapping his shoulder. "He's done right by you so far, hasn't he?"

"Yes," she said, trained to respond to all questions.

As Bruno and Dax whispered to each other, the latter reached out behind him, offering his hand. She took it and was whisked out of the room. Downstairs, there was no sign of Rita. Bruno went off towards the back deck without saying goodbye and Dax took her out the front door.

Out.

Just like that.

He led her across the driveway to a convertible in the covered car port.

He opened her door without waiting for her to get in and rounded the hood to get in his own side. The engine roared to life, and he donned his sunglasses while she still stood, staring into the open car.

Laying his arm along the back of the seat, he raised a questioning hand. "What?"

"I… I don't know, but…"

"What?" His impatience flared. "Do you think I'm gonna run off with you? Don't worry, we'll be back before dinner."

The idea he laughed at was the one she'd considered. He should laugh. If she struggled just getting into a car, how would she survive on the run?

"It just feels… weird."

"It will," he said. "You've been in that place for nearly two months."

Had it been that long? Damn. Yes. He was right. So much for not being brainwashed. Being herself with Dax gave her the impression that she'd avoided succumbing to their training. A part of her knew she wasn't allowed to leave, and that part was in charge.

Memories of the basement faded in. "I won't get in trouble, right?" she said on an awkward, self-conscious laugh.

"What kind of trouble?" he asked. "I'm your Master, remember? Your owner. Did you forget?"

"Okay," she said, still wearing the stunted smile.

With a dry mouth and shaking fingers, she took one wavering step and slid onto the warm leather seat.

"Are you nervous about being punished for leaving or worried what will happen to you out there?" he asked, bobbing his chin in the direction of the great wide world, his attention sticking to her.

"I don't know," she said. "I didn't realize I felt this way."

"It'll come back to you. No one will punish you for leaving here. I'm the guy in charge and you're with me."

"And out there?"

"Nothing I haven't faced before," he said. "Like I said, you're with me."

Why did that make her feel better? He wouldn't abandon her.

The journey started off quietly. Breaking the silence, Dax fiddled with the stereo until he found a tune he wanted to hear.

"It will take about an hour to get into the city," he said, putting both hands onto the wheel. "Just relax and enjoy the ride."

"You are a good ride," she said. He flashed her a smile, then produced another pair of sunglasses from his door for her. The sun was shining, the breeze was cool, it was a perfect California day. "Have you got any more fights lined up?"

"You are not coming to see me fight. Mauri wouldn't

let you."

That gave her the perfect opener. "Am I going to meet him?"

"Today? No. Today I'm taking you on my rounds. It's about time things got back to normal."

"You don't usually do rounds," she said. "Do you?"

"Before you I did," he said. "I have a job. I don't just sit around holding women prisoner all the time."

"That's reassuring," she said. "What do you do?"

"You'll see today," he said. "Have you ever been arrested? Any probation or outstanding warrants I should know about? Any criminal history?"

"Nothing serious," she answered. "Have you?"

"Don't be surprised if Mauri knows everything there is to know about you when you do meet him."

He hadn't answered her question, but the Mauri statement was more interesting. "How would he—"

"Mauri's family have made a lot of money doing what they do. He has the resources and connections to do pretty much anything he wants. If you filled out information for that phony job, they'll have your full name and social security number. The rest is just leg work. Most of that can be done at a desk these days."

They'd know everything. "Why would they want to know about me?"

"Because they chose you," he said. "And Mauri likes knowing everything about people he welcomes into his family. Including any trouble they bring with them."

"The only trouble I've been around recently is you."

"And they know all about that," he said, squeezing her thigh before sliding his hand further under her sundress.

"Just how much do they know?" she asked. "They know we're sleeping together, but do they know the details? How does Bruno fit into all this?" Being away from that house gave her the freedom to ask the questions she'd been too afraid to ask before.

"Mauri and Bruno have been friends for years. They worked together for Mauri's old man when they were kids. Bruno knows everything that Mauri does… just about."

"And you? How do you fit in?"

"I've been working for Mauri since I was a kid. He caught me pickpocketing him, which was amazing because I was pretty good. I'd been doing it to feed myself for years. Stealing from spectators at fights and getting in the ring to fight for money, was how I kept myself alive. Mauri caught me, pinned me down, I thought I was dead. I had no idea who he was."

"Did he hurt you?"

"Took me home with him and fed me, asked about my family, my history, and kept on asking until he knew everything about me. After that, I never left, I grew up in the mansion, not out front with the Stark boys as an official member of the family, but in back, with the household staff. They trained me up, looked after me. As soon as I could, I started to graduate through the ranks of Mauri's team."

"Doing what?" she asked.

He shrugged. "Anything he asked. I sold, I couriered, I did everything."

Being away from the house seemed to offer him a freedom too. "And now you do this?"

"I do what Mauri asks me to," he said, maybe sensing her aversion.

"Why didn't he send you out here alone to deal with me? How many other women have you beaten into submission for him? Do you treat them all like you treat me or do you follow Bruno's method?"

"You're the first. I mean it's the first time I've been involved in anything like this. I enforce a lot, and I interrogate for information, that can take days, sometimes a week. But like this, a woman? No, I've never done this."

"But Bruno has?"

"I don't know. I am trusted in the family; I know a lot of their secrets. But there's no way I know everything that's for damn sure."

"Why now?" she asked. "Why did they ask you to do this now? Why not just leave me out here with Bruno if he's more trusted than you? He's obviously more sadistic."

"You're unique from what I figure. No one has done

this before. And Bruno, I told you, he can't get a hard-on."

"So your purpose was purely sexual? You were selected because your dick functions?"

He shrugged again, still watching the road. "Best I can figure, yeah, and because they trust me. I've had Trystan's women before. The punk won't get queasy about it, you know?"

"Trystan's women?" she repeated. His jaw ticked. "What has he got to do with this?"

"Trystan's the guy you met in Vegas."

"Yeah, I know who he is," she said, picking his hand from her thigh to toss it away. Twisting in her seat, she pinned a glare on his profile. The prickle circling her spine told her there was more to this. "I figured out he was the one who wanted me snatched. But I am not his woman. I haven't even seen him for the whole time we've been out here. I haven't seen him since that night in Vegas."

"He's in Europe," Dax said. "Has been since the day we brought you here. He'll be back in a week or so."

"The deadline," she said. "The deadline for going back to the city?"

"What are you talking about?" he asked, flashing her a frown.

"I overheard you and Bruno talking. He said we were going back to the city. That after we went back, we'd be off the hook. I thought you were here against your will too, that they were forcing you to do this."

"Forcing me to fuck you? Yeah, it's a hardship."

"Dax, be serious, what is going on? I thought you were teaching me a lesson. I thought Trystan wanted you and Bruno to teach me some lesson. Just like you said about him holding a grudge."

"He does," Dax said. "He picked you because you rejected him in Vegas. It was a disrespect; he wouldn't stop going on about it."

"And the deadline? I thought by then I was supposed to have learned my lesson, that I'd be freed."

From the concern in his double-take, she was off base. Way off base.

"Freedom is…" he said. "At some time, we will get the call to take you back to the city."

"And then what?"

"You move into the mansion."

Her chest tightened and like he'd just sucker punched her, she shrank back against her side door. "No," she exhaled. "Am I supposed to service his men? Be another Rita? Follow commands?"

"No, Rita is sport, a Stark employee, there for the guys pleasure, or whatever," he said. "Everything you were told is true. You're going to live a life of luxury and privilege."

"And you? What are you going to do?" she asked. "We move into your room in the mansion and then what?"

But he was already shaking his head. "I don't live in the mansion."

Breathing grew more difficult as panic set in. "Wh… wha… why not?"

"Because I'm a grown man and Mauri isn't the only guy I work for. I couldn't live like Brad and Trystan do, in the mansion, always under supervision."

"You're going to take me to the mansion and just leave me there? What am I going to be? A homecoming gift for Trystan?"

"I don't know what I'm gonna do with you yet."

Clearly, he wasn't ready for this discussion, and it was getting away from him.

It was indefensible that she'd been kept in the dark; they'd been sharing a bed for weeks.

"You're not thinking about leaving me there," she said. "What happened to all that crap about caring for me? Didn't you mean it?"

"I meant it," he snapped. "But this isn't as easy as—"

"I already told you to make a choice," she said. "And I'd appreciate you telling me up front if that choice isn't me."

"Don't get your panties twisted up, I'm gonna figure this out."

"How exactly?" she asked, crossing her legs away from him. "And how many times will I have to swallow his spunk before you do that?"

The car jolted forward when he sped up in what appeared to be an involuntary motion. "He's not gonna lay a finger on you, and you're not gonna let him if he tries."

"Uh… forgive me but isn't that how we got into this mess?" she asked, happy to be snide. "I've been playing the role of brainwashed Manson girl in front of Bruno because I thought I was doing both you and me a favor, running out the clock until the deadline. Until freedom. I didn't even mind being your fuck-bunny. It was fun and you're incredible in the sack. Screwing you broke up the monotony between trips to my prison cell. All this time you were playing with me. You're even sicker than Bruno."

"No," he said. "Why would I do that?"

"Maybe because it would be fun to see what Trystan would do to me when he found out I wasn't as obedient as you and Bruno said? Was that the point of this? To make me so pliable you could just hand me over to him? What was your plan? Were you going to tell me to do whatever Trystan asked just to save your hide? Did you expect me to do with him all the things I do with you just because, why? I'm such a slut?"

"You're no slut. I've been around sluts all my life and you're sure not one of them."

"Don't change the subject or try to flatter me now," she said. "I want to know, were you expecting me to go to him willingly to do you a favor?"

"This isn't my ideal scenario either, Minx. Do you think I planned on falling for you?"

"What did you plan?" she asked. "To steal some woman, fuck her up as much as you could and then hand her over to that pervert?"

"No," he said. "Maybe. I don't know. Do you know how long it's been since I cared about anyone or even really cared about myself? You go through the motions… you just… you…"

"Survive?" she said and sighed, remembering what he'd said about breathing in and out.

He'd been following the orders of Maurice Stark for so long, he never stopped to consider if those orders were moral or if he even agreed with them.

"Look, the way I see it, you're fine until Tryst gets home. We'll get this worked out before he's back on US turf, okay?"

"Great," she said, not reassured. "You're not the one facing the prospect of a lifetime of rape. At least on the plus side, I probably won't live very long. I'm telling you now, I won't submit to him. No, I won't. I don't care if they get pissed at you because you didn't do your job right. I will not have sex with him, not voluntarily."

"Good," Dax said. "I don't want you to. If you ever find yourself in that situation with him, or with any other guy, you fight your damndest, babygirl. This is mine." Grabbing her knee, he dug his fingers in deep to haul her toward him. "From the tips of those toes to the roots of your hair, Minx, even that damn clever mouth."

"That's your strategy? I fight them off? Wow, Dax, you're not a planner, are you?"

"You're giving me a hard time?" he asked. "I've kept you safe and let you off the hook. I could've taken you down to that basement anytime and given up on you, but I didn't."

"While your balls were being played with, you had no reason to," she said. "Now that you're being held to account it's not so much fun, is it?"

They sped up again. Fine by her. Being stopped by the cops wasn't going to do her any harm.

"I have time," he said, maybe like he was trying to convince himself. "We play it cool and keep it together for a while longer. I'll talk to Mauri, he'll see—"

"What? That you don't want anyone else to play with your toy? He'll tell you it's nice to share, Dax. You'll do what your surrogate daddy tells you to, and I'll be the one sailing down shit creek on my own."

"That won't happen! I'm going to keep you safe!"

His outburst stunned her into silence. Five miles must've gone by before she spoke again.

"You want us to keep doing what we've been doing," she said, trying to be logical and not let fear rule. "I'm supposed to trust that one way or another you're going to keep me safe, is that it?"

"Yeah," he murmured. "That's it. Give me some time to figure this out."

"Okay," she said, their anger got them nowhere. Walking away from Dax, without giving him a chance, could be suicide. He might be her only hope. "I'll give you three days. After that, if we're not safe together, I'm on my own."

"Okay," he said. "That's fair…. You're not going to run now? Are you saying this to keep me from…?"

"From what? Tying me down?" she asked. "No, I'm not just saying this. But if you don't trust me, I have no reason to trust you."

"I trust you."

"We need to have faith or else we'll ruin each other."

"We stand together, or we die," Dax said. "Can you play the game for a little while longer, Minx?"

"My stamina is better than yours."

He laughed. "Now we both know that's not true, but there will be time to prove it later."

"If I let you," she said, wondering if they were going to turn into Bonnie and Clyde.

"You'll let me," he said. "I know how to work you now, Minx. I know your buttons."

If there was no future, hanging around for another three days could be cutting escape too close. "What we have, Dax…? Is there a future?"

"I don't want you to go anywhere," he said. "Having you around is… cool."

"Cool," she said, taking her eyes to the windshield. "Typical manspeak for not wanting to reveal too much of yourself. Fine. Let's just get through today."

"Mauri will understand," he said, skimming his hand to her inner thigh. "I'll talk to him and work this out and then we'll be together."

"And Trystan?"

"He'll be a little shit because he always is. Mauri will keep him in line."

Was that true? She had no way to know. All she had to rely on was Dax's word. Her reluctance to leave him reinforced just how much she cared about him. Fitting into life with the Starks as Dax's girl might be difficult, but she'd rather do that than try to fit into it as Trystan's girl. As far as she was concerned, that would never happen.

TWENTY-THREE

TO SHOW HER WHERE it was, Dax drove them to the Stark mansion and stopped at a broad wooden gate. Why? She didn't really know. Maybe he meant to ease her into the idea of spending time there. His offer to take her inside and show her around was a hard no. A step too far. If she went inside, there was no guarantee of getting out again.

After the brief spell parked outside, Dax drove on until eventually they ended up in an industrial area, pulling up alongside a grey concrete warehouse on a lot that appeared to be vacant.

"What's this place?" she asked when he turned off the engine and got out of the car.

"This is where we prep the product. Come on, get out."

"I don't want to go in there, Dax," she said, shaking her head. "Who is in there?"

"No one will hurt you. There's nothing to worry about, I already told you that. Come on, you have to know what we do."

"Why? Why would Mauri want me to know?"

Dax came around the car and crouched to rest both forearms along the sill of her door. "Because as far as he is concerned, you're gonna be part of the family. He wants to know we can trust you… and also thinks you're gonna be the mother of his future grandchildren. You know, the kids who'll take over the family business."

"I'm supposed to give birth to felons," she said. Opening her door, he took her hand to pull her out. "I've heard of planning for the future, but that idea takes the cake."

"Do you want kids?" he asked, leading her towards a dusty brownish red door on the side of the building.

"I don't think now is the time to talk about it, tough guy. We could get our heads blown off at any second."

He laughed. "I do this almost every day. Any guy who takes a shot at me will have his kneecaps ripped off. Trust me, these guys aren't gonna hurt me."

"That's you," she said, on alert, worried there could be a sniper or security guy ready to hate on her. "I'm just some chick they don't know."

"The guys in here aren't what you're expecting," he said, pushing open the door to guide her inside.

The air was pungent, noise rattled somewhere in back, but it was the humidity, or rather the lack of it, that was most startling. The space was almost empty. He led her into another room, some sort of recreation room. Couches. TV. Thankfully, no human beings.

"We're at the end of a shipment. Everything was taken out last night. We'll get another one in a few days. There's been a hiccup, Mauri's taking care of it."

"Thank God, I was worried for a second," she said, absorbing the details of the well-kept space.

Air conditioning, check. Fridge, check. A series of mismatched couches and a wide screen TV were the cherries on top.

It was on the tip of her tongue to ask if they could hang out there together, alone. Just be two people anywhere except that beach house.

That idea was crushed when a far door opened, and a guy came in. Tall but quite weedy, he wasn't the hardened thug she'd been expecting… like Dax said outside.

"Hey, Zoom," Dax said. "You need to be quicker off

the mark. You don't have company back there, do you?"

Wow, so severe. That wasn't quite anger, more like an aloof authority, carrying an unspoken warning. Just like in Vegas when he'd threatened her without using negative words.

"No," Zoom said. "Wasn't expecting you today… I called Serg."

"Why?" Dax asked.

Judging by that reaction, Zoom's statement obviously held some significance she didn't understand.

"One load wasn't picked up," Zoom said, scrutinizing her until she caught him. His attention flicked to Dax… for a few seconds anyway. "Who is she?"

"Not for you," Dax said, leaving her to go grab Zoom's shoulder. "Who was it? Who missed it?"

"I… I gave Serg the details, you said, you said to report to him while you were… I would've called you but—"

"Yeah. Yeah. I'm here now. I'm on it. It's just sitting back there?" Zoom nodded. "Okay. Don't do anything until someone is in touch. Stay here."

Dax let go of his shoulder.

Zoom tried to smile. "I never go anywhere else."

Apparently unamused, or maybe just uninterested, Dax stalked back to snatch her hand, tugging her outside and back into the car.

"What is that place?"

"It's where we cut the coke," he said, starting the car again. "It's cut and packaged there. Supposed to be picked up once it's divided."

"But someone didn't pick up their share?" she asked as he maneuvered out of the industrial site. "Why would that be?"

"Someone is lazy, scared, or dead, those are the only three reasons."

"Maybe someone kidnapped them, and they're stuck somewhere having a whole lot of incredible sex." After glaring, he drew his gaze away. "Serg works for Mauri too?"

"Yeah, he's an okay guy, once you get to know him. He's been running things for me while my attention has been split.”

“You trust him?”

Dax glanced at her and then the road. “With the product and the job,” he said. One side of his mouth turned into a smile. “Not with my girl.”

“Another rapist friend,” she said. “You know you should really expand your social circles, baby.”

“What do you think you are?”

“I’m a refreshing experience,” she said. “I haven’t decided yet if you’re beyond redemption.”

“If I got any better, babygirl, you’d have died and gone to paradise.”

He didn’t often make jokes and they were almost always dry, but she was getting used to his more laid back, friendly side, though that didn’t stop her from goading him.

“If I was in heaven, you wouldn’t be the one delivering me to ecstasy,” she said. “I heard you’ve already paid your room deposit in hell.”

“A room with a view,” he said, flashing her a smile. “I might be able to talk to my peeps if you’re interested in the lot next door.”

“I thought I belonged under you. Is that lot still vacant?”

“Not anymore,” he said in a deep purr that made her tingle.

The implications of that kept her mind busy on the ride to their next destination. Compared to where they stopped, the isolated warehouse was a day at the fairground. Dax came around the car to take her out of it like before only this time without the pep talk.

Graffiti covered old, rundown apartment blocks. Broken windows and fences surrounded groups of youths in baggy pants wearing cheap jewelry, hollering at each other. This was what the “*wrong side of the tracks*” looked like.

Instead of going in the front of the single-story structure, Dax took her through an open chain link fence beside it. Moving around the back, they passed a barking dog tethered to a side wall and a group of heavy, tattooed men on a picnic bench. Nothing affected Dax; he carried on through a swing door at the rear into a short corridor.

"Dax," she said, hoping for an explanation.

He didn't stop, just reached back and locked his fingers between hers. As reassurance went, that was pretty good. His long, calloused digits with their bumps and scars were so unique that their thickness provided security. That comfort lasted until Dax shoved aside the strands of a metal-link curtain and entered a room full of jeering men, sitting around a long table.

The smoke-filled room reeked of cigarettes and greasy food, but as soon as Dax walked in the half dozen men shut up.

"Boss, man," a blond at the head of the table said, getting up.

Though her eyelids flared, she managed to restrain her instinctive urge to gasp. The blond guy had to be nearly seven feet tall.

"The place is falling apart, Serg," Dax said. "What you doing sitting on your ass when we've got a hold up at the factory?"

"I'm on it."

"Doesn't look like it," Dax said, unintimidated by the man's bulk.

Each guy present didn't look like the sort to mess with. They were varying grades of thug and hooligan… she recognized one or two from the party at the beach house.

The phone in Dax's back pocket rang. While striding into the corridor, probably for privacy, he dug out the cellphone and answered it, leaving her alone with the goons.

Her initial discomfort dissipated when a thug on the right spoke. "Are you the boss's new slut?"

Okay, so she was supposed to be the submissive slave in front of Bruno. But Bruno wasn't around, and it just wasn't her nature to show weakness when confronted with attempted intimidation.

"If I am, you're taking a risk in speaking to me like that," she said.

"The boss has never brought a girl here before," another said.

"Insult me," she said, "and you'll find your nose embedded in the back of your skull, not your ignorance satisfied."

The men can't have been expecting such a reply, if they'd expected any at all.

When Dax came back in, they were still suspended in silence. "I'm getting out of here," he said. If he noticed the atmosphere, he said nothing about it. "Get to the warehouse. I'll join you there in a while, Serg… Minx."

She took his statement of her pet name as an indication to follow when he departed. In the outer corridor, he linked their fingers again and held them against the small of his back.

Outside, they passed the inked group without a word and eventually got back to the car.

"What was that place?" she asked.

"Out front is a bar where most of the guys hang. It's a good place to check if you're looking for someone."

Didn't really seem that she'd ever be looking for any of Mauri's guys, but whatever. "Where are we going now?"

"Back home," he said.

"You said you'd go back to that warehouse. You already drove me out here and now you're going to drive back to the beach house just to drop me off with Bruno? It seems like a long way to—"

"Bruno's on his way to the restaurant where Mauri is eating."

"So I'll be alone? Is Rita there? What will she and I talk about? The only thing we have in common is your cock… I suppose we could talk about that for an hour or two."

"She's never seen my cock," he said with a flourish of a smile.

"She did this morning."

"Never before that," he grumbled.

"So you screwed her in the dark every time?"

"Are you jealous, babygirl?" His hand was back up her dress at her inner thigh. "I've watched Bruno put his hands all over you."

"And Trystan too," she said, curious as to how he felt

about the night they first encountered each other.

"We're not going back to the beach house. There's been a change of plans. Mauri wants you at the mansion."

All good humor drained out of her, no doubt the color did too. "What? Why?"

"He didn't say, just told me to take you over. He's not there. You won't have to meet him."

"Is Trystan there?"

"No, he's still in Europe."

"Are you sure?"

"Yes. I told you he won't get his hands on you. Trystan's the most unreliable SOB you'll ever meet. We could get lucky and he stays in Europe another six months."

"Or he makes a surprise return."

"I'm never gonna leave you anywhere you'll get in trouble."

Having faith in him consoled her. "I have a talent for that. I could get myself in trouble in an empty building."

"No doubt about it," he said. "I'll take you to the mansion. Someone will show you around and give you a room… I don't think they'll put you in Trystan's suite."

Revealing vulnerability churned her stomach, so she tried to disguise her anxiety. "You haven't shown me your place, maybe we could go there first."

"When Mauri calls and tells you to do something, you don't do anything else 'first,' you do what he's told you to do."

"To the detriment of anything else you might be doing? What if we were having sex?"

"I probably wouldn't have answered the phone."

"Probably?"

"Depends how well you were doing. As long as I'm entertained, you've got nothing to worry about, babygirl."

"Entertained," she said, twisting to lean closer and press her palm to his fly. "Is that how you usually feel when we're in bed together?"

Using sex to manipulate him seemed dishonest, given their confessions of feelings, but her options were limited. Tracing her lips on his neck, she urged her breasts against his solid arm while rubbing her body on his in time with her hand kneading his now stiff cock.

"I'll drive the scenic route to the mansion if you get your mouth down there," he said, turning his head to kiss her quickly.

"I'll get my mouth down there and you can fuck my throat 'til you fill my belly, if you take me to your place."

He let her keep going for a few more seconds before moving her hand from his groin to curl her fingers around his knee.

"We have to go to the mansion. If we go to mine, they'll come over to find out what's going on."

"So we tell them," she said. "Isn't that what you said you were going to do?"

"Yeah. I haven't had a chance to talk to Mauri in private. I have to talk to him first."

"You'll get that chance, if you take me to yours."

"Mauri won't come over. Even if he did, he wouldn't be alone… there's a line of respect, babygirl—"

"Don't say babygirl to me in that patronizing tone," she said, extricating herself from him, putting space between them. "I thought you were a man, Dax. I guess I've been sucking too hard on those balls you carry around in your pants, I seem to have more 'nads than you do."

His fingers worked the steering wheel, squeezing and twisting around it. "If you start running your mouth, you're gonna make me do something we'll both regret."

"I'm not afraid of you, Dax. Do your worst. You are the fighter here."

Accelerating hard, he fired the car into a rest area and slammed on the brakes, bringing the vehicle to a lurching halt.

"Have I ever hit you?" he asked with a snarling rage.

"Well, the spanking—"

"That's a different thing and you know it. Have I ever hit you in anger?"

"No," she confessed, confused by his fury. "But you just said—"

"Let's get one thing straight, babygirl. Just because I don't do things your way doesn't mean I'm a coward. I do things my way. You better get damn used to that, fast, because from now on that's how you'll be doing things as well."

"I'm supposed to sit tight in this guy's big house because you tell me to? And if his men choose to take turns with me—"

Seizing her wrist, he wrestled her back to his side. "I've already told you that won't happen."

"Let go of me!" she protested, trying with her other hand to get him off her, to no avail.

"I've claimed you, Minx. You're mine."

"Claiming me in private means nothing," she hissed. "Are you afraid of them?"

"Mauri's given me everything and now I'm stealing his son's girl."

"You're ashamed of your feelings for me?"

"Yeah," he said, without hesitation, his scowl deepening. "I vowed to never screw Mauri over and that's what I'm doing. So, yeah, I'm gonna send you in there and you're gonna play along just like you have been. I'm not gonna embarrass Mauri. We're gonna handle this right and give him the respect he deserves. That way, when I tell him what's going on, he might be open to the idea of not forcing you to be with Trystan. Mauri shouldn't be inconvenienced just 'cause I can't get the scent of your skin off mine, or that vision of your goddamn smile out my head."

"Because he's not the one who has done anything wrong, we are," she said not meaning a word of it, which she figured Dax knew except he didn't hint at acknowledging her sarcasm.

"Yeah. We are. This was never supposed to happen. It's not Mauri's fault touching you makes me wanna slam the door and lock us up alone and naked all day. It's not his fault that whenever you look at me with that goddamn unimpressed pout I wanna go out and find myself a no-bell, no-forfeit fight. I'm a guy always in control. That's what Mauri knows. I've worked hard for him, I have. I'm the problem-solver, not the problem-creator and you, Minx, are one major head-fucking problem! One I could do without!"

"Do you love me, Dax?"

His grip loosened with the jolt that question gave

him; his adrenaline was coursing. "You looking for a fucking ring?"

"No, but this is a rough call for you. From what you've said, this situation could rip your family apart. You'll have to dishonor the man you consider your father to be with me. If you're not sure you love me, then is this worth it?"

Her question could backfire, but it should give him some clarity, which might push him into action.

"So if I don't plan to keep you forever, what? You'd rather marry Trystan?"

Marry? That's what this was about? It didn't matter. She'd fight so hard, no way she'd live to see the altar.

"I don't want to cause conflict in your family if you're going to dump me in six months," she said. "That's just moving the problem down the road. Then I'm the bad guy and I've lost any hope of protection."

"You won't get the chance to fuck around with other dudes," he said. "It's my job to make sure that—"

"What does that have to do with—"

"The only thing you could do to change this is fuck around. I won't let that happen."

Her question wasn't about sex. "Do you love me? Don't tear your family apart and ruin your life unless you're sure. You'll only end up resenting me."

His face hardened, but his eyes left hers. In every passing second, she prayed he was accepting his feelings for her were deep and true.

"If you love me, we have to get out of here now," she said, linking their fingers. "We don't have to go back to that place, we can't reason with the illogical." It was illogical to assume she would marry Trystan without putting up a fight. Why did the Stark family believe she would? They were too used to getting their own way. "Let's not walk into another of their prisons, I might not get out of this one, Dax. Baby, let's just go… please?"

"No," he murmured. His eyes crept back. Stony and cold, they littered ice across her. "Mauri's gonna listen. This is gonna work out."

Thrusting the car back into gear, he screeched away

from the rest area, sending a scattering of loose chips firing up behind them. Their speed grew in time with her anxiety.

"Where are we going?"

"The mansion," he said, his focus fixed out the windshield.

"But… if we go in there—"

"We're going in there," he said. "You're right. If you force me to betray him and leave with you… I will end up resenting you for forcing my hand. Mauri gave me a job, to get you to the mansion, and I've never let him down yet."

"You're not letting him down," she said, swamped with the dread of panic. "We didn't intend for this to happen and—"

"And I'm gonna explain that to him. Mauri will get it, he will."

Who was he trying to convince? "Why do you need them so much?" she asked, witnessing his determination rise. "Why can't you walk away with me?"

"Because they're my family. Mauri didn't have to feed me, train me, and watch out for me, but he did. He's a good guy. You've never even met him, you don't know him, not like I do."

"I'm scared, Dax. I don't want to go in there and never see you again."

"You will see me again. You're gonna keep playing along, just like you have been. You're a good actress."

"Implying what?" she asked. "Are you accusing me of lying about my feelings for you?"

"Maybe. Best way to save yourself, right?"

"You don't believe that. Are you scared of loving me? Is that why you cling to them? You can't really believe I don't feel for you, I do, Dax. It's no easier for me to admit that than it is for you to admit it to me." The closer they got to the house, the faster her words came. "Please, Dax, I do, I love you. I don't want to go in there, I want to get out of here with you. Please, Dax, baby, please don't take me in there."

They turned the corner and drove through the already open mansion gates, silence fell.

Pressed to the back of her seat, she dug her nails into

the leather by her thighs, frozen in futile terror of what was to come. Part of her couldn't fault Dax for not trusting her completely and being torn in his loyalties. If he had dropped Mauri in a heartbeat, she'd have questioned how deep Dax's respect for Mauri went. And how long Dax's loyalty to her might last. Despite that, she couldn't forgive him. He would leave her there to her fate, whatever that may be.

Past the tall, swaying trees and the lawns, which were being watered by an immense sprinkler system, she saw a large white house accented with deep red and dark grey. When Dax stopped the car in the long portico, she immediately jumped out. She didn't get far, he caught up with her by the trunk.

Grabbing her arms, he slammed her down on the searing metal using his bent body to restrain hers. "Where do you think you're going, Minx?" he growled into her hair. "You're going in there to be a good girl."

"No," she huffed, spitting out her hair and turning her head to rest her cheek on the trunk. "I won't. It's over, Dax, I trusted you for too long."

"You've got no choice," he snarled into her ear, using his pelvis to lock her in place. "You disobey them, ruin my rep, big deal, that's not what you should worry about. They'll fucking torture you if you disrespect them. Do you remember being starved and dehydrated? They'll beat you, might even rape you... you remember what that kinda fear is like, don't you?"

"You're a fucking jerk!"

Undulating his hips, he rubbed his erection on her ass. "That anyway to talk to the man you love?"

"I didn't mean it," she sneered. "You were right, I was using you."

He laughed. "No chance. I know that you meant it, Minx."

Clamping her wrists in his hand, he pinned them at the small of her back and lifted her skirt to coil the fabric around her imprisoned hands.

"No," she said. "No, don't think about—"

The first smack silenced her. She gritted her teeth for the second.

His body bowed over hers, covering her bare derriere. "You've got to stop misbehaving."

"Don't you dare put your hands on me again you sonofabitch."

"The girl who loves me will take what I give," he growled, smoothing his palm down her ass to slip two fingers into her panties, to stroke her clit in circular motions.

She squeezed her eyes closed, trying to prevent the rush of blood to her pussy.

"You love it, babygirl, and you know you do. No one else can make you feel like I can. You're ruined for every other guy. You'll do whatever I say and still beg for your reward."

"Go fuck yourself," she snapped.

"I plan on fucking you, again and again because you are my girl, Minx," he said through clenched teeth. "How many times have I told you to trust me?"

"You can't ask me to do that when you're dumping me here."

"You're going in there to keep your mouth shut. I'm not bored of you yet; I want more of you. You're going in there to wait for me."

"Wait for you?"

He flipped her over and pulled her to her feet to cart her toward the door.

As they approached, it opened. He yanked her against his side. "You're going to wait for me and you're going to trust me, understand?" he whispered.

Looking over her shoulder, their eyes met. The ferocity he returned was calm fortitude. With him at her back and the thugs coming out of the mansion, she had little choice except to accept his terms.

The grip on her arm was swapped from Dax's hand to another man's. With a last glance back, she was swallowed up by the Stark mansion.

There was no going back.

TWENTY-FOUR

FOR TWO DAYS, Ivy speculated as to what was going on behind the scenes. Much of the grand mansion was still a mystery. On arrival, they led her up one side of a double staircase, took her to the back of the building and put her into a bedroom containing an oak sleigh bed. An upgrade from the foam mattress in her cell.

But no freer.

A princess in the ivory tower; alone and waiting for rescue. She had her own shower room and Rita brought food, other than that Ivy saw no one.

Late on the second day, Rita came to her room again, this time with Serg in tow.

"We're going upstairs," Rita said. "Mauri wants to talk to you."

Serg and Rita took her out of the bedroom, through corridors, presumably to wherever Mauri was located. At last it was time to meet the Great and Powerful Oz. Her fizzling anticipation didn't know whether it was rooted in fear or excitement.

Without word from Dax, all she could do was maintain the façade of obedience. The dream scenario was Dax speaking to Mauri about their feelings. Maybe this meeting was the reprieve. By tonight, she could be back in Dax's arms, safe in his apartment.

If their last conversation was a barometer of where their relationship was headed, it was as likely Dax had chosen Mauri Stark instead of choosing to be with her. In that scenario, her future would be bleak. Dax once told her she'd never win against him if they were on opposing sides. Unfortunately, that was probably true.

She, Serg, and Rita stopped at broad double doors, Rita opened one but didn't go inside. Serg urged Ivy forward.

Inside the large office, Brad sat at the desk, addressing two men sitting opposite him. There were men at the window too. Three of them. One of whom was Bruno. He and the man closest to him stopped talking to look at her while Serg closed the door at her back.

Dax. Dax was the third man. Opposite Bruno. His back to her, he hadn't seen her yet. Did he know she was there?

Dashing over, she made sure he'd notice by falling to her knees at his side, as Bruno instructed her to do. The asshole could think that was her motive. In truth, she needed to confirm if her ally was still her ally. She didn't care that the men in the room laughed, she looked up, waiting for Dax to look down, which he eventually did.

"Get up," Dax murmured.

She rose.

"No, leave her down there," one of the men guffawed, "see what else she'll do."

"Ivy."

Turning toward the voice, Brad came toward her, hand out. Without touching him, she looked at Dax.

"It's okay," Dax said with a roll of his eyes.

She gave Brad her hand and he raised it to kiss the back. "You guys can excuse us. We have family business to discuss."

The men began to file out and Dax went right along with them. Ivy watched his every move, but he didn't look at her again. A compulsion to join him, to stay at his side despite their cross words, overwhelmed her. Except while Brad held her hand, she had no choice except to stay put.

"Would you like something to drink?" Brad asked when everyone was gone. She shook her head. "There's no need to be nervous. You're part of the family now. You've proved yourself."

A door at the back of the room opened, in walked a tall man with dark grey hair and a suit that matched. With a confident air, he went to the desk as Brad led her to the chair opposite. As they got closer, she noticed white flecks through the grey hair and his equally grey eyes.

"Ivy," the older man said, offering her a hand. "I am Maurice Stark."

Brad handed her over. The men exchanged a look, then Brad evaporated from the room.

"Please, take a seat," Mauri said after he let her go.

Keeping her eyes front, she backed up until her calves hit the leather chair and she dropped into the seat.

"It's a pleasure to finally meet you," Maurice said. "I have heard a lot about you. You are just as beautiful as I have been told."

From this friendly manner, she guessed Dax hadn't said anything about their relationship.

"Thank you," she whispered.

"Do you know why you are here?" She shook her head, not wanting to reveal what Dax told her. "My son, Trystan, wants you to join the family. Formally. You have seen some of what we can offer. The Stark family are very successful. We own a dry-cleaning firm and a haulage company. As you can see from where we are, we live comfortably. Bruno assures me you will be happy to accept our invitation, is that correct?"

What Ivy needed was time alone with Dax to find out if there was a plan. If not, she was on her own. If that was the case, all bets were off. Whatever happened, she'd find a way out of there by any means necessary. Not that she'd been ignoring chances to escape. Her windows didn't open, and her bedroom door was constantly locked. Every time, she checked, just in case.

The life of a Stark wife would be one of extravagance.

She would never have to worry about paying a bill or being alone or in trouble. Still, that wasn't enough to offset being Trystan's wife. The trade wasn't worth it. He wouldn't be a good husband or a good father, and he wouldn't treat her well. She would sacrifice luxury for principle, because there was no better reason.

In that moment, she wasn't in a position to say any of that to Mauri. As deep inside the dragon's lair as one could get, there was nowhere to run to, so she went with plan B.

"I… I do what my master tells me to," she said, portraying herself as weak and vulnerable, lulling him into a false sense of security.

Never hurt to give a guy like Mauri an ego boost either. Men like him believed in their powers of intimidation.

"Your master?"

"Dax."

"Ah," he said. A broad smile adorned his face. "You like him?"

"I must admit, I've… I've been a little lost without his direction over the past couple of days."

"But you will do as he tells you?" Maurice asked, peering closer. "If he instructs you to join the family, you will?"

"He is my owner," she said, blinking a couple of times, managing a meek smile. "I want to make him happy."

"Good. That's excellent," Maurice said and stood up. "That is all that I wanted to hear from you, Ivy. You can go back to your room now."

Springing to her feet, she nodded once, and went toward the door. Being allowed to return to her room along gave her a chance at a quick getaway.

Except she wasn't. Serg waited on the other side of the office door. He took her back to her bedroom, locking her safely inside. Where was Dax? Could she believe he would find a way to get to her?

TWENTY-FIVE

ONCE HE FINISHED up with Mauri, Dax anticipated going home. As he pulled on his helmet and kicked away the motorcycle stand, he glanced up and there she was in the window. Ivy. Right there. Almost within reach.

It was too tempting an opportunity to pass up.

Setting the bike back on its stand, he shoved the helmet over one of the handlebars and stalked back up the stairs, determined the conversation wouldn't last long.

He wasn't allowed to touch her anymore. That didn't mean he couldn't grab the bag of things cast aside by Bruno from the beach house and stop by her room on the way out.

Having grown up in the house, it was familiar. Her room was in the staff section. In a quiet, not heavily trafficked area. No one guarded the bedroom. No one had to. The Stark mansion was secure. Any attempt to get out of there alone without being noticed would fail, especially when she didn't know the layout, not like he did.

In Mauri's office, her skin had been pale and her spirit dampened, but there was no doubting her fire still burned. She had fight in her, and damn if she wasn't hotter than he remembered.

Picking the bedroom lock took no time at all, just as

locking it again on exit would. If he wanted to go downstairs and get the master key, he could, but he didn't want to waste time.

Opening the door, he strode in, dropped the bag, and kicked the door shut behind him.

She gasped and whirled around, then sighed. "Geez, Dax, you scared me," she hissed.

"Have you been visited at night by anyone else?" he asked, suddenly concerned he hadn't fulfilled his duty of protecting her as promised.

"No," she said. "That's why you scared me."

The satin night gown thing she wore hung on lace straps and was short enough that he could admire the length of her legs.

"Are you going to give me shit?" he asked.

"I should," she said. "You brought me here, you left me here... I thought..."

"What did you think?"

"I didn't know what to think, Dax. You let me see who you are, and I fell in love with that man, but... then you throw up the shutters and become what they want you to be. What they made you to be. I don't want to be with that man. I want to be with the man who won't let go of my hand all night. I want to be with the man who turns me over his knee when I piss him off. A guy who'll kiss and caress me all night, who makes me feel valued. All I've ever wanted is to belong somewhere. I realize now that it's not about where, it's about who."

He'd expected anger. She was definitely hurt and maybe confused, but she wasn't the only one. She came over, raising her arms as though to put them around his neck.

Capturing her wrists before they got there, he held her forearms together, keeping their bodies apart. "We can't do that," he said.

Being with her, kissing her, was what he wanted to do. But if he let her lay those lips on him, he'd lose control.

"If you're not here to have sex with me, why are you here?" she asked, shaking her hands free from his.

Sensing her becoming defensive, he had to defuse the

ticking bomb, or they'd end up in another fight. He didn't have the time to soothe her after, or the inclination to appease her. Okay, so maybe he didn't mind appeasing her. That did things to him that he always had time for. The after was one thing, the during was something else. If she started screaming bloody murder, and he was caught there, they could both get into serious trouble.

To put her at ease, he reached for honesty, and was surprised by how easy it came. "Because you're damn beautiful and I can't keep myself away... Come here." Grabbing up the bag, he caught her wrist and tugged her toward the bed. "Lie down."

"Are you kidding?" she asked. "You won't let me touch you, but you want me to get on the bed?"

"I want you to get naked too," he said, shirking his jacket and tossing it aside. "Come on, babygirl, let me have some fun."

"What does that mean?" she asked, slipping the lace from her shoulders to let the satin shimmer to the floor. "You want to torment me into frustration and leave me hanging?"

She crawled onto the bed, giving him a bare ass view, he shivered as he licked his lips. Not touching her would be the toughest thing he'd ever done. He knew how perfect the glove of her body fit his, and how the slick heat of her clamped around him when he took her to climax. He'd never experienced anything like it.

Dumping the bag on the bed, he unzipped it. "Lie on your back and relax." She rolled to her back, lying horizontal on the bed, from one side to the other, and pulled her knees up to let her legs flop apart. For a moment, he forgot his own name. "That's just perfect," he said, still unable to take his eyes from her pussy.

"Dax, we need to talk. I told them that I'd do whatever you said, but—"

"We'll talk when I'm through."

"Through with what?" she asked, watching him draw the pink, metallic, bullet-shaped object from the bag. She clamped her legs together. "What is that?"

"Just relax," he said, taking his place on the bed

beside her.

Lying on his side, he touched the tip of the toy to the inside of her knee when she loosened her muscles enough to let them part by an inch.

"I don't want you to…"

He turned the base, the gentle buzz it emitted silenced her words. Very gradually, he traced the cool metal down the inside of her thigh, letting the vibrations loosen her up. When the leg closest to him relaxed onto his, the contact was almost enough to shatter his resolve, despite the denim barrier of his jeans keeping flesh from flesh.

"Does that feel nice?" he murmured, and she nodded. "Close your eyes."

She did as told. The thump of blood rushing into his dick began to ache. Telling himself that he had no intention of using it, he unfastened his jeans for a little relief… though not the right kind of relief.

Taking the smooth stimulator to the apex of her thighs, he used it to separate her folds and circle her entrance. "How does that feel?" he whispered.

"Mm hmm," she said, nodding her head, tipping it closer. "Kiss me, Dax."

"No," he said, resisting her attempt to find his lips. "I can't fuck you, babygirl. I'm sorry."

"You can," she breathed in a hardly audible whisper. "Please, Dax, I want your dick in me."

"Don't talk."

If she said much more, or asked too many times, he would give in.

Of their own volition, her fingers curled around his cock. As quickly as he felt the urge to remove her digits, it abandoned him. That neat, smooth palm of hers felt too good wrapped around him. Those delicate fingers stroked him with such strength of entitlement he dipped down on instinct, lowering his lips toward hers. Only a centimeter from their goal, he stopped. He wanted to fuck her. Fuck. Goddamn. He wanted to fuck her. But he couldn't. If he did, he'd never leave, never leave this room or this woman.

Sliding the vibrator through her slit he pushed it into

her clit. She arched, purring against the pleasure it delivered.

"That's nice," he said. "Your beautiful face, that happiness, that delight, that's what I needed to see."

"I need you," she said, squeezing him tighter in her fist, working her hand up and down. "Break the rules, Dax, come on."

"I want to see you come," he said, letting the buzz almost leave her.

On her squeak of protest, he circled her clit and took the toy back to her opening to slip it just inside.

She gasped, her face contorted. He'd never been so jealous of a stupid piece of metal. It felt nothing at being inside her, yet that was where his own bliss existed. Observing gratification pass over her face, and her hand clasp her own breast to tease her nipple, the pulse in his dick kicked up. His hips moved in time with her fist, matching how she bobbed up and down against the toy teasing her g-spot then drawn out to stimulate her clit.

Both climbed toward the peak of their pleasure, he turned up the vibrator as she sucked in a breath, panting and writhing, getting closer and closer. Increasing her grip until when her orgasm hit, she yanked on him, making it impossible to maintain his composure.

She screamed out his name, her hips braced up in a fixed seizure of tightened muscles. His convulsion of climax roared into shore, he reared onto his knees and grabbed her hair to angle her head.

"Open," he demanded.

She turned her head to comply, letting his seed spill onto her tongue while she rode through the aftershocks of pleasure. With himself in hand, the tip of his cock bounced on her lips as he finished the jerking to ensure he'd emptied all of himself. In a haze of endorphins, she swallowed him down, her tongue coming out to lick the last buds seeping from him.

Spent, he lay with her, and despite his previous words, he gathered her naked body against him, holding her through her own post-coital harmony.

Their peace was too good to shatter. Unfortunately, reality crept over him. That shouldn't have happened. And she was loud at the end. Someone might have heard them.

"I'm having breakfast with Mauri in the morning," Dax said. "Alone. I'm going to talk to him."

"About us?"

"Yes," he said. "This can't go on anymore. He has to know that... the wedding isn't gonna happen."

When she turned, he loosened his embrace so their eyes could meet. "Do you mean that?"

"I won't let Trystan have you," he said, stroking her hair from her face.

"Will Mauri let us be together?"

He took a long breath. The truth was, he didn't know how Mauri would react. He'd never let the old man down; disappointment was an experience he'd been spared.

"He's reasonable, so I sure hope so."

"And you'll come back for me?"

"By tomorrow afternoon, I promise," he said. "You won't spend another night in here alone."

If he didn't leave then, he never would. Logic didn't make kissing her head and climbing off the bed any easier.

"You're leaving already?" she asked, pushing onto her elbows.

The sight of her naked body, with the vibrator still rolling loose beside her ass, was almost too tempting to resist. Why the hell was he leaving such a fucking perfect picture? He had to stop admiring her or he'd never walk away.

"I'm gonna come back," he said, doing his jeans again and retrieving his jacket from the floor. "Sit tight for one more night, babygirl."

She nodded and smiled. That kind of trust was rare. He'd never expected to witness it, let alone have it entrusted to him.

"We're going to be together, Dax, aren't we?"

"Damn straight."

Locking her in felt wrong, but they had to keep up appearances for another night. At home he'd think more about what to say to Mauri. He had to believe Mauri would listen to reason because if he wouldn't... the choice was just unthinkable.

TWENTY-SIX

BY THE TIME BREAKFAST rolled around, Dax was amped and more than ready to have the conversation. He was going to get his girl today, no two ways about it. He couldn't leave her locked up anymore. She trusted him, he couldn't let her down, he wouldn't. Watching her get married to Trystan would tear him apart. For his own reasons and the pain it would cause her.

Feeling resentment toward Mauri was new. He didn't like the way it built up inside. Seeing his girl hadn't eased the torment. All it did was remind him of what she'd been through and his role in her ordeal.

"What's eating you?" Mauri beamed over the breakfast table. "You've done an excellent job."

"I have?" he asked, his mind elsewhere.

Obviously, Ivy made a good impression.

During her conversation with Mauri, had she been resigned to her fate and fully intending to marry Trystan or was it another fake out?

"The girl is magnificent. Eager to do anything to please you."

"She is?"

What the hell was wrong with him? Where was his

head?

"Yes," Mauri said, pushing back in his chair. He'd never seen Mauri display such open happiness. The smile on his face was unique to the point of unsettling. "She will marry Trystan providing you tell her to, which you will. At the moment, she is dependent on you. We can wean her from you to Trystan. All you have to do is make it clear you want her to marry Trystan."

"About that…"

Mauri carried on. "Trystan will be home tomorrow."

That startled him. "Tomorrow? That's earlier than planned."

"Yes," Mauri said. "But he and the girl have to get the marriage license together in person. So he'll get back tomorrow, they'll pick up the license tomorrow or the following day and be married by the weekend."

The smile. The joy. No, elation. Maurice Stark was beyond thrilled. He hadn't known it was possible. If he said anything about his feelings for Ivy, the exuberance would turn to anger. When Mauri was angry, someone paid the price. If Mauri chose to be angry at him, he could take it, but the anger wouldn't be aimed at him.

Mauri would believe Ivy had manipulated him; that he was just a dumb schmuck to fall for it. More than that, Mauri would discover Ivy wasn't quite as brainwashed and compliant as he'd been led to believe.

If there was one thing Maurice Stark despised, it was being made a fool of. Disrespect was an enemy. Didn't have to look far to find where Trystan got his grudge-habit from, or rather who. If the Minx got the full force of Mauri's wrath, there would be no way to counter it and protect her.

TWENTY-SEVEN

THE LONGEST DAY of her life had started out like normal, with Rita delivering breakfast before Serg brought the treadmill into her room. During her workout, her focus on the door was so absolute, she ran twice the normal distance.

It would open. Dax would come back for her.

Luxuriating in the shower after her exertion, she fantasized about Dax joining her, telling her everything was taken care of, that they could celebrate being together under the hot spray.

She'd drawn every task out, killing time, waiting.

Still. No Dax.

Books and DVDs in the entertainment center struggled to hold her wandering interest.

Dax would come.

He would.

Dax said breakfast with Mauri, right? Shouldn't that be at the beginning of the day? Maybe he meant brunch.

Lunchtime came and went. Maybe Mauri rescheduled, pushed the meeting back due to something unforeseen.

At three o'clock, her bedroom door opened. In her haste to leap from the bed, the book she'd been reading was tossed aside.

The burst of expectation was met with disappointment. No Dax.

"You're wanted downstairs," Rita said. "What are you wearing?"

She glanced down at the strapless white sundress. Funny how she'd put it on with such hope that would be the day Dax would take her away from the madness.

"Why do you care what I'm wearing?" she asked, digging her ballet pumps out from under the edge of the nightstand to stick her feet in them.

"You need something that's quick and easy to take off," Rita said. "Come on."

That didn't sound good. Rita was already leaving, Ivy hurried to follow her out anticipating that... yes, Serg was there to accompany them to wherever they were going. Mauri's office was upstairs. This time they went down, so no Mauri?

Maybe Dax was waiting for her. She stayed close to Serg and Rita, eager to reach their destination. Disappointment had been difficult to fend off all day. Optimism was her only choice. Believing in him was her last chance.

When they went through a heavy door, she held her breath in anticipation of what would be waiting on the other side. What she didn't expect in the first-floor space was an array of full-length folded out mirrors standing behind two unknown women.

"You are the bride?" one of the women asked. "I'm the seamstress, I have to fit you."

"Fit me for what?" Ivy asked.

The door closed, sealing her in with these women.

The second woman rounded the portable mirrors. The swish of material sent a corkscrew of dread and alarm twisting under her itchy skin. The two women beamed with joy and pride and didn't seem to register her anxiety.

"Your dress!"

The second woman brought the gown into view and held it up in triumph. "It's just beautiful, you made a fantastic choice."

The swathes of white silk and lace bugged her eyes. She hadn't chosen anything. Someone else had chosen the dress, just like someone else had chosen the groom.

"We'll help you on with it," the first woman said. "We have lingerie for you to try as well. You can make a selection today. I hope you're not modest, though with a figure like yours, why would you be?"

As she slipped out of her clothes, the women paraded lingerie in front of her. She did her best to be civil but couldn't imagine they missed her hostility. For some reason, they spent an age doing her hair; styling it in long, large curls and using half a can of hairspray to keep the diamond tiara in place.

In what felt like a blink, she was wrapped in the dress. The ballgown style had a tiered skirt and a tight corset that clenched around her breasts and hung on capped sleeves. It was a beautiful dress. No one could deny that. But it wasn't her style. The dress screamed "look at me!" She'd be happier as the casual observer rather than the center of attention.

"We're supposed to take some pictures," one of the women said, pulling out a makeup case and carefully applying some liner, shadow, and mascara.

"Pictures?" Ivy asked while the woman worked. "Why would you need to—"

"Mr. Stark wants to see how you look in the gown," the second woman said, fastening earrings into Ivy's ears and hooking a necklace around her neck.

One pulled her this way, while the other pulled her that. Trussed up like a model at a beauty pageant, the pressure mounted. These women were probably used to gushing brides happy about the prospect of being gussied up.

For her, the whole experience was uncomfortable; she didn't like being preened like a Barbie doll. Dressing up and looking good was fine, when the choices were her own.

Resigned to the fact these women had a job to do, she let them finish with the make-up and accessories and then stood static while they oohed and ahhed.

"Perfect," one of the women said.

What was that glaze in her eye? Was she about to start

crying? Sheesh, she was sensitive. In her line of work, she must see dozens of women in wedding gowns all the time. Maybe the tears were part of the sales pitch.

"I'll get the camera," one woman said, hurrying for the door.

"No," said the other. "The veil! What about the veil?"

"Did you bring it?"

"It's in the car. One person can't carry it alone because of its length. The last thing we want is for it to be soiled or torn this close to the big day."

"Oh yes, yes, of course," the first woman said and snatched Ivy's hand to give it a pat. "You wait here, we'll get everything we need and be back in a jiffy."

They rushed toward the door together.

"Oh," the second woman paused while the other opened the door. "Don't sit down, the dress will crinkle."

Once they were gone, her first impulse was to plant herself on the floor. The petulant act would wrinkle the dress, but she didn't care. She didn't care about the dress, or the wedding, or anything else the Starks had planned for her.

"Take it off."

Inhaling what could be her last breath, she spun around so quickly that the dress swooshed. Lurking in the shadows of the far corner was a figure. A person. If he hadn't come into the light just then she might have been afraid.

"Dax."

"You heard me," he said, sounding far from pleased. "Take the damn thing off."

Marching over, he grabbed hold to wrestle her to the side of the room, trapping her flat against a tall dresser that stood to the height of her shoulder.

The hard wood bit into her, but Dax persisted, pinning her to it. "Why are you doing this?" she asked. "What's going on?"

"I told you to take it off!"

Forcing her to turn, he tugged at the lace holding her corset together. With him not being the most delicate of men, the rip of material was inevitable. He freed the lace and yanked at the corset that hung on its sleeves.

Holding the garment to her chest, she struggled around to try and look at the damage. Not that it mattered, the dress was already ruined. "What have you done?"

With his grip biting into her upper arms, he jerked her around to face him. "You were right," he said and shook her. "Goddamn it, Minx, okay? You were right!"

And he didn't sound happy about it. "Right about what?" she asked, trying to reach for his jaw.

In his agitation, he recoiled from her touch. "I couldn't do it. I couldn't tell him. He'll never accept this. Mauri will never accept us, not like this. He'll never understand."

Oddly, she wasn't surprised. "You came here to tell me we're over or to help me go free?"

Hope budded. Swallowing, she couldn't let it flower, not until she knew his intentions.

"There is no free," he said, looming closer, his eyes narrowing to slits. "You will never be free."

"You want me to marry him?" she asked, struggling in his grip. "You actually want me to walk down that aisle, just to make your life easier? So that you don't disappoint your surrogate daddy?"

"I'm here to take you with me," he said. Absorbing the shock, she stilled, even her breathing stopped when his hand slid onto her cheek. "I'm here to take the chance of losing everything I've ever had."

"Oh, Dax—"

"But I don't want you to be confused," he said, snatching hold of her again, his grip even more ferocious. "It isn't freedom. You will never be free. If you walk out of here with me today, then you belong to me, forever. You won't be allowed to leave me. You'll be my girl. Mine. I won't let you marry him. I won't watch you walk down that… If we leave here, now, you will do what I say. Everything I say. With me, you are completely mine, every part of you. Every single breath that you take will belong to me. You are obligated to be at my side. You've gotta accept I will never let you go free."

"Dax," she said on a sigh, allowing herself to smile.

"It's their prison or mine, your pick, Minx."

"Yours," she said. "Being with you is no prison. I want to be with you too."

Encouraging him to ease off, she let the corset fall and went to work loosening the skirt. When it collapsed to the floor like a sunken soufflé, she balanced herself with the help of his arm to step out of it. Her own clothes were on a chair, just a few feet away. When she tried to go to them, Dax wouldn't let her go.

Glimpsing at him, curious about the delay, the answer came in the form of a bulge in his jeans.

"You're going to have me forever," she said. "There's time for that later. But the dress women—"

"Right," he said, letting her go to shove her away, making a point of averting his eyes.

Flattery kept her smile in place, but she wasn't wrong about wasting time.

Tugging up her strapless dress, she shoved her feet in her shoes and was back at his side in a flash. "How do we get out of here?"

"The same way I got in," he said and seized her hand.

In the darkest corner was a smaller door to a short corridor with a stairway at the end. They didn't go as far as the stairs, he took her through a narrow door, definitely not any kind of official entrance, and there in front of her was a motorcycle. Outside. They were outside.

"You're kidding," she said when he handed her a helmet.

"Do you want to leave or debate mode of transportation?" he asked, throwing a leg over the bike. "Showing up on anything other than my bike would raise suspicions. Come on, Minx…"

Her apprehension evaporated. Determination flooded in. He was right. If the choice was getting on that bike with him or going back inside… well, that wasn't a choice.

"Take that shit out your hair," he said.

The tiara, which probably cost a small fortune was quickly cast aside to the pebbles at her feet. She yanked on the helmet, got on the bike and wrapped her arms around him. In the hot, humid air of the day, the seat was hot under her ass.

She quickly tucked her skirt under her thighs and hung onto him again.

The bike roared to life. The deep vibrations racked her body, warming and arousing her in unexpected ways. Again, something to explore later. Holding herself tight against him, she closed her eyes as they sped away from the mansion toward a back gate she hadn't known existed.

Relief poured through her. Not just relief at being freed from her prison, but relief that Dax had come to understand the depth of his feelings for her. Now they could be together and make what they had real.

TWENTY-EIGHT

THEY RODE FOR LESS than an hour before pulling off the highway, traversing residential and commercial streets to a storage area. He parked the bike and unlocked a garage while she stood eagerly anticipating what might be inside.

"Are you okay?" he asked, stooped ready to open the door.

Her grin burst. "Yes, Dax, I'm… God, I've never felt like this."

Straightening up, he frowned. "Felt like what?"

"So… exhilarated and high and… it's like… to finally be free and to be with you—"

"I told you, you're not free," he said, backing her up against the outer wall of the storage unit.

"Oh, all that stuff about being your prisoner, it's just foreplay, tough guy. I want to be with you. I don't feel like a hostage with you. This is what I wanted all along. I wanted us to be together, and now we are."

Sliding her hands up his chest, she was about to beckon a kiss when he spoke again.

"You haven't asked the rest of my plan."

"Plan?" she asked, loosening. "I thought the plan was to get out of there and we did that."

"It's not that easy," he said. "We have to…"

"Have to what?"

He backed off and opened the garage door, revealing a car inside, among other things. Wheeling his bike past the car, he stowed it at the back, covered it with a tarp, then went to a metal cabinet to stuff supplies into a backpack. When that was in the trunk, he drove the car out of the garage to stop it beside her.

"Get in," he said, leaving the car to lock up the garage again.

"Do you have a plan?" she asked, having assumed they would leave the state and the Starks behind.

"Yes," he said. "My plan is to make sure they can't follow through with their plan."

"Okay," she said, sliding into the car, grateful to find a bag of snacks on the seat and shades on the dashboard. "I thought we already did that by leaving that house?"

"No," he said as he got back into the car and showed her a key.

"What's that?" she asked, retrieving a sandwich from the bag.

Breakfast was the last time she ate and even then, her hunger was for her man, not food. Now she was famished.

"The key for the storage unit. No one else knows this place exists. If I'm not around, if something happens to me, everything you'll need to disappear is in there."

That didn't bode well. She didn't like the suggestion he wouldn't be around but watched him slip the key into his wallet and return it to his back pocket. Taking off from the storage compound, they got back on the interstate. She munched on her sandwich, happy to finish it and one of the bottles of water before getting back to their conversation.

"I'm ready," she said, stowing her trash in the door compartment.

"Ready for what?"

"For you to tell me the plan. So out with it, what's the plan? Why isn't leaving enough?"

"Because I don't plan to stay gone," Dax said. "We're going back."

"When?"

"Tomorrow, maybe the next day."

If she could jump out of the car and run, she probably would. "What? Are you serious? No! I am not going back there."

"Yeah, you are," he said. "I'm not gonna run forever. After we show Mauri we're serious about this, he'll understand. He'd be pissed if we did this for the sake of sex. That'd make him think we're playing for sport, you know? You won't have to go back to the mansion. I'll take care of it. I'll go over there and show him I'm not cross-eyed over a dumb tramp I'll forget about next week."

"No! I don't want you to go there either. If you do and he's pissed at you, God knows what he'll do."

"I've been a part of his family for twenty years, Minx. I'll make him see sense."

"You couldn't make him see it this morning. Either he vetoed us being together or you didn't tell him at all. What makes you think the situation will be any different in a day or two? If you needed more time—"

"There was no more time," he said. "Trystan is coming back tomorrow. Mauri wanted you married by the weekend. Why do you think there was a sudden rush with the dress?"

A chill went through her. Married by the weekend, to a man who'd assaulted her, to the cause of her abduction, her imprisonment, her violation. Shit. Dax cut it close, he'd got her out just in time. Gratitude overwhelmed her.

"Why will the situation be different in a couple of days? Trystan will be mad, won't he? Mauri might not listen to you and if Trystan's in his father's ear… We could end up with more trouble—"

"It doesn't matter," Dax said.

"How can you say that?"

"Because he'll have no choice. He'll have to accept that we're together. That you're mine. He won't be able to do anything to keep us apart, he'll know we're serious."

"How will you prove that to him?" she asked. "And where are we going now? What's the point in leaving if we're just going back?"

"We have something to do."

"Okay," she said, settling against the seat. What could she do to deter him? If he had a plan that would work, there was no point arguing. Dax knew the Starks. The alternative was going back to marry Trystan. "What is this important thing we have to do?"

"There's only one way to guarantee Trystan can't marry you."

"What's that?" she asked, thankful he'd found a silver bullet.

"You have to be married already, before he gets the chance."

"I have to be married," she said, repeating the words that took a few seconds to sink in. "Dax… what are we going to do?"

"We're getting married."

If lightening struck her, or aliens landed in front of them, she couldn't have been more surprised.

Sitting up straight, she fixated on his profile, but he ignored her shock. "We're what?"

"It makes sense," he said. "I don't plan on letting you go. If you're married to me, they can't force you to marry him."

Logic wasn't the number one reason to get married. Then again, most men didn't propose in the way he just had either. "We're getting married?"

"Yeah."

"Just like that. We're getting married?"

"Why not?" he asked. "You got a better offer on the table?"

"What?"

"You're twenty-nine, you've done all your screwing around, right?"

"Dax!" she exclaimed, otherwise lost for words.

"I told you it straight up. You chose my prison. That meant agreeing to doing things my way. You're going to marry me. You have no choice."

She couldn't figure out if his cool manner was

arrogance or dominance. His suggestion—which wasn't really a suggestion at all—didn't offend or repulse her. In fact, it made a lot of sense. But before she could agree to it, one thing had to be certain.

"Do you love me, Dax?" she asked, causing him to glance her way.

Sunglasses shielded his eyes, concealing them from being read. "After everything I just did, you have to ask me that?"

"I want to hear the words. I need to hear your answer," she said.

Just as she'd been taught to vocalize her answers at the beach house, she needed to hear him admit it aloud.

"I wouldn't have risked losing everything if I didn't."

"That's not saying it. That's implying it. I've known you for two months, Dax Harrow. I know there's nothing you're afraid of. So if you can't say three silly little words—"

"Goddamnit, babygirl, of course I love you!"

Satisfied, her lips curled, and her hands settled in her lap. "You're such a romantic, Dax," she teased. "I'd never have pegged you as the mushy type."

"Shut your mouth and get over here," he said, opening his arm to her.

She slid across the seat and kissed his jaw, then his cheek, prompting him to turn his head and steal a lip kiss too. As her head rested against his torso, his arm settled around her.

"We have a few hours until we hit Vegas, get some sleep. You'll want to be fresh when we get there."

"Won't you want to sleep?" she asked, nuzzling closer. "I can drive some of the way if you want."

"It's not that far," he said. "I can handle it. You handle the wedding night."

Which meant he wanted her to do the work in bed later. After all he'd done, that seemed like the least she could do.

"Okay," she said, turning her face to his body and closing her eyes. "But if you need me to keep you awake, let me know."

"I will."

She listened to him inhale her hair and her smile crept up again. That morning she'd woken up with a glowing hope that had faded as the day got older. She could never have imagined her day would turn out this way.

TWENTY-NINE

VEGAS WAS THE SAME. It was the only constantly-changing, exactly-the-same city she'd ever experienced. While the buildings and attractions transformed, a buzz existed in the air as you moved down The Strip. That buzz was always the same.

Dax parked at a hotel and checked them in under a pseudo-name, he'd then given her ten minutes to freshen up. She tried to tempt him into the shower with her, but he'd been insistent they'd have time once the deed was done.

Either he was nervous and getting cold feet, so he wanted it over with, or he was eager to have them bound together. Picking up the marriage license took no time at all. Somehow, Dax had everything they needed, including her ID. Brought, or rather stolen, from the Stark place.

He'd quizzed her on whether it was genuine, or if she was using an alias. Her name was real. Given he was the one involved in criminal activity, it seemed if anyone had a right to suspect the other of duplicity, it should be her. Except Dax made such a big deal about their marriage being completely legitimate that she couldn't really doubt him.

Vegas might be cliché to a lot of people, but it was where they met. It meant something to her. They went to a little white chapel advertising a drive-thru window. Dax drove past that to park. Apparently, they were going inside.

The night was bright neon, the city alive with possibility. Droves of people came hoping to win the jackpot. She was probably the only person in the whole state of Nevada who felt like she'd brought her jackpot with her.

She reached for the front door handle of the chapel, but Dax caught her hand and drew her away from it. In the shadow of the awning above, he pushed her to the wall and rested an arm at the side of her head. His own bowed head gave her cause for worry.

"What is it?" she asked. If he had decided he didn't want her, she might be forced to go back to the Starks', back to Trystan. "Dax?"

Cupping his face, she brought his stooped form up enough for him to meet her eyes.

"I need you to say yes," he murmured.

"What?"

"I… I did something stupid, before I came to get you at Mauri's."

"Something stupid?" she asked. "What did you do?"

"It seemed like a good idea… at the time, but… now I'm embarrassed to admit I did it." He got on the defensive. "And I'm not the type of guy to be embarrassed, I mean fuck the world. I don't give a shit what anyone thinks—"

"What was her name?" she whispered, sick at the thought of him touching another woman. "Where did you meet her? Did you go looking to get laid or did it just happen by accident?"

Warring emotions overcame her. Technically, until today, they hadn't been together. Except at the beach house, he'd admitted caring for her. Was it all bullshit? She wanted them to have a future and wasn't sure she had the right to be sick and angry. But technicalities didn't erase the mental images of him being intimate with another woman.

He frowned. "What?"

"Was it after you were with me last night?" she asked. "I told you to fuck me. You could've had me. Why would you—"

She stopped talking when he sank down in front of her, fumbling something from his inside pocket. Unsure what it was, she was about to ask when he popped open a box and showed her a single solitaire diamond ring.

"I bought you a goddamn ring, Minx. I didn't fuck around on you."

In surprise, her jaw relaxed. "You bought me a ring," she said, trying not to swoon because his scowl told her he wasn't happy about this humiliation. Covering her mouth with both hands, she concealed her soppy grin. "Oh, baby."

"Just say yes or no so we can get this shit over with," he grumbled, lowering his attention to the ground.

He'd be worried someone would go by, catching him in the humiliating position.

For all his stomping and strutting, he did respect her; this act proved that. "I say yes," she said. "Yes, yes, yes."

He took the ring out of the box and handed it over so she could slide it on. As he stood, it looked like he was about to toss the box away. Grabbing it before he could, she leaped up into his arms and kissed him.

Oops. Big mistake. Within half a beat, he had her pressed to the chapel wall. Crouching, he ran a hand down her thigh and lifted it up to coil her limb around his hips. There was a busy street just behind him. They were at the main entrance to a no doubt frequently used establishment. Trouble was that their passion had been contained for too long; her kiss had reawakened his want.

"Let's get this done," he said, backing off, holding her hips. "Once this is done, that's it, right?"

"Yes," she said again, admiring the ring on her hand. "Let's get married, Dax."

"Then no one can take you away from me."

Was that his biggest fear? He led her into the chapel as she considered the gravity of that. The details didn't matter, Dax dealt with everything. All that mattered was he hadn't let go of her hand; his determination hadn't wavered.

Once they were joined in matrimony there was no way Mauri could make her marry Trystan. Not only was Dax protecting their love, he was protecting her freedom as well.

This could cost him his family, everything he'd ever known, but he'd made the choice, just as she'd told him he would have to. He'd chosen her. That put it on her to ensure he never regretted his decision.

THE WEDDING WAS QUICK. Their eyes and hands remained locked throughout the ceremony. When it came time to say "I do" neither of them hesitated. This was it. They were man and wife; she was Mrs. Ivy Harrow.

Romance wasn't completely lost on Dax, though tradition certainly was. As was proven when he opened their hotel room door and strode in, preoccupied by other things. Ivy didn't step over the threshold. She caught the door before it closed then cleared her throat.

Dax glanced back, still stuffing the keycard into his wallet. "What?"

"You're supposed to carry me."

"Why?" he asked, tossing his wallet onto a side table. "What's wrong with you?"

"There is nothing wrong with me," she said, torn between losing her patience and laughing. "It's tradition."

"What's tradition?"

"That the groom carries the bride over the threshold. Come on, Dax, you're not getting the best start with your husband duties."

"No?" he asked, swaggering back. "Maybe I'll gain points when I perform other duties."

Crouching down, he tossed her over his shoulder and hoisted her into the hotel room in the most un-traditional way possible. When he threw her onto the bed and kicked off his shoes, she decided tradition could go to hell… except the consummation part.

"Maybe I'll play hard to get," she teased.

"You don't have a choice about putting out," he said, yanking his tee-shirt off over his head.

"I don't?"

"No."

"Because we're married now?"

"That," he said. "And until we've consummated the marriage it can be annulled. We don't want Mauri pulling that one, do we?"

With the deed done and out of the way, he was much more relaxed. It was nice to see him in his comfortable self. In front of Bruno, and the other mobsters, he was cold and aloof; it suited the image. With her, it was a different story.

Like being back in his bedroom in the beach house, where they could tease and argue, they were safe with each other. The masks came off, the games ended, and they could just be. Dax gave her safety. All her life she'd existed in an unsecure state, never sure when or where the next paycheck was coming from… or if she'd have enough money to pay bills and eat the next day. Now in this love, none of that mattered. Every challenge would be faced together, she finally had somewhere to belong.

"I guess I have no choice," she said.

Sitting up, she pushed down her dress, elevating her hips to shimmy out of it. Ironically, she was still wearing the wedding day lingerie from earlier. When she lay back down on the bed, Dax remained standing. As much as she enjoyed basking in his flattering gaze, she worried about how the day's events had affected him.

She had no interest in imprisoning him. "If you're having second thoughts…" she said, wanting him to know he could still back out.

"No," he said, loosening his jeans. "I'm wondering why we didn't do this a month ago."

"Because someone was sure it would work out in the end," she said, holding up her arms to invite him down onto the mattress with her. Still, he didn't come. "It turns out that you were right, just maybe not in the way that you thought."

"We've still got a long way to go."

"I know," she said, sitting up to pull down his jeans, hurrying things along. "Let's not worry about that tonight."

Taking hold of the thick appendage hanging before her, Ivy kissed his head and ran her palm along the length of his shaft. Taking him in both hands, she licked and sucked at his penis until the beads of his pre-cum were dripping out onto her tongue.

"You keep doing that and I'll end up consummating with your face," he murmured.

Ducking down, he picked her up and raised her higher until her head landed on the pillows. He came down on top of her, already massaging her breasts. It didn't take long for his fingers to be joined by his lips. He sampled her nipples from every angle and with every part of his mouth.

The heat of climax teased at her. She gripped his waist, bringing her legs up and around him, as high as she could, hoping he would take advantage of the invitation. But he shifted his position higher to kiss her mouth.

Goddamn, she could feel his cock poking and stroking her abdomen. What a tease. "Just fuck me, Dax," she exhaled, dragging her nails up and down his back.

He kept on kissing her mouth. Frustration clenched her teeth, barring his tongue's entry.

"You're tense," he said, pressing moist lips to her cheekbone, then her ear. "Are you nervous, babygirl?"

He knew exactly what was wrong with her because he was the one doing it. "You said I could handle tonight's action," she said, remembering his words in the car.

Trying to push him onto his back was futile, she'd never be able to overpower him and needed him to choose to submit.

"Maybe later," he said. "This here is a husband's job."

On the night they met, if someone asked her if Dax was the commitment type, she'd have bet her life against it. Now knowing about his two decades of dedicated work with Mauri, and about how long he'd been frequenting fights on the underground circuit, she knew different. This guy was determined and loyal, and was happy to throw himself into what he loved full force.

"We're actually married," she said, gazing at the ceiling beyond his shoulder. "We're married." How could she be married? It would take some getting used to. She jabbed the heel of her hand into the pressure point of his shoulder to get his attention. "You're not gonna screw around on me."

"Was that a statement or a question?" he asked,

teasing her nipple between his teeth.

"A statement. If your dick thinks about sniffing around any other pussy, I'll chop it right off and carry it around in my pocket. I mean it, Dax. I don't care how big and hard all your friends think you are, you are not allowed to—"

"Geez," he said, abandoning his work on her body to look her in the eye. "Married ten minutes and the bitching has started already. Keeping you happy is gonna be a full-time job, Minx. I'm not interested in going out there to chase tail."

"Good," she said, broadening a smile, tracing the stems of ivy on his bicep. "Not many guys would do what you've done for me tonight, Dax."

"I haven't done anything yet," he said, prodding his engorged head into her folds. "You keep waffling shit, puts a guy off his game. In fact…"

He didn't finish the thought. Instead, he rolled off the bed with his usual catlike finesse and pulled something from one of the closets. Rising onto her elbows, she tried to see what he was raking around for. Whatever it was, he hid it behind his back on his return to the bed. The view of his intimidating erection nodding at her as he walked ran her curiosity out for a second.

Straddling her hips when he crawled over her, she expected immediate, intense action. "What have you got for me, big boy?"

"It's not for you, it's for me."

Intrigued, her eyebrows slid upward but were quick to snap back down when he brought his hand around to reveal a strip of black cotton elastic. He unwound it with a single flick, doubled it then tied it around her head, gagging her.

"That's much better," he said, gripping his cock and stroking it while his other hand petted and pinched her breast.

Grumbling behind the gag, she tried to point out he might need her mouth, but he couldn't decipher her words. When his lips curled with satisfaction she relaxed, sinking into the bed.

"There's a lot of shit coming, and we don't know how it's gonna go down," he said, dipping to bite her nipple so hard she squealed at the jolt of torturous pleasure.

Her whole body seemed to be connected by strings. Every fiber linked to another apparently unrelated point through invisible rods of rubbery steel that conducted the current of his touch like zipping electricity. Each caress made her want to scream and purr at the same time.

"There's one thing I'm sure of, one thing you should worry your little head about while I deal with the rest of the crap going on in our lives." She couldn't ask him what because of the gag, waiting for an answer was her only option. "Every night your bed, and your pussy, are going to be filled by me. I'm going to fuck you every night and every chance I get. You don't need that spirit of yours to defend yourself anymore, Minx. It's mine. Every part of you is mine. The spirit that loves to spar with me and spit out at the world, that belongs to me now too, and I want you to use it. You're going to use it to think about sex, use it to pleasure yourself on my dick every time I give you the opportunity."

Again, she tried to grumble, instinct drove her to fight, to tell him she didn't need to be looked after. She wanted to yell she would be at his side to deal with any shit that might come their way. He wasn't out in the world alone anymore. Except with the gag in place, nothing but grunts and mumbles came out. Despite trying hard, all she succeeded in doing was dribbling on herself.

Dax might have taken it the wrong way. He laughed and bowed to lick the saliva trail at the corner of her mouth, then raised his mouth to her ear. "Does that turn you on, babygirl? The idea of dedicating your life to my cock make you drool? That makes your husband very happy, I'm gonna make sure you get constant access."

Tumbling off her body, he stole a pillow from under her head to prop up his own then bucked up to make himself more comfortable. After, he scooped her body over his, kicking her legs apart. She didn't have a chance to straddle him comfortably or find her own place. Intent, he jerked her body down while thrusting upward; he plunged in so deep, the intrusion bruised her sensitive cervix.

But he kept on going, holding her at the perfect height for maximum offensive impact. He fucked his way up into her. Driving faster with each push until her legs became so weak, she struggled to match his fervor.

Her alive body webbed with pain and equal all-encompassing pleasure; she almost forgot the muzzle over her mouth. Each time he stabbed into a new, responsive spot, she squealed or called for him.

Their eyes met. The chill of those ice blues brought her to instant crashing climax. Inhaling a breath so deep the gag was sucked into her mouth, she fought to huff the syllable of his name. Her love forged on with his relentless onslaught, desperate to reach his own summit.

He shoved her down, putting her on her back between his thighs. Searching for her bearings, she wasn't anchored until he was above her, charging into his bliss again. Every inch of him occupied her and then… he stopped, locking his eyes to hers, he stayed still.

Mumbling, she tried to move, fearing what might be wrong.

He locked their pelvises and just stared. "I'm gonna fuck you all night."

That didn't mean he couldn't come. The longer he remained there, the more she was convinced he was pacing himself. Whether it was a test of stamina or restraint didn't matter, she wanted him to have completion, to be wild and crazy and hers.

"I'm the last man who will ever be inside you. Mine is the last dick your pussy will ever swallow."

Wow, that possessive reality was… Wriggling, she wanted to kiss him, to reassure him and to remind him her pussy would be the last his dick would occupy too. But his hand slithered between them to torment her clit, undulating his fingers while gently rocking his pelvis.

Shit… that felt too good. All coherent thought abandoned her. Dax was all that filled her head, her heart, and her existence. This man had chosen her, married her, because he loved her so much, he had to protect her from being taken by another guy.

The pulse of his throbbing dick sent her over the apex of pleasure again and this time he couldn't resist. She clamped around him so tight, he couldn't move, she wasn't sure either of them breathed. As his slick seed pumped into her, she felt every quiver of him.

Holding onto the moment, she didn't move. That was exactly where she was meant to be, exactly where she belonged.

THIRTY

THEY ORDERED ROOM SERVICE, watched some bullshit TV, and had sex again. After that, they went down to the casino for a while. Every time she caught a sideways glance at her husband, the moment seemed unreal. How could he belong to her?

Anyone on Dax's trajectory cleared the path so he could walk in a straight line without interruption. Yet, he was oblivious to the intimidation he exuded. He strode on the same way he would on an abandoned beach or a crowded sidewalk. His superiority was more than just a case of his height and formidable form. His expression was clear, he didn't scowl, yet managed to maintain an intensity that made him inscrutable.

He existed in a bubble. No one could penetrate it; no one would dare enter the personal space restricted behind the invisible barrier. It was as if he had his own transparent security team ensuring no one could touch him. No one except her.

For some reason, he'd accepted her into his bubble while keeping others out. Not that history mattered, they were married, no other woman would be allowed into her husband's inner bubble because she'd make sure he never needed anyone else.

After a few drinks and some flirting at the bar, they returned to their hotel room. Tomorrow could prove to be a big day if they went back to California. That was a big "if." She planned to take another swing at talking him out of it.

"Your legs working this time?" Dax asked, opening their door.

"What?" she asked, strutting past him, giving him no choice except to hold the door open for her.

She went all the way into their big bedroom with the massive bed they'd test drove already. Although it wasn't exactly a suite, the bathroom was big enough to have a double shower cubicle and a Jacuzzi tub. Dax's initial offer was the GoldSpring, in fact it was the first place he stopped when they got into town. The last thing she wanted to do was face her former colleagues.

"Tradition isn't my thing."

"No white picket fence in our future?" she asked.

Sitting on the end of the bed to slip off her shoes, she'd need to buy more heels if the rest of her life was going to be spent on Dax's arm. Being so much shorter meant when they were walking together, she couldn't kiss him or whisper in his ear without first having to tug on his arm like a child looking for the acknowledgement of a parent.

"Get ready for bed," he said, striding past her toward the bathroom.

Leaping to her feet, she seized the moment to appeal to his better sense. Soon they'd be engaged in the physical and talking would be the last thing on their minds.

"My aunt lives in Florida," she said.

From the peculiar look on his face when he stopped to peer at her, he didn't follow her line of thought. "So?"

"So…" she said, creeping toward him. "Maybe we could go visit her. Go to the beach and laze in the sun all day."

"We're in the fucking desert now," he said as she curled her fingers around his wrists. "And I've seen you in a bikini enough to last me the rest of my life."

"We could find ourselves a topless beach. I could leave the bikini at home."

He frowned. "Why would I want you parading around in front of other guys? If I want to see your tits, I snap my fingers."

"Oh, it's not as easy as that," she said. "You forget I'm not your captive anymore, there's no basement to relegate me to. I can be as mouthy as I want."

Sidling closer, he lowered his face. "Didn't I prove earlier that I control that mouth? I can prove it again right now."

"No way," she said, her smile slinking upward. "I'm wise to you now, big boy. There's no way you'll be keeping me quiet again any time soon. Next time you screw me, I'll scream until my lungs bleed."

"Screaming is acceptable, your back talk is not."

"You married a woman with opinions," she said, elevating herself on her tiptoes. "Opinions that you just love to contradict."

"Because they're wrong," he said. "Keep your opinions to yourself and spend more time listening to mine."

"Why would I do that?"

"Because mine are the ones you should be spouting. My opinions should be your opinions. A wife should toe the line that the husband orders her to."

Although he delivered the instruction with sincerity, she laughed. No way could he think a piece of paper would make her Miss. Compliant. Bruno hadn't managed it with physical abuse and imprisonment, Dax wouldn't achieve it with marriage.

"That so?"

"You're gonna be a good wife," he said, touching a fingertip to the underside of her chin.

"So I should meet you at the door with a kiss after a hard day of enforcing? Have your favorite meal cooked and on the table every night?"

"A blowjob at the door and a good spanking over the dinner table is what I expect."

"Why would I need a spanking," she pouted, hooking two fingers into his jeans belt loops. "I might have been a good girl."

"Unlikely," he replied, walking himself forward and forcing her to walk backwards until he'd barged her all the way to the bed. "You've already been bad, and we've only been back in the room five minutes."

"I have?"

"I told you to get ready for bed, what does that mean?"

"I don't have any jammies," she said, squeezing out from the restricted space between him and the bed to cross to the closet that contained his sports bag. "I don't suppose you packed me anything to wear."

"Your birthday suit is all you'll ever need in my bed, Minx. Stop the fucking teasing and get over here."

Having already tugged out the sports bag, she opened it to see if he had packed any clothes for her. The item on top broke the spell of seduction. With a rubber band looped around to keep them together, the large stack of a dozen or so zip ties stared up at her. She took them out of the bag and held them up.

"What's this?" she asked, rising from her crouch. "Why do you have these?"

"They're mine," he said as though they held no significance.

"Why did you bring them? Why do you need them on our wedding night?"

Until that moment, she'd never considered herself an insecure person. The unfamiliar wave of timidity and doubt came with a flourish of nausea.

"I plan to be prepared," he said.

"For kidnapping other women or—"

"None of your business," he said. "I do what I want, I don't answer to you."

"No, you answer to the man behind the curtain. You have all this respect for Mauri Stark, but all I see is him sending you out to get your hands dirty. I haven't seen him do any work at all. He's taught you to subjugate and—"

"What's Mauri got to do with this?"

"You feel the need to go back there, to apologize for falling in love with me! I mean how dare you think that—"

Storming over to her, Dax snatched the zip ties and tossed them onto the bed. "We're going back there, if I have to sling you into the trunk of the car and—"

"No! We are not going back to those people. I was dragged to that beach house and held prisoner so that you and your buddy could make me into the perfect wife for… for him. But it didn't turn out that way, did it? You were my only sanctuary," she said, uninvited tears burned her eyes. She gritted her teeth and carried on, determined not to let them fall. "I don't know why you let me in, why you chose to show me mercy when—"

"Ah, hell," he said, turning his back on her. "Don't get into all that romantic hero bullshit. You were a decent lay who—"

"That doesn't explain this, now," she said, going around, so he had to look her in the face. "You married me! You brought me here to marry me for a sole reason: to stop Trystan from marrying me. You've made it impossible because my name is already on a piece of paper with yours."

"Yeah, I get it. We did the commitment bullshit already, now strip for me, put on a show."

Backing up to sit in a corner armchair, his relaxed pose was one of a man waiting to be entertained, and in a far more intimate way than a standard lap dance.

"I'm not going back there, Dax," Ivy said, unwilling to let the issue go.

"I already told you, I'll go to the mansion and—"

"No. I'm not going back to California to watch you turn yourself inside out for them. It's not worth it."

"It's not worth it for you maybe," he said. "But after everything I've done for you—"

Tilting her head, she let out a whine, "Aww, yes, thank you so much for making me strip naked in front of strangers. Thank you for forcing me to parade around doing your chores. I especially loved the part where you left me down in that dungeon to rot for days, happily allowing your buddy to grope and ogle me to his heart's content. Is that what I have to look forward to in our marriage?"

"It's not gonna be like that, babygirl. I'm gonna talk

to Mauri, make him see—"

"I've heard this before, Dax," she said, shirking her sarcasm. "You weren't man enough to stand up to him then. Why should I believe you are now? For whatever reason, you're afraid of him—"

"I am not afraid!"

"Whatever, Dax," she said, crouching to pick up her shoes. Before she was even upright again, he was out of his seat, coming toward her.

"What the fuck do you think you need those for?"

"I'm going to take a walk," she said.

"No, you're not," he said, lashing out to grab her wrist.

She tried to pull away, but his strength was far superior. "I am not your captive anymore, Dax. You have to learn you won't always know where I am. We won't always exist in the same space. Let me go, please."

With one yank, her body clashed into his. "I told you you'd never be free," he snarled.

He got hold of her other wrist. Knowing she couldn't pull free, she tried to back away. But he followed, carrying on until she fell backwards over the sports bag discarded on the floor.

Dax's muscles bulged as they contracted to seize her weight. Catching her wasn't kindness, he hauled her up and slammed her against the closet, wrenching her upstretched arms so high that the tips of her toes almost left the floor.

"Let me go," she whispered, sensing this was about more than them being physically apart.

"No," he huffed, growing more sullen. "You're mine. You stay. You go where I go."

"You can't truly love me until you trust me, Dax. You have to be able to watch me walk out that door and know I'll come back to you."

"No."

"Do you think I'm going to run away? I'm not. If I didn't want to be with you, I wouldn't have married you. I want to be with you."

"Vegas is a dangerous place."

"Uh-uh," she said with a shake of her head, her shoulders beginning to burn. "That excuse won't fly with me, I can take care of myself, Dax."

"Like you did the last time we were in Vegas together?"

"I got myself out of there, without help from you or any of your friends…" Despite trying to tug down her arms, she had no chance of freeing herself. "Now let me go."

"You're not walking out that door."

"I am."

Whoever won this battle of wills, would struggle to claw back power in enough time to have a say on whether they journeyed to California.

"You're gonna stay here, strip, gimme a show. You're gonna open your legs for me and spend the rest of the night screaming my name."

"Don't hold your breath," she murmured.

Undeterred, and perhaps in an attempt to win the war, he snatched her mouth with his. The usual frisson of arousal zipped through her bones, but the punishing kiss was one of power. He was trying to exert authority over her, she had to break through this conditioned behavior. He'd been taught to be tough, to be the best, to overpower and crush an opponent. It was on her to teach him they were on the same side and that not everyone was his enemy.

The only person he seemed to trust was Mauri and she couldn't see why at all. Although she had never witnessed them interact, Ivy couldn't imagine what Mauri Stark had done to deserve such reverence; she had quite the towering idol to compete with.

"No," she said, but when he squatted to wrench her up, her legs twined around his hips.

She told herself that the maneuver was to offer relief to her aching arms, but in truth she just wanted to feel the reassuring bulge insisting itself against the yielding flesh of her center. Giving in to him would be easy. She could let him fuck her or let him take her to bed for a slower joining but teaching him that she could be distracted by sex set a dangerous precedent. She tried to push him away, but his grasp remained strong.

"Your body wants it," he said, sucking just above her pulse point. "My naughty Minx wants me to take control. You want me to force you, to ram my cock up into you. What you want babygirl is a dose of my sweet medicine right deep inside that dripping pussy. That will cure this defiance."

"You don't want me compliant," she said, flipping his sentiment back on him. "If I whimpered and whinnied and bowed down to worship you and your dick, you'd get bored, you said it yourself."

But what he wanted was to keep her there, to seduce her into forgetting the declaration she was leaving the room and him alone in it. Getting some air, being free to move, was her given right. Until the Starks took over her life, it was something she'd taken for granted.

Freewill was the most important thing in the world. It sickened her to watch how her mother and sister pandered to the men in their lives. Both were so insecure and totally firm in the belief they needed a man to be a complete person; that somehow, they wouldn't survive without one.

Ivy didn't need a man to survive. Working hard and paying her own way was just fine by her. She could make it on her own… except now she didn't want to. Since meeting Dax and experiencing what they had together, she'd learned one vital distinction between herself and her mother and sister. Ivy didn't need Dax, she wanted him.

Tilting her chin, she rested her cheek on his, rubbing back and forth as she whispered, "You want my mouth all over you, all over your body and your mind. I challenge you; it turns you on, tough guy."

"You're no challenge," he said.

Whipping around, he carted her to the bed. Instead of taking them down onto it as they were, he sat and wrangled her around to lie over his knee. Slinging her dress up out of the way, he took hold of the mono-line of her G-string and with a single pull, snapped the feeble thread. His large palm covered one cheek, he squeezed and skimmed across to the other. If caressing her was his only intention, there'd be no need to remove her underwear. Their horns were locked in a battle for superiority. Tearing off her panties had been his opening act of dominance.

Straightening her body, trying to roll away, her effort was obstructed by his thick thigh locking her legs between his, presenting her ass to him.

"It's nice owning something as sweet as this," he said, pinching her cheek where it met her inner thigh.

"You married me for my ass?" she asked. "What if I get fat and lazy some day?"

"Not gonna happen," he said, loosening his clamp on her legs enough to grant himself access to her sensitized center. "I'm gonna be part of your work out every day."

"We're married now," she said, struggling to prop her head up on her hand because her body hung limp over his leg. "I'm allowed to say that I have a headache."

"Say it all you want; it's not going to stop me from doing this."

How would bending her over his knee combat a headache? His fingertip glided into her, only as far as the first knuckle, but it reminded her of his occupying force.

"I said no, Dax, what does that mean to you?"

"That I'm not trying hard enough."

Her sarcasm was lost on him, or his distraction was too much for him to concentrate on two things. His dull murmur sent a jet of arousal cascading through her with the force of haphazard shrapnel impaling her body. As much as she hated him for having such intense power over her, she loved him for it too.

His casual words threw her off-balance. For a few seconds, she forgot they were fighting, forgot everything in deference to surrendering to him, exactly what she didn't want.

Dax shifted their positions. Laying her on the very edge of the bed, he pushed her knees up to part her legs wide. When he kneeled on the floor between her thighs, he revealed his plan to eat her before fucking her. He licked his fingers and ran them through her pussy, up and down a few times then he slapped her vulva and lowered his head. If she let his mouth close over her, there was no way she'd walk away.

Seeing an opportunity, Ivy pushed her heels into the bed and levered herself backwards, away from him. Crawling the width of the bed, she reached her strewn shoes and pulled them on before chancing looking at him.

"I have to do this, Dax."

Still on his knees, he dropped his elbows to the mattress, examining her. "Did you come with me just to get away from them?"

"What?" she said, pierced by hurt. "No."

"If you did, you need to tell me now. An annulment is still possible if we both deny—"

"Dax," she said, edging to the door. "I promise by the end of tonight you'll know what true love is. By the end of tonight, you're going to trust me."

"If you walk out of here, I'll never see you again."

Her hand fell to the door handle; a horrifying thought struck her. "You would leave me because I go for a walk?"

"If you walk out of here, I don't believe you'll come back."

Warmed and reassured, despite his anticipation of betrayal, she smiled. "I'm going to teach you to trust me. You're going to see love doesn't come with conditions, not like those Mauri put on you. You think you owe him something because he took care of you and yes, that was nice of him. But it wasn't selfless, he did it for a reason. He did it to shape you into this man. A man who would do anything for him, no matter how distasteful."

"I wouldn't do anything for him," Dax said. "There are conditions on my respect for him too."

"Such as?"

"I wouldn't let him keep the woman I wanted… I wouldn't let him hurt you."

"But he is hurting me," she said. "Watching him push you, a wounded animal, into these corners and torturing you into doing his bidding… that hurts me. I won't stand by and let him tie you into ever tighter knots. I love you and wouldn't ask you to do anything that might cause you pain."

"Like walking away from the only family I've ever known?"

"If you tell me it's a deal breaker, I'll come with you. But they're going to tear us apart, Dax, and they'll love every minute of it."

"I won't let them do that."

"Yeah, you will," she said. "Today proved it. You couldn't tell Mauri how you felt, then propose to me like any other guy would. You couldn't even trust yourself to bust up the wedding to stop Trystan from having me. You brought me here to marry me because that piece of paper we both signed is the barrier to Trystan marrying me. It won't allow Mauri to talk you out of your feelings. No one could talk me out of loving you, I didn't need a piece of paper to back me up."

"So why did you sign it?" he sneered. "If I'm such a weak, pathetic mess—"

"Because I love you, Dax. I couldn't walk away from you. I'll always do whatever makes life easier for you, no matter the personal cost. Putting someone ahead of yourself, ahead of your own wants and needs, that's love. If this was about me hating Mauri, I wouldn't hesitate to come back with you. I don't want to go back there because of what they'll do to you, not what they'll do to me."

"No one will hurt you."

"We'll see, Dax… There are all kinds of hurt."

She opened the door, and he sprang to his feet. "Ivy," he whispered.

Her name on his lips was rare. "I will come back to you, Dax. You're going to know love and trust because I'm going to keep giving you both until you recognize them. I will come back."

The discussion could go on all night, but actions would teach Dax the truth about her, so she walked out of the door before he could say anything else. While striding down the corridor, she half expected him to follow her, but he didn't. She went down the stairs and out onto the Strip to take a long breath of the sticky air.

Until being out there, she hadn't had a destination in mind. Vegas was once her home, there were old haunts she could visit. One person came to mind. One person she definitely wanted to see. There may never be another opportunity. She walked away from the hotel containing her husband and marched on with determination in her gait.

THIRTY-ONE

HER EXPEDITION TOOK LONGER than anticipated. Partly because she had no money, meaning no cab, and also because it took her longer to find her target.

After her reassurances she'd return to her husband, she didn't want to be gone for too long. Playing games with his insecurities would be cruel. That was the opposite of her intention. Being true to her word, returning to him of her own volition, without coercion, would go a long way towards showing him they were secure. Together by choice. Didn't that mean something?

Without a key she couldn't get into the room. Knocking didn't rouse Dax, no surprise there. He slept like the dead. The receptionist eventually handed over another key after asking a zillion questions.

In the room, she figured sucking him off had worked to wake him up before. She stripped down and crawled into their bed. Their empty bed.

Clambering out of bed and turning on all the lights, she explored every corner. Dax was gone. The sports bag was gone too, but there were clothes on the bathroom floor. Did that mean he hadn't checked out? The receptionist hadn't implied he had. So Dax had split, leaving her to pay the bill with her non-existent cash?

The shoe was on the other foot. She didn't like being the insecure party, unaware of her love's location or if he was coming back. Though she'd meant to teach Dax something about them, she'd taught herself a lesson too.

Would he come back? Should she go out to look for him? Vegas wasn't a place where you could easily find anyone. Just locating an exit or an elevator to get to your room was hard enough. Locating someone in a melee of noise and constantly moving bodies was near impossible.

She put on the tee-shirt from the bathroom floor, surrounding herself in his scent as she crawled onto the bed. With no way to get in touch with him, all she could do was wait and hope. On leaving, she'd asked him to trust she'd come back. Now she had to do the same.

LESS THAN AN HOUR after she lay down, the click of the lock propelled her out of bed to race for the door. The slice of light from the corridor that accompanied his entrance illuminated his battered features. Her shocked gasp startled him around. Before the door had clunked back into its frame, her body was plastered to his.

"What happened?" she asked, cradling one side of his face, soothing her fingers over a bruise above his cheek bone.

"You're here?" he said, ignoring the concern in her voice. "What are you doing here?"

Her fingertips slid down to his bloodied lip. "I told you I'd come back," she said, slipping the strap of his bag off his arm and letting it fall to the floor. "Come here."

Holding his hands on her hips, she guided him to follow until she seated him on the bed. Leaving him there, she dashed over to turn on a lamp, then retrieved ice and a napkin from the minibar. Climbing onto the bed at his side, she rested her knees on his thigh and wrapped the ice inside the cloth, rubbing it before pressing it to his cheek.

"Tell me what happened," she said, aching at the sight of her man bruised and in pain.

"You came back."

Lowering the ice pack, she was amazed at his incredulity. Was he oblivious to the bruises? The way he transfixed on her was… like she was an apparition invented by his mind.

"You don't have concussion," she said, threading her fingers through his hair. "You're not hallucinating. I really am here, Dax. I came back, just like I told you I would. I don't want to be free from you. I'm always going to find my way back to you."

Swiping her nursing hand aside, he seized the back of her head and clamped their mouths together. The metallic taste of his kiss didn't deter her. He wrapped his arms around her and tried to navigate them down on the bed. If he got her onto her back, she'd let him follow through. Going all the way would be bliss, it always was, but she had questions. Communication was crucial to trust. They had to be open with each other. Tonight had been a leap of progress in proving to him she could be trusted physically. But they weren't all the way and had to build on that.

"Tell me where you were, tough guy," she said, climbing into his lap to stop him getting her on her back.

"I went out looking for a fight," he said, brushing his blood from her lip.

"If any other man said that to me, I'd think he was crazy," she said. "You mean a fight, a real fight." He nodded. "You didn't kill anyone, did you?"

"It's against the rules," he mumbled.

Guessing how tumultuous his thunderous mood would have been, she would have forgiven him for forgetting.

"Fighting is how you vent your emotions," she said. "What state did you leave the other guy in?"

"I was sloppy with the first guy; he went down too quick. The second took more time, I played with him. The third, he was a big fucker, no style but enough substance to knock me to the deck a couple of times."

"Three," she said, leaning away. He grabbed her hips to pull her against him. "You fought three different guys? How many guys will they let you—"

"One," he said. "You're only supposed to fight once

a night in the ring when you're headlining."

"So how did you manage—"

"This is Vegas, babygirl. There's always a fight going on somewhere; bookies make big bucks."

"People bet money on you getting hurt?" she said, revolted. "They're actually hoping that you'll be hurt and—"

"Few people who know anything about the sport bet against me," he said, sweeping her hair back over her shoulders. "My name means guaranteed income."

"Which is why they'll let you fight more than once?"

"I went to three different joints."

"And they didn't see your bruises?"

"These came from the last guy," he said. "That's why I came back. I figured I couldn't talk my way into another fight."

"If he hadn't beaten the crap out of you, would you have kept fighting all night?"

"Maybe," he said and shrugged. "I figured you'd be long gone. And he didn't beat the crap out of me. I still won for you, babygirl."

"You didn't win for me," she said, thumping both hands into his shoulders. "You go out there and get yourself hurt because you believe that you deserve it."

"If that was true, I'd lose. I fight because I'm good at it."

"Because it's something you can control," she said.

"And for the green," he said with a backwards nod. "You should see how much is in that bag. I can rake in a fortune for you."

"I don't want money," she said. "I want you to see forty."

"Murder is against the rules."

"So it's never happened? No one has ever died in these fights?" His silence said it all. "See, that's what I'm worried about. What if you fall and hit your head?"

"I'm not gonna fall and hit my head," he said with a smirk that made her want to smack him.

"You think it's funny," she said, tossing the ice to his groin, then dug her nails into his wrists to yank them away so she could get off him and the bed. "You know, the best way to make me feel better is to take me with you and show me what it's all about."

"You weren't here," he said.

"I'm here now."

"Give a guy a minute to get over the last bout," he said, dropping onto his back on the bed, his feet remaining on the floor.

"Not tonight," she said, flitting to the bedside. "The next time."

Crawling up him on the bed, she laid her cheek on his heart. "I want to be there."

"You won't feel better," he said, drumming his fingers on her temple while his held her tight against him. "Watching will only piss you off."

"I thought you were good," she said. "I'll only be pissed if you're a wimp. Are you a wimp who can't handle himself?"

"No," he said with a scoff of a laugh. "But how will you feel when I let a guy twice my size hit me?"

"Why would you let him hit you?" she asked, with a hand on each pec she pushed up to look down at him, but his eyes were closed. The resistance in his chest grew as he braced to take her weight. Even now when he was tired and hurting, he didn't complain. "Is that what you did tonight? You let him hit you because you wanted to be hurt? You think it's easier to deal with physical pain than emotional." Her heart broke. "I told you I would come back."

Her whispered words opened his eyes, maybe he'd heard some of her hurt too.

"I'm amazed you did."

When her smile slunk up, it was eventually joined by his. He was grateful? Relieved? Maybe grateful she'd left in the first place, because now he got her point. Trust was not easy for him. Hopefully, he had peace of mind. As for the rest? She'd have a long time to prove her loyalty over and over.

"Suck me off," he said, mischief in his tired, smiling eyes.

Oh, it was relief. She wanted to climb inside of him

and stay there, in that place, safe forever.

"How is me taking my medicine going to make you feel better?" she teased, lowering enough to kiss the stubble on his jaw and chin.

"I've been saving the good stuff."

"We had sex earlier," she said, brushing her lips over his. "After all of your exertion, you probably have a headache."

The fact they could laugh together despite the horror the surrounding their lives boded well for their relationship. Marriage was impulsive. Their future was still a big question mark. The sacrifice awed her; he'd done it to protect her. Trystan wanted to marry her to punish her. Dax wanted to marry her because he didn't want anyone else to. To prevent a woman from marrying another man, a guy had to marry her himself.

"I'll work through it," he said, closing his arm around her and flipping them around so she was underneath him. "You're wearing my tee-shirt."

"Is that a problem?" she asked, accepting his kiss.

"Yeah," he said. "You're supposed to be naked in my bed."

His jesting ceased when he inhaled and parted his lips on hers. She had no room to breathe let alone talk so couldn't be expecting any kind of response. His gratified groan was joined by the grinding of his hips down on hers. The pace increased, there was something so satisfying about taking their time to learn each other's moans and maneuvers without time or people hanging overhead.

Bruno wasn't downstairs listening in or expecting a blow by blow after the fact. Tonight they had the gift of freedom. No one was keeping them there against their will. No one knew they were there.

Her hand slipped into his jeans before a noise in the hallway broke their kiss. Dax didn't look at her for explanation, but he was on alert for something.

"Wait here," he mumbled and moved to leave her.

She snatched his tee-shirt in her fists. "No. You're not going out there. It's just some drunk guy or something.

Stay right here." Levering up, she kissed his chin and raised her knees to angle her core around the length she'd just freed from denim.

"There's no reason for a drunk guy to be right outside our door," he said. "I'll come back and fuck you when I've chased away the fool."

No one had knocked. Given their circumstances, she wasn't happy to let him stroll out there unprotected. "Don't you at least have a gun or something, just in case you need it?"

"I don't carry a gun," he said, leaving his shielding spot over her body and standing up to straighten his jeans.

"What kind of a thug doesn't carry a gun?"

Muttering, he buttoned his jeans. Just as he was about to head for the door, he stopped to scrutinize her

Mad, she didn't really notice that his focus was on the apex of her thighs. "What?"

"If some dude is about to burst in here with trouble on his mind, I'd rather that your gash wasn't on show." Jerking her thighs closed, he nodded once. "Better."

"Why don't you have a gun?" she asked, scrambling up to kneel on the bottom corner of the bed, closest to the door.

"I know how to use one and I've carried them before. I just don't do it regularly."

"Why not?" she hissed, trying to keep quiet and satisfy her curiosity at the same time.

Dax pressed an ear to the door and held up a finger. His frown deepened then he backed away from the door. "If someone walks in to shoot you, you don't usually have time to hunt for your piece before you die."

"That's a reason?"

With annoyance, his attention snapped to her. "I don't need to carry my own gun because if it comes to it, I just take the gun from the guy who brought one along with the trouble."

Mr. Bigshot fighter was quick and nimble, he had the experience to observe someone's movements and assess their weaknesses. If someone's sole purpose was to kill, having a gun wouldn't save the target. The hitman could shoot while you slept, a house full of guns wouldn't stop that.

Dax's logic was strange yet justified. Watched him creep back toward the door, she experienced an invigorating esteem for her husband. His background meant he didn't need to be capable with weapons, he was one.

Still, she was surprised when Dax opened the door fast, maybe he was hoping for the element of surprise. The man on the other side of the door wasn't holding a weapon, he had a phone to his ear. Dax glared at the man who was only a few inches shorter than him, but far skinnier. The guy paled, and his mouth stopped moving.

"You're a sonofabitch, Benny," Dax said, grabbing the guy by the throat to yank him inside, slam the door, and thrust the guy against it, squeezing his throat.

The man sputtered and choked. Although Dax's arm was tensed straight, Ivy knew it wasn't Dax's intention to kill the stranger.

Sure enough, Dax's fingers relaxed. "You followed me back here?"

Benny wheezed in a breath. "There's big bucks out for you, in the inner circle."

"Mauri's looking for me?"

Benny nodded. "Yeah, yeah, said you went AWOL. I was knocked out to see you at Tig's tonight."

Dax probably would have laughed if he wasn't his intimidating routine. "Mauri's looking for me and you thought that you could bring me in?"

She stayed on the bed, not saying a word.

"No, no, not me, Ravager. I would never… No, I would never think… I mean I could never—"

"Quit stuttering and tell me who you called, Brad or Bruno?" Benny's eyes flicked to her then to Dax and back to her. "Forget her."

"Yeah, yeah, I… never saw nothing, Ravage, nothing."

This Benny guy was obviously low level and clearly scared of Dax. Still, if he knew Mauri and Brad, he was in the loop somehow. Usually, it was her default to avoid any interaction with criminal sorts. Being poor didn't mean being dishonest. The underground circuit of fighting, syndicate drug dealing, and money laundering hadn't been on her radar. Learning the complex hierarchy would take time.

Avoiding criminality didn't mean being squeaky clean either. Her experiences were petty in comparison to how Dax had grown up. Throughout her life, she'd had associations with people struggling with addiction issues, criminal records tended to follow when her friends got in too deep. Bearing witness to the repeated downfall of anyone embroiled in that was a good part of the reason she'd always avoided the slippery slope.

"Who did you call, Benny?" Dax asked.

"Bruno."

Dax's head tilted when he inhaled through his nose. Even she couldn't tell if that was a positive or negative reaction.

"We're going back tomorrow."

"Sure," Benny said. "Sure. Sure."

"You calling me a liar?" Dax asked with a thread of disdain that tightened his fingers around Benny's throat again.

"No! No, you're not a liar, man. You're a stand-up guy, yeah, I know that."

"Get back on the damn phone and tell Bruno we're on our way back. They can call off the dogs."

"I… I will…" Benny said, relieved and grateful for getting out alive and with all of his teeth.

Dax opened the hotel room door and threw the wimp of a man out, then he whipped around to glare at her. "We have to go now."

"Tomorrow," she said. "You told me tomorrow. We were still talking about if we should—"

"We have to go back," he said. "They're my family and that is my life, my life is there. Mauri has connections all over the country. If we run, he'll find us. We have no reason to do run. We'll tell him we got married, that we're serious, and he'll get it."

"He'll get it," she said, not convinced.

Their return to California was inevitable. Nothing she could say would sway him.

"We can fix this. Trust me," Dax said. She had asked for his trust, so couldn't flout his when he offered it and asked for the same in return. "Mauri will be shocked, but he'll let me talk. He'll let me fix this."

"Fix it how? By running his errands for the rest of your life? What about me?"

"I'll look after you. You don't have to worry about—"

"What?" she snapped. "You going to jail for life or getting yourself injured in a fight?"

"Mauri has excellent lawyers, there's no way that—"

"He could ruin us," she said, climbing off the bed to go to him. Slipping her hands under his arms, she wrapped her around around his ribs. "If he doesn't understand or let us off the hook, who is to say he won't use those lawyers against you?"

"I trust him," Dax said, cradling her head in both hands. "He's gonna understand. You asked me to trust you, and now you're going to trust me. Get dressed."

He left her in the bedroom and disappeared into the bathroom. The shower went on. Ivy remained on the spot. Just a few minutes later, he was back in the room, dressing in clean clothes, ready to get moving.

Flinging everything into the sports bag, he clicked his fingers, beckoning for the tee-shirt back to pack it too. Whipping it off, she handed it over to put on the dress and shoes she'd been wearing on their arrival.

"You haven't slept, will you be okay to drive?" she asked.

He slung the bag over his head, across his body, then tucked her under his arm to hurry out of the room.

"I've survived on less sleep for longer," he said. "We'll check out and get home, this is gonna work out. We're gonna be fine."

From what she could see of his profile, his iceberg blue eyes were focused straight ahead, his jaw was tight. He wanted to believe what he was saying, but he didn't like unknowns. Everything in their future was just that: unknown.

THIRTY-TWO

THE JOURNEY BACK to California was quiet. The sun was up by the time they got there. People were starting their days when she and Dax hadn't finished theirs yet. Her offers to drive were rebuked. She couldn't blame him for refusing, even she wasn't sure whether she'd flip a U-turn and haul ass in any direction thàt didn't lead them to Maurice Stark. The man had a power over Dax she didn't understand.

Back in the busy streets of LA, Dax pulled the car into a space on the street and turned off the engine. He left the vehicle and grabbed the sports bag from the trunk. She got out with no idea where they were going so waited until he came over and threw an arm around her.

Dax held her tight against his body. She looped an arm around his waist and rested her head on him, letting him take her to wherever they needed to go. A few paces down the sidewalk, Dax guided her up the stairs of a stoop and through a communal entrance. The stairway was clean and freshly painted, decent but nothing fancy.

On the first floor, he led her to a door with a number four on it. Fumbling with the keys, without loosening his grasp on her, he flicked through them to locate the right one and stuck it in the lock.

Until that moment, she hadn't realized just how eager she was to see his apartment. The increased pulse of her heart made her squeeze closer to his side. She turned her face into his body, preventing herself from hurrying him.

As ever, Dax was expressionless when he shoved open the door to usher her inside. A couple of closets led off the internal hallway. A bedroom was visible through the open door at the end, but it he took her in the opposite direction.

Left of the front door was the main living space. Dining table, open plan kitchen, nice. To the right of the table was a huge, light, airy space.

The broad windows drew her closer. Gauze curtains hung over a door. Rushing in that direction, she peeked through the curtains to see a broad deck which hung above the sidewalk below. The car they'd arrived in was just in view beneath. Grabbing the door handle, she tried to slide the door aside, but it was locked.

Spinning around, she leaned on the glass. "Can I go outside?" she asked, wondering if she'd always be asking him for liberty.

"In a minute," he said. "I've gotta shower and get over there."

"What are you going to say to him?" she asked.

There was no need for build up to this conversation. They had rushed back to this city to face down the demon on their tail. Both knew exactly who she was talking about.

"The truth," Dax said, tossing the keys on the table. "I don't want you letting anyone in here while I'm not here."

"Okay," she said, believing that was a sensible request when they didn't know who was on their side yet. Having never lived in LA herself, she didn't expect visitors. She had no plans to call up a posse of friends or to have a rave while he was absent. "Do you want me to come with you?"

He shook his head. "No."

"It doesn't feel right, sending you over there to deal with this alone. We're as responsible as each other, I mean… I fell in love with you first… I kissed you first too. I guess you could argue that this is all my fault."

"If things start to go south, I'll tell Mauri that," he

said, though he remained aloof his smile slipped up.

Moving across the room, she got to his side, and it felt right to encircle him in her arms. He edged back to perch on the dining table and nestled her in the vee of his thighs just holding her.

"Should we have a contingency plan?" she asked.

"In case I don't come back?" he asked. "I won't get hurt."

"I don't trust these people as much as you do."

"These people," he said. "Are the closest thing I've ever had to family."

"I'm your family and I love you," she said, leaning back to look up at him. "I would never make you come to me and grovel."

"I'm never gonna steal your girl, am I?"

"I was never his and you know it. This… it's all a power play and I don't understand why—"

"Don't start again," he said, nudging her away to slip out and head toward the bedroom.

Ivy followed in his wake, through the entryway. She expected him to go into the bedroom she'd seen. He didn't. Perpendicular was another bedroom she hadn't noticed.

When they entered, she might have spent time exploring the room with its large bed and closed doors. But Dax started to strip, distracting her with his sculpted body.

"Are we going to have sex?" she asked, not meaning to sound quite as formal as she had.

"No," he said, entering the bathroom. "Let me fix this mess with Mauri, then we can think about the honeymoon."

A honeymoon wasn't anywhere on the agenda. Dax had already said traditional wasn't his style. They had a lifetime ahead to figure out each other's styles. At least, she hoped they did. Fixing the problem with Mauri would be the first step on that path. Even if Mauri accepted the marriage, they would still be a part of each other's lives.

While Dax showered, she snooped around the bedroom and found no indication he'd had women there recently. No women's clothes left in the closet either, which gave her some relief.

Intending to depart the closet, she turned to learn she was barricaded in the room. Dax filled the doorway, naked except for a small black towel around his hips. The combination of that, his black hair, tanned skin, and the noir ink on his arms made her shiver. The bruise on his cheek only added to the danger that he exuded.

For a second, her apprehension fled. It was almost incomprehensible that man was her husband. He belonged to her. The reminder made her smile.

"Are you sure you don't have time?" she asked, slinking toward him.

He took her shoulders and moved her out of his way. "If we go to bed, I'll never get to the mansion tonight. Let me get this out of the way, babygirl. I'll take care of you after."

"You should sleep," she said, concerned for his wellbeing. "You've been on the go all night."

"I slept a bit, I'll be fine."

He slept a bit after they consummated their marriage, before they went down to the casino. A lot had happened since then.

"You'd be better if you rested before you went over there."

"If I drop the towel and get into that bed, are you gonna let me sleep?"

Hmm, good point. She couldn't make that promise. Chewing on her bottom lip was enough to convey that to him.

"I said rest, not sleep," she said. "I could climb on board, take on some of that tension you're carrying."

Passing her, he retrieved clothes and began to get dressed. "If I leave you in bed without fucking you raw, I'll be carrying more tension, babygirl… You're just trying to keep me here. If you've got plans to keep me under your thumb, you're gonna be disappointed."

Slipping out of her dress, she accepted his determination. Subconsciously, her greatest goal was to keep him there where she could keep an eye on him, where he was safe. Long term, he wasn't ever going to be under her thumb, of that, she was sure.

Naked and happy that he was admiring her figure with a satisfying bulge in his jeans, Ivy pushed out her chest and crept toward him.

"You would do anything to keep my pussy happy," she said. "If you want guaranteed entry any minute of any day, you're going to have to make sure the rest of me is smiling too."

Propping a hand on the shelf behind her, he created a barrier around her, crowding her into the restricted space. "I put a ring on it, babygirl. It's mine whenever I want it. I own you."

"And I own you right back," she said, raising her arms in a round sweeping motion to hang them around his neck. "If I demand your cock, you better give it to me."

"I'll give it to you good, on my terms."

When he moved fast, snatching her hips to whirl her around, she gasped. He bent her over to grind her ass on his groin. "This better be a prelude to something."

"To making you wait," he said. "Get yourself into that bed and sleep. When I get back here, we're gonna be consummating all over the apartment."

When he got back, she would insist he slept, she might even make him something to eat. But for now, the illusion was good enough.

"You're going to let me sleep in your bed while you're not here?" she asked. "Should I expect a zip tie around my ankle?"

"No footpost on the marital bed, I'll fix that soon."

"I'm not calling the bed you slept in with God knows how many whores our marital bed."

"No whores, just you."

Maybe he hadn't lived there long, or he never had women back there. Learning she was unique gave her the drive to push back into his crushing caress. The line of his dick nudged her ass as he rolled her hips back, squashing them together.

"You could fuck me fast, right here, tough guy," she panted, hanging onto the closet shelf for support.

"Yeah, I could," he said, giving her ass a hard smack

then backing away.

She still couldn't breathe, so staying put in the same position, she tossed her hair out the way and turned only her head to seek him out still using the shelf for support. Her chest heaved as she tried to pull in oxygen. He'd got her riled into one hot mess and was going to walk out the door anyway.

"Dax," she whispered.

He glanced back, a satisfied smile spread across his face. "Think about how crazy you're gonna be for me by the time I get back."

With nothing to think about except the arousal he'd sparked in her, yeah, she'd be hornier, maybe he was hoping that would lead to fewer questions. That logic seemed too complicated in the face of her need to be united with him.

He came back and tipped her chin up to kiss her lips, brushing her hair away from her cheeks. "You think about my cock, babygirl. Just keep thinking about it, about how bad you want it rammed up inside that snatch I put my brand on. You think of that and nothing else, you'll do just fine."

He kissed her again and left, still wearing that smug smile. She couldn't be angry, not while so scared for his heart. The distraction he'd put in her head would be enough to ease her concern about what he'd walk into, at least for a while. If he thought she'd and delay her own gratification, he was mistaken.

The front door shut, and she closed her eyes, thinking of exactly what he'd told her to until she was panting and ready to explore. The shower was her next stop. Dax hadn't told her to wait for him. Pleasuring herself then didn't mean she wouldn't be up for some collaborative fun later. The distraction was welcome, she just wished he was there to deliver it to her in person.

THIRTY-THREE

DAX TRIED TO FOCUS on the image of his wife undone, hanging on that shelving unit like she might melt to the floor if she even considered taking her own weight. That bliss could only live in his mind for so long. He needed to get his game face on. Talking to Maurice would be tough, they'd better be talking alone instead of with Brad or Bruno present. No matter how it worked out, the conversation was unavoidable. The time had come to confess all; there was no going back.

Trystan couldn't marry. That didn't mean the prick would appreciate that news, not at all. It would be better if the brat was still a continent and ocean away, in Europe. Dealing with one problem at a time would be easier. If he didn't know already his once-prospective bride was AWOL, he would very soon.

Dax didn't fear Trystan. He'd bet the squirt wouldn't take the chance of raising his fists to him. Everyone in their circles knew about his hobby, and how long he'd been doing it. If Trystan wanted to challenge him to a duel, that was fine and might be one fight he'd let his girl tag along to.

Usually, he went everywhere on his motorcycle. Driving up to the mansion alone was a novelty. He'd have to get used to using the car now he had Ivy in permanent tow.

Marrying her had been the only thing that made sense. The minute he'd had the idea, nothing would have deterred him from following through. What he'd said about there being no tradition, or white picket-fence in their future was true. Ivy wasn't interested in that. Yes, things were going to be bumpy, but they would find their rhythm, so long as he could get Mauri to accept the situation. If he didn't… what would come next?

No one stopped him from entering the mansion, though he only saw newer members of staff. None of them would be clued in on the inner secrets of the family. What had happened with Ivy would be classified as a secret.

Heading straight for Mauri's office, he knew better than to seek out Trystan. The guy was too highly strung to see reason. Maybe he'd have to apologize for what had happened, but he would never regret it.

Bruno was the only one in Mauri's office. He paused and the two of them just stared at each other.

"You're some dumb prick, you know that?" Bruno said eventually, swinging out of his seat at the side of Mauri's unoccupied desk. "You let her go free, didn't you? Sent her off somewhere to—"

"I know where she is," Dax said. "I came in to talk to Mauri."

"I'll bet you did, but I gotta tell you… he's not a happy guy. For you to shit on this family after all they've done for you… You're one ungrateful fuck—"

"I didn't shit on anyone. You don't know what the fuck went on."

"The hell I don't," Bruno said, raising his voice and storming in closer. "I was there, every damn day in that house. You were supposed to be whipping her into shape and you let yourself get led around by your cock. You're a fucking pussy. I knew it the minute I saw you, dumb squirt of a little kid. I knew you'd cause trouble; knew you weren't worth nothing. I told Mauri, told him to leave you, that's what we should've done."

"You hid your contempt so well," Dax retorted, subtly widening his stance to absorb any blow the other man might deliver. Getting into a full-blown fight, here in Mauri's office, wouldn't be smart. If Bruno lashed out, the only option Dax was to take the hit then get Bruno down, on his back, to pin him until he calmed down.

Because he was in the wrong, he'd let Bruno vent his anger, but the guy was no saint. Dax wasn't close to at his best. Maybe Ivy was right to order him to bed, though the mix had something else on her mind when making the suggestion.

"You've fucked this up royally. That fucking bitch is gonna pay for causing this shit—"

The crimson rage didn't register. Without thought, he acted, grabbing Bruno by the throat to force him across the room, bending him backwards over the desk before the cunt knew he'd spoken out of turn.

They'd gone halfway across the room, the impotent bastard trying to kick out while clawing at Dax's wrist.

The red shrouding Dax's vision wouldn't let him loosen his grip. "Don't ever speak of her that way. You show my wife some respect or respect is the last thing I'll show you."

He hadn't meant to declare his union with Ivy, but the minute he did Bruno's eyes got widened and he relaxed, not in a battle with consciousness but in deference to disbelief.

The back door of the office opened, and Brad came in. Dax released Bruno and backed off. Bruno coughed and rubbed his neck. Brad wouldn't care about his comfort, or anyone's comfort. Around there, men had to be able to handle themselves, and they handled things as Mauri believed men should.

At least the others did, few challenged Dax anymore. After fighting his way through most of his teens, he'd taught staff children how to defend themselves. That had carried right on through to the ranks of Mauri's workers. Everyone knew Dax could handle himself and that he trained most days. The chances of anyone else winning a fight against Dax were zero. Especially when his wife was the prize.

"Dad's on his way," Brad said, remaining by the open door, hands in his pockets. "Where is she?"

"Doesn't matter," Dax said.

Brad had always been hard to read. Dax hated that about him. Sometimes Brad could surprise an enemy by showing them mercy, or he could shock a friend by turning on them. That kind of erratic nature left a person unsure where they stood, exactly as Brad wanted.

"He married her! He fucking married her!" Bruno declared marching past Dax toward Brad.

A stunned look of incredulity flashed on Brad's face. "Did you?"

Dax nodded once because he wasn't going to lie. He'd come to tell Mauri the truth. Everyone in their circle would know it by the end of the day.

Ivy's declaration that he intended to apologize to Mauri for falling in love with her stung him deep. She wasn't the type to be easily hurt or to wilt for the purposes of drama. The idea she could think he was ashamed of loving her… Except he could understand how she got that idea: from him. From the way he acted toward her and his feelings for her. It wasn't a bombshell she believed he was ashamed of her… of them.

"Yeah, I did," Dax said, giving voice to the truth, looking Brad in the eye.

If there was one thing, he'd make sure of, it was that no one ever believed him ashamed of his wife. She'd never feel undervalued again. He didn't have the skills to be the best of husbands. Their future wasn't certain, he had no idea what the future held, and hadn't begun to figure out the details. Maybe he didn't need to do it… alone. Ivy would be there with him through every kink.

He'd learn how to be better for her. She'd held up a mirror to him in a way no one else ever dared to and he'd be eternally grateful to her for that.

"Why the fuck did you do that?" Brad asked, taking a snapping step in his direction.

Brad rarely lost his cool, his strong reaction was intriguing, but there was no time to address it.

Mauri came in and they all shut up to look at the patriarch. "All of you get out of here," he said, fixated on Dax. "My boy and I have to have talk."

THIRTY-FOUR

NO ONE QUESTIONED Mauri when he gave an order. So although it probably irked him, Brad slunk out of the room, Bruno at his heels.

Mauri didn't sit at the desk, as he did when conducting business. He gestured to the vast leather couch in the corner, Dax accepted the silent invitation to sit on it.

"It's a shame, we haven't had one of our talks in a while. We should get back in the habit, shouldn't we?"

"Uh, yeah," Dax said, growing up he and Mauri talked regularly.

The private audience with the patriarch was envied by others. He hadn't realized the importance of that relationship until they'd lost the routine.

"Do you want a drink?" Mauri asked, opening a palm toward the Waterford.

It was too early in the day to be mixing martinis or sipping scotch.

Dax shook his head, rubbing the back of his neck. "No."

"Coffee?" Mauri asked. "You look tired."

"I've been on the go a while," Dax said.

Brad got his ability to disguise emotion from his

father's side.

"I can tell," Mauri said, coming over to seat himself in the armchair perpendicular to the couch. "Something is troubling you."

"Hmm, yeah, why would you think that?" Dax said, leaning forward, elbows propped on his parted knees, his hands clasped between them.

Talking back to Mauri? Not something he'd have done before the Minx came into his life.

"You've been in the ring."

As his bruises showed. "Yeah."

"You let your opponent disrespect you."

Calm Mauri's lack of mentioning Ivy amped him. This was the receiving end of Mauri's displeasure. The old man was toying with him, like a cat with a mouse. Playing the prey didn't work for him.

"Yeah, he got a few hits in, he was bigger than me."

He set his jaw and tightened his fingers around the other fist, almost overwhelmed by the urge to pummel something.

"That's never mattered," Mauri said. "You use their size against them—"

"Am I here to talk tactics?" Dax exclaimed, shooting to his feet. "Because if that's the only thing on the table I'd rather come back later."

"Sit down, Dax." He did. "I don't know why you're here at all, boy."

"Benny told me you were looking for me; I always come when called."

Saying it aloud made his blood congeal. In the early days, Ivy referred to him as a lapdog; more and more he could that truth. Whether she meant it or intended to anger him, it didn't matter. Running Mauri's errands had been his way of life since he was a kid. He never thought to stop and question what he was doing or even if he wanted to be a part of this at all.

Worse was the sickness churning in his abdomen, there because disappointing Mauri tore him up. The control his surrogate parent wielded probably wasn't healthy.

Definitely wasn't healthy. Gaining the acceptance or pride of a parental figure had never figured in Dax's conscious mind. Yet, shaming and disappointing Mauri somehow made Dax feel like less of a man. His self-worth was tied to the opinion of this one man. How had that happened?

"The girl was alone with the seamstresses yesterday. They left to retrieve something, when they got back, she was gone… We couldn't find you and you were the last one seen leaving this property… Do you want to tell me where she is?"

"She's at my place," Dax said.

Concealing the truth would put Ivy into hiding forever and she wouldn't go quietly. Her obvious objections would leave him only one choice: he'd have to restrain and imprison her again. She wouldn't see that he was doing it for her safety.

The truth was undeniable. If he wasn't honest, wouldn't that imply Ivy was right he was ashamed of them? Hopefully the difficult path would lead to everyone getting used to the way things were going to be. Now that he had Ivy, he had every intention of letting the world, meaning every other guy on the face of the Earth, know she was taken. She was his. No other man would get near her again.

"That's good," Mauri said. "Trystan will be back tonight and that gives us plenty of—"

"I married her."

Saying it out loud was freedom. A weight floated from his shoulders, he sat straighter. Even the crackle of anger coming from Mauri's didn't diminish the relief.

The ire floated away. Mauri smiled, he actually smiled and then he laughed.

What the…?

"Ah, you're clever," Mauri said, still enjoying a laugh. "Funny too. Sharp."

"It's no joke," Dax said, slowly shaking his head.

With each passing second, Mauri's amusement faded. "You can't be serious," he barked. "You can't be. You know her purpose was—"

"I asked her, she said yes, we did it," Dax said, glossing over a few details. "I'm sorry, Mauri. I know you had a deal with Trystan but—"

"There is no but," Mauri said, pouncing out of his seat. "You went to Las Vegas, he found you in Las Vegas."

"Yes," Dax said, knowing that Mauri was referring to Benny.

"Then you can get it annulled. I'll delay Trystan and once the paperwork is—"

"I'm not getting it annulled," Dax said, standing up, noticing for the first time how he towered over Mauri. "I love her."

The ringing in his ears grew louder with each passing second.

For the longest time, Mauri said nothing, he just stared, then his attention dropped. "She doesn't belong to you. You cannot have her. The family—"

"She's part of the family now," Dax said. "Just not in the way you wanted. Tryst can go fuck himself. I'd slit her throat and mine before I'd see her go anywhere near his bed."

"Jealousy," Mauri said, angling his head to peer at him. "Is that what this is about, boy? You don't want him to play with your toy?"

"She's no toy. She's my wife."

"And why is that? Why did she say yes to you? Do you think she wants to be married to you? That she actually loves you?"

"Yes."

With a whisper of another laugh, Mauri softened, and gave him a pat on the arm before sitting, gesturing for Dax to do the same. "You have been played. You're not the first man to fall for a great rack and a sob story. I'm surprised she managed to manipulate you, very surprised. I knew you didn't embrace the cruelty necessary to bend her will, but you've always been cold. Even as a child. You never cried," he said, drawing in a breath and settling back in his chair. "You never asked why or whimpered. You did the job. You were given a task and you completed it. I suppose your father conditioned you from a young age to do that. He taught you how to fight and put you into that ring to make him money and you did."

Often children and weaker fighters would occupy the

ring to put on a show before the main fight of the night. It was entertainment and gave the bookies a chance to make more money. Back then, Dax had been something of an anomaly, far younger and scrawnier than the other kids, he learned to be fast and disguise every weakness.

"What happened back then is nothing to do with now."

"No?" Mauri asked, arching a brow. "Growing up in this house, in the back kitchen with the other staff children, you never complained. You always knew your place."

He was the only child to get alone time with Mauri, even Mauri's children spent more time with their mother. Dax was special, he was the chosen one, though he'd never asked why.

Despite being the obvious favorite, asking for more never occurred to him. Lesser men had been cast out for greed. What he had was enough, had been enough. He'd always believed serendipity found him the day Mauri offered him the chance to repent for his crime.

"And I've stepped out of it," Dax said. "Is that what you're saying?"

"She has given you something the rest of us couldn't." Devotion, loyalty, respect, the choices were varied. "Status. No matter how we valued your work, you were never going to be the most powerful man in the room. Not with Brad, Trystan, Bruno and I on your fringes. No, she saw exactly what you wanted and gave it to you to save herself."

"Ivy fell in love with me before she knew what was going on."

"She knew she was being held captive and that you may have held the key. She manipulated you, my son."

"No," Dax said, shaking his head. "Why would she have married me if—"

"Marriages are easily undone these days," Maurice said. "She likely planned to stick around while you smoothed over things with the family and planned to leave you, divorce you, after Trystan moved on to other things."

He didn't want to hear that. Didn't want to think it could be true. Except Ivy had pointed out she'd been the one to initiate so much between them and had even taken the lead in seducing him on their first night together. Any time the possibility of manipulation crept in, the idea fled in the moment her body accepted his. Everything about her soothed his ego, he'd let her do it.

His face fell into his hands. What was truth and what was not? Ivy, a smart woman in dire straits, would've done whatever was necessary to survive. The Starks had been his family for twenty years. They always stood by him, just as he stood by them. Had he been ready to give up his family for a woman who, Mauri was right, might choose to leave him in three months?

Mauri's got him through; the old man never let him down. Even though the fighting didn't fit the Stark image, he'd been allowed to continue it. Mauri never appeared shamed by it and never questioned his loyalty. Somehow, meeting Ivy forced him to do both to the man who had nurtured him.

"What do I do?" Dax asked, rubbing his face up his fingers until Mauri came into view again.

"Bring her back to us," Mauri said. "It's unlikely Trystan will marry her now. Clearly, she isn't as obedient as we thought. If she tries to manipulate him or gives him trouble… well…"

Trystan had no restraint and was so erratic there was no telling what he would do. If Ivy spoke to Trystan the way that she spoke to him, well, the chances were high she'd get a beating. Having another person wielding that kind of power over her, she would push back hard. Trystan would see that as disrespect, he'd want to show her who was boss, and he equated sex with power. Trystan would beat her and rape her and keep her until he got bored, until she was truly broken, if he didn't kill her first.

"You don't want him drawing attention to the family," Dax muttered.

"I don't." That was enough to divulge Mauri's thinking. If Trystan killed Ivy, whether on purpose or by accident, the family would have a body to get rid of and a lot of unanswered questions. "Keep her for today," Mauri said.

"Give me a chance to talk to Trystan and bring her over here, say midnight."

"And then what?" Dax asked, glad he would have the time to talk to Ivy and get the truth out of her. All he'd thought about was his love and how it would affect him to see her with another man. Had she played him for a fool?

Midnight was a daunting time. There wouldn't be many eyes around to witness whatever happened. If Trystan was understanding, Ivy might get out alive. Unlikely.

Mauri looked tired, worn out. He'd believed Ivy was the answer to his aggravation. Through the years, Mauri put up with a lot of Trystan's immature antics, but he was getting bored and desperately wanted Trystan to grow up. They'd been on the cusp of that happening and Dax had dashed all hope.

"I can send Bruno for her if you are uncomfortable—"

"No," Dax said, rising to his feet. "I got us into this mess, it's my responsibility to get us out of it."

"Good," Maurice said and actually smiled as they walked to the door. "I wish Trystan was as responsible as you. I'm proud of you, Dax."

He hadn't expected those words to come out of Maurice's mouth, certainly not on that day. "Proud?"

"Yes. You made a mistake; we all do that sometimes. Now you've had this experience you'll never let it happen again." All good humor left Maurice and he stopped Dax from opening the door. "Are you?"

"No," Dax said, understanding the undertone.

"Family should always come first and that's what I'll be explaining to Trystan. We shouldn't let a woman come in between brothers, should we?"

"I'll deal with it," Dax said, experiencing an emotion drain more profound than anything before.

Before finding Ivy, he'd believed himself numb. Now being with her with the prospect of losing her on the horizon, numb didn't come close to describing the lead in his veins.

THIRTY-FIVE

IVY HADN'T MEANT to fall asleep. The bang of a door opened her eyes, revealing that was exactly what she'd been doing. Rolling onto her back, she stretched and closed her eyes again, anticipating her husband joining her.

Except he didn't.

And she couldn't hear anything to indicate what he was doing.

Sitting up in the middle of the vast bed, she was confused to see him in the doorway of the closet, doing nothing.

"What happened?" she asked. "Did you fix it? Did everything get worked out?"

"I think it did."

"Wow, really? I'd have put money on it going the other way," she said. Awash with relief, she sighed out a smile. "Do you want me to cook you something and you can tell me what happened?"

"No," he murmured.

Should she laugh or get up and run away?

His static form wasn't giving much away. "Are you okay? Was it rough? Was he pissed?"

"Brad was pissed, so was Bruno."

"And Mauri?"

"I knew I could count on Mauri."

Their relationship must be stronger than she'd given it credit for. No way had she expected Mauri to be understanding. Dax wasn't upset or angry. At least, she didn't think so, he was still just standing there.

"What are you thinking about, tough guy?" she asked, resisting the urge to exhale a nervous laugh.

He grabbed the neck of his tee-shirt and pulled it off, then bent down to unlace his boots and kick them away. Uncertainty evaporated after he shirked his jeans.

The full-frontal view of his healthy form curled her lips. "Never mind," she said, untwining herself from the sheet.

Dax brought his bodacious body onto the bed where she waited, arms open wide. As he ascended the length of her, he snagged the sheet, sliding his open hands up her arms, tickling the delicate flesh. Her almost laugh faded when he clamped her wrists around the headboard and used the sheet to tie them in place.

Lying naked, stretched out on the warm bed was uncomfortable. The naked part was fine. Being restrained by Dax, no problem, though he tended to tether her leg rather than her arms. Being unable to touch him, the lack of freedom, those weren't so relaxing.

"You horny, baby?" she teased, trying to kiss his mouth.

He took it away to press his face into her throat instead. Clasping her breasts, he proved his ownership there before skimming his palms downward. With one punishing jerk, he opened her thighs and shoved himself into her. Wincing at the unexpected intrusion, she wished her hands were free. The man on top of her wasn't touching her with the same respect he'd shown last night.

"Dax—"

His mumbles cut her off as she strained to hear his words. Often, he mumbled when he was buried in her. She'd never figured out the message.

He licked down to a nipple, which he took in his teeth and pulled upward, stretching her skin, making her yelp. She was all for rough play, except his frown suggested he wasn't having fun and, to be honest, neither was she.

"Dax—"

"Shut the fuck up!"

Pulling out, he flipped her body over, crossing her arms in the binds, burning her shoulders with the twist. The position was uncomfortable, but she got over it fast when his hands landed on her ass. A gentle finger slap was followed by a full hand smack, then he squeezed.

"What the hell is going on, Dax?"

"If I've gotta get rid of you, I'm getting the most I can out of you first."

"Rid of me," she repeated.

As the words filtered in, she tried to see him over her shoulder; the awkward position made it impossible.

Dax's shins pressed into the back of her thighs, holding her there, legs still spread wide. Parting her ass cheeks, he drew a finger down between them and pressured his thumb on her rear opening.

"No," she said, lacing her words with warning.

"We're married now," he said, without any hint of love. "I get to have all of you."

"I said no, if you force the issue, it's still rape. I don't care if we've known each other ten minutes or ten years."

"Making me happy in bed has been your priority since the start of this."

"I care about making all of you happy, at all times," she said. "And you should care about the same thing. It will not make me happy if you violate me. You're supposed to love me."

"Supposed to," he said. "Is that what you're supposed to do too? Supposed to make me believe you love me?"

"Please talk to me," she said, panic rising. "What went on with Mauri?"

"We're going over there tonight," he muttered, brushing her hair away from her back. "You're gonna be introduced to the family."

"I've met them all," she said, almost growling, frustration was growing within her. "Why did you say you were getting rid of me? How can you get rid of me and take me over there?"

His body came down on top of hers. "Never mind."

The burning rod of his erection emblazoned itself on her butt.

Grabbing her hair, he twisted it in his fist, forcing her head up and back. Still, she couldn't see him.

Pouring disgust into the mist of his poisoned breath, he came close. "Disrespect is the greatest of enemies," he snarled into the shell of her ear. "You are disrespect, Minx."

"I'm your enemy?" she asked, incredulous. How did he get to that conclusion in such a short time? When he left, her worry was for his safety, not for their relationship. Idiot. She should never have let him go back to that place alone. He wasn't as secure in their relationship as her. Given his attitude, her confidence may have been misplaced. "What did he say to you?"

"Forget that. Don't talk about my family. Don't even think about them."

"Dax, this isn't you. I love you and you know I do."

He yanked her head back causing her to gasp for air.

"How can I believe that? You wanted freedom and you got it... by using me."

"Is that what he told you?" she spat, angry at those who'd manipulated him, turning him against the one true happiness he'd had in his life. "That bastard told you I seduced my way out of Trystan's bed and into yours?"

"Yeah, it's pretty damn clear when somebody says it to you like that."

Honesty meant going all in. "Fine, believe that if you want to, because you know what? It did kind of start that way. I thought about it, thought I needed an ally, I was in fear for my life. When you come from the streets, you're used to doing whatever it takes to get by."

"So you turned to turning tricks? Fucking me for liberty instead of green?"

"You had an ulterior motive too," she said, squashed under his body, his hand still twined in her hair, her arms stretched to the headboard.

Everywhere hurt, though nowhere more than her heart. It wasn't the most civilized position to argue, but he needed to exert dominance over her. Right then, she resented the hell out of him for it.

"My ulterior motive was to fuck you, and you knew that."

"Your ulterior motive was to groom me for your buddy. It's sick, Dax. I didn't know that when we started sleeping together. Hell, I thought you were being coerced too. I actually thought there was a chance you were being blackmailed or bribed to be so cruel to me. I see now it's what you have to do to fit into your family."

"Damn right, and we're proud of it. No one disrespects us and gets away with it."

"According to you, I did," she said, spitting a section of hair from her mouth when it tumbled from her matted locks above. "According to you, I got you all the way down the aisle. I must have some serious skills in the sack. You actually believed that the marriage thing was your idea."

Grunting, he thrust her head into the pillow. His body weight disappeared. She tried to see through her hair, but her field of vision was so narrow, the effort was useless. Figuring he must've left the bed, she tried to shift onto her back to untwist her arms. Except she'd barely gone a quarter turn when he snatched her hips and forced her onto her chest again.

"I don't want to look at you," he said, holding her down.

"That's called guilt, Dax. You know you're wrong and you can't look at me because hurting me hurts you."

"It's not going to hurt for long," he sneered and opened her thighs again, resuming his caress, moving from her rear opening to her front one, pushing his fingers through the pleats of her body.

"Fuck my pussy all you like, Dax," she said. "Maybe some of that frustration will give us both a head start, and you'll be through before I have to think about faking it."

She had never faked orgasm with him before. But with him in this kind of mood, she couldn't really see herself being able to relax and enjoy any intimacy.

"If you're so pissed at me, why would you want to have sex?" he asked.

Her heart grew sick. "Because if you're gonna get rid of me, this might be the last chance I'll ever have to be with you."

"My thoughts exactly," he grumbled.

Because she couldn't see him it was a shock when he plunged into her. Their conversation hadn't meant much in the way of foreplay. She wasn't really ready for him. Her hissing curse didn't stop him from pulling back and sliding in, on a path much easier to forge.

She closed her eyes and tried to loosen the clamping tension low in her gut. He slid in and out, gaining pace. Other than the occasional spank, he didn't touch her. There were no fingertips on her spine, no kisses on the back of her neck, or stroking of her thighs.

He kept going at it and cursed a few times until his pace slowed. After a few more advances, he withdrew and vanished from between her legs.

"What are you doing?" she panted. "You weren't done. I wasn't done."

He didn't say anything, just flipped her over and freed her arms from their binds. Anger saturated his expression. What would she do if things got violent? Against a man like this, she wouldn't stand a chance.

His body lunged for hers and she braced, but his mouth was the only thing that made contact. It found hers in a kiss so deep and punishing, the sickness in her heart metastasized to all of her cells. With her hands free, she could touch him. Finally.

Cupping his face, she ran her hands into his hair and to the back of his neck, caressing his shoulders, his arms, and his ribs, all while he kissed her mouth. The severe force of his kiss seemed to be his way of chastising her for everything she'd made him believe. Her words and actions had all been true, but Dax didn't know that, he didn't trust her.

This time when her legs parted around him, they did it by choice. And when he slid his unsated passion into her, he pushed all the way, as far as he could go, only to then still, controlling their kiss with a hold on her chin.

His other hand was busy bracing his body over hers. She wanted to believe he was being considerate, that it was a sign of care, but it wasn't. If he wouldn't touch her with his hands, he wouldn't touch her with the rest of himself. It was too intimate. Apparently, he didn't want to be reminded of a time when he had faith in her.

Eventually his pelvis rose then came back down and he was making love to her slowly. Maybe he realized it too, because he jerked away from the kiss and rose onto his knees, pulling her pelvis up with his.

"Come," he demanded, pushing into her, the awkward angle hurt her neck but gave the blunt head of his fat cock the perfect aim to pound against the g-spot hidden inside her.

"No," she said, unwilling to follow his order just because he gave it.

Maintaining hold of her hips with one steadying arm, Dax licked the tips of his free fingers and began to rub her clit. "Come!"

"No!" she retorted. Her rebellious nature didn't want to give him the satisfaction, but the more he worked her inside and out, the harder it became to resist him. "No, geez, Dax, don't!"

"You want it. Don't you fucking dare deny how hot you are for it."

His panting increased. Her teeth clenched. All she needed to do was hold out longer than him. Once he tipped over the edge, she could relax. "You're a fucking jerk!"

"Squeeze my dick with that tight snatch, Minx. Come on, girl. Do it now!"

"No," she said, but it was too late.

The burst of bliss cascaded throughout, clamping the invader in place with the spasm of her intimate muscles.

He cursed and huffed, smacking the side of her ass, but she couldn't let him go, the vice of pleasure was wringing every drop of her worth into holding onto him. Letting him go now could mean letting go of him forever, her body didn't seem to be willing to do that.

"Fuck, babygirl! Fuck! Fuck!"

Were those words of pain or pleasure? Whichever it was, the heat of him filling her up betrayed he'd gone over the cliff as well. Sparkles on the inside of her eyelids joined the ones pulsing in her head and the ringing in her ears.

Lying there, dizzy, her blood pressure had just plummeted through the floor. Just as her muscles loosened, they contracted again. The aftershocks of orgasm left her twitching and squeaking as he tried to retrieve his probably bruised dick from the prison she'd locked it in.

The bed bounced when he collapsed onto it beside her. Still, he didn't touch her. With her eyes closed, she didn't know if he even looked at her. Lost in their own ecstasy, it took a while to come around to replaying the mess, or rather what had come before the pleasure she'd tried to deny herself.

Opening her eyes, her head flopped to the side. "What now?"

Blank, Dax stared up at the ceiling. "Get some sleep," he said, without moving. "You're gonna need it." Reassured he wanted to rekindle their intimacy, her smile almost made an appearance. "Trystan will wanna play with you all night."

Any thoughts of happiness evaporated as did all feelings of goodwill. Endorphins retreated and the weight of pounding panic returned. Bucking up, he got off the bed to stalk out of the bedroom without giving her another thought.

She had lost him. He was going to turn her over to them. She wouldn't go quietly. No. In fact, she had no intention of going at all.

THIRTY-SIX

IVY SHOWERED AND CHANGED into her only available clothes. In need of money, she went hunting for Dax's wallet. Seeking out his jacket in the closet, it was as she stuck her hand in his pocket that he walked in.

"What are you looking for?" he asked.

He must have used the other shower because his hair was still damp, and she could smell his soap.

"I need some money," she said with no intention of hiding the truth. "We're married, right? What's mine is yours?"

"Why do you need money?"

"I need a change of clothes and transport."

"For what?"

Unimpressed by his lack of expression, she tried to match it with her own. "Did you think I was going to hang around and let you hand me over to them?"

"I didn't ask what you wanted. I told you what was happening."

"That Trystan wants me in his bed? Thanks, but no thanks, you know?"

His wallet wasn't in his jacket. The hunt continued to the laundry hamper. His jeans from earlier in the day were in there.

"You're not walking out of here.".

"What are you going to do, Dax? Hmm?" Throwing the jeans back in the hamper, she reached around him to pat his back pocket. "Bingo," she said, snagging the wallet. He didn't stop her from taking it. On opening it, she figured out why. "Twenty bucks, that's all you've got?"

"It's enough to get you a pack of condoms and to the nearest street corner."

"Funny joke," she said, taking the money anyway. "Yeah, I'll start whoring myself, 'cause after being with you what's the difference, right?"

"You used me to get what you wanted, why not do it to some other poor schmucks out there?"

"You know, I can't figure out if you actually mean the bullshit you're spouting or if you really are gonna let your daddy issues wreck our relationship."

"What relationship?"

Of everyone involved, she was the least to blame for things taking this turn. He'd been fine before seeing Mauri, now things were all fucked up again.

"I'm getting out of here," she said. "This is all some sick, twisted bullshit."

If his head was so fogged that he'd comply with Mauri's demands to take the woman he loved over there… Eventually he would realize his mistake, by then it would be too late. If Trystan had laid so much as a pinkie finger on her, she would never forgive Dax for throwing her to the wolves. It just wasn't in her.

Managing to swan past him, she kept the twenty flat in her palm. "Where are the car keys?"

"You're gonna steal my ride too?" he asked, trailing after her out of the closet into the bedroom.

"Consider it division of marital property," she said, holding open her other hand. "Where are the keys? Come on, hand them over."

"I switched it out for the bike after I left the mansion," he said. "Do you know how to ride a motorcycle?"

Not yet. If she had to figure it out, she would. She matched his look of angry satisfaction with her own. "Maybe

I'll find myself a pimp who gives out perks with the job."

Dax's ridiculous comparison of her to a hooker was unjustified. Completely unjustified.

"Like a company car?"

"Or a private jet," she said, bobbing her brows.

"You're not that good, honey."

"And Mr. Smart Ass Tough Guy is back. I think I'll take a pass on spending time with him. You know how he can be," she said, spinning to make a beeline for the door.

"He tends to be right," he said, his voice following her into the entryway. "You're gonna learn when to keep that mouth shut, Minx!"

"Unlikely," she said and turned the handle to open the door, but it only got an inch.

His hand came over her head to thrust it back into its frame. "You're not going anywhere," he said.

About-facing to glare up at him, she was trapped in the confines he set with his body. One of his hands was above her head, his forearm resting downward, his other hand touched the door by her hip. He came in closer.

"What are you gonna do?" she smirked. "Are you going to hurt me, Dax? Are you going to use your mad skills to beat me? Pummel me with your fists until I'm drowning in my own blood."

His chin moved, fury mated with disgust and his eyes grew narrower. "If I have to," he whispered like the words tasted foul on his tongue.

Closing the last inch between them, she pushed onto her tiptoes to get as close to him as possible, searing her own disgust into him. "I don't believe you," she whispered. "You wouldn't lay a finger on me in anger, you never have."

"I'll drag you through to that bedroom and spend the afternoon whipping your ass until you can't sit for a week."

"And if I told you to stop?" she said, already aware of the answer. That made this anger flickering back and forth between them all the more upsetting. Their love was still there but he couldn't handle it. He couldn't turn his back on people he believed himself indebted to. "If I told you to stop, you would. If I told you I was in pain, you would cure me. You would never see me hurt, Dax." She softened slightly. "And that's why you're going to let me walk out of here now. Because if you don't, you have to take me to them. You know if I go in there, they'll never let me walk out again. Let me leave now or spend the rest of your life knowing I'll never forgive you.

"You love me, and you hate yourself for that because it means disappointing the only person you've ever really respected or admired. I wanted to fight for this. For us. I married you because I wanted to make it work. But you have to be stronger. I thought you were stronger. I can't make the decision to commit for you, only you can do that. If your commitment lies with them, this marriage will never work."

"You're staying."

"Then you have to turn me over to them. Knowing what that means, are you prepared to do that?"

The lie was easier to believe. It gave him an out. Getting rid of her would make all the problems in his family go away, at least as far as they related to her.

Their locked gazes didn't flinch. Cool frost cracked around his irises. She wanted to see them soften, to hear him whisper he was going to take care of it. For real this time. How nothing would make him give her up and he'd never let them hurt her. But that was a fantasy, those words weren't in him. The Starks gave him his identity. They made him who he was. Everything in his life was tied to them.

Sure, he had his own place, his own life. He even said that he'd worked for other people. But the Starks had been there for him, loved and sheltered him, when no one else had. Asking him to turn his back on them, for her, was too much.

"Let me go. Just make up some excuse about me sneaking out while you were asleep. I promise I won't cause any trouble. It's that or you take me to them and watch Trystan, maybe some of his men, torture me. I don't care how much you say you resent me or how much you imply I lied to you. If you have to watch me swallow his spunk…"

His eyes closed slowly showing she didn't need to finish the thought.

His hands slid down and he took a single step back,

giving her enough space to fumble behind her back for the door handle. It clicked out of place, and she'd begun to sidle around it when he opened his eyes and spoke.

"Keep your head down, Minx."

"I plan to," she said and before he had the chance to change his mind, she slipped out of his apartment.

In the same moment she left, she wanted to go back in and pretend like nothing had happened. Like everything was as it should be. That wasn't possible. Leaving was the only option. Yes, she loved Dax, and they were still married. But until he realized what it was to be without her and until he could look at the Starks in a new light, they would never be able to be together.

In time, maybe he'd come to see that. She went down the stairs and out of the front door onto the sidewalk. Until he got there, she had to be vigilant. That meant leaving the state and maintaining a low profile.

Without chancing a glance upward, she slunk into the first alleyway to get out of sight of the apartment as quickly as possible. When she was out of view, she stopped to glance at the twenty-dollar bill in her hand. Sliding it into her other palm, she revealed what was nestled under it: the key to Dax's storage unit.

She needed money, transportation, and a change of clothes. The twenty would get her most of the way to the storage unit, she would walk the rest of the way. In that garage was water and transport, and maybe even a change of clothes. She didn't feel guilty about taking the key, or advantage of Dax's belongings. He was her husband and would want her to be alright. Worst case scenario, he came looking for the key, to challenge her for it back. That might give Dax the excuse he needed to come and find her. So long as she held the small piece of metal, she still carried a piece of him with her.

THIRTY-SEVEN

MIDNIGHT CAME AND WENT. Dax hadn't got to the mansion. He was on his way, sort of, it wasn't like he was hiding out. Waiting for the meeting made him edgy, so he'd gone to the bar to hang out with the crew. Only a few minutes after getting there did he acknowledge being social wasn't the draw, he came for the booze.

When the meeting time rolled around, he was too wasted to drive. Good sense dictated he shouldn't dare go near his bike. But, with every intention of going to Mauri's, he rose from the back corner couch, where he'd been slouched, observing his men enjoying their evening.

Staggering towards the door, he blinked, trying to clear the double vision. It had been years since he'd got himself drunk enough to know it affected his performance. Damn, he regretted picking up the Scotch bottle… that wasn't the only thing he regretted.

The reminder ignited the angry urge to drink again. Pausing, he rested a hand on the doorframe, sliding it up as his head dropped. He'd been an idiot. A complete and utter idiot. Believing Mauri when the Minx… he'd jumped on the excuse, unable to believe such a dynamic woman could want anything to do with him beyond sex.

Hadn't he only ever been worth what someone was willing to pay for him? That was the sad truth: he'd accused her of being a whore when the title suited him better. He sold his skills to the highest bidder, panting like an eager dog for Mauri's praise and acceptance along the way. Maybe that was the true reason for his drinking.

He was a coward. It was no more complicated than that. The Minx was right. He hadn't wanted to stand up to Mauri. Ivy gave him ample opportunity to make this right, she was patient, and now he'd lost her.

Mauri didn't want things to change. Well, he wanted Trystan to change. Ivy was the golden ticket, the miracle cure supposed to make that happen. Except she wasn't Trystan's miracle cure, she was his.

Curling his fingers into a fist, he readied himself to take out his frustration on the wall. Someone stepped in and got hold of his arm. Instinct should drive him to fight, but did it matter? He didn't have his wits about him or care what happened to him, so when the guy pulled him out of the room, down the corridor and out back, he just fumbled along. If someone wanted to kick the shit out of him, he should probably let them, it would be karmic retribution.

Instead of a punch, he was thrown to the outer wall. Again, he blinked, this time to clear the pulse of pain in his skull.

"You're not getting on the bike."

"No choice," Dax said, resting his head on the concrete to bring the interfering person into focus. Serg.

"You got a choice," Serg said. "The cops pull you over when you're in this state, they'll keep you."

"Who gives a fuck?"

"You got product on you?"

Dax could barely remember getting to the bar let alone whether he'd been working before or after. "Maybe."

Checking his pockets would expend energy. No point when he didn't give a shit.

"Then a lot of people care. You gonna tell them where you got it?"

Once again Mauri was being prioritized over

everything else. "Get off me, man," he said, giving his colleague a full body shove.

Catching his footing, he carried on in the general direction of where he thought he remembered leaving the bike.

"You shouldn't have let her go."

Serg's statement made him stop. "Didn't," he called back over his shoulder. "She bailed on me after I fucked her. Bitch snuck out while I was taking a nap."

Talking about Ivy like that made his jaw ache. She wasn't a bitch, and she didn't sneak. If there was one thing he knew about Ivy for sure, she didn't skulk. She walked into a room with her head held high and exited it in the same way. She wasn't a chicken-shit, no-good—

"Rita thinks different."

"What the fuck does that tramp know?" Dax barked. "And when the fuck were you talking about it?"

"She thinks you got yourself in over your head. Says Trystan's girl had something on you."

"If a bitch won't keep her mouth shut, fill it with something," Dax snarled, grabbing the chain link fence for stability. "You're fucking Rita, right?"

"Everyone's fucking Rita," Serg said. "I'll take you to the mansion." Dax heard the jangle of keys; he still hadn't bothered looking at his associate. "I heard Trystan was back."

Dax's tongue curled in his mouth. Suddenly, it wasn't so difficult to stand up straight. His posture grew and the self-pitying effects of the alcohol began to subside. "He is?"

"Yeah," Serg said, moving past.

With new purpose, Dax went with his colleague and got in his car. Why take the chance of killing himself on the bike when there was still so much to say to his surrogate little brother? Maybe the alcohol had been a good idea after all. His inhibitions were lowered. Let the drunk man speak with a sober tongue.

THIRTY-EIGHT

SERG SAID HE WAS GOING to get coffee. Dax didn't care, he was on a mission. The house should be awake waiting for him and Ivy to arrive, though he didn't know the actual time. None of that mattered anymore, there was only one thing he wanted to do. Taking the stairs two at a time, he flew up them and along the hallway to Trystan's suite. Adrenaline counteracted the alcohol, as had always been his experience.

It wouldn't have mattered whether the door was locked, Dax was going through it either way. But it was unlocked, so he stormed straight in. Trystan was in one of the armchairs by the window, Brad sat in the one opposite. Rita was there too, on her knees in front of the slouched Trystan.

Brad had a glass in his hand, casual, loose, definitely not drunk. Anyone else might find the scenario shocking, but he'd lost count of how many times he'd been the one in Brad's spot. Carrying on a normal conversation while the bastard got his cock sucked by some pretty little thing.

"Rita, bail," Dax said.

The woman sat back on her haunches, wiping the moisture from her swollen mouth with the back of her hand. "I'm almost done."

"Now!"

His fury got her up. While tucking her exposed breasts into her dress, she scurried out of the room.

"Have you got a thing for fucking my bitches?" Trystan asked.

Yes, thank you, the prick had anger of his own. Good.

Trystan straightened out his slacks and shirt as he stood, putting himself away to start on over, except Brad leaped up to grab hold of his brother.

"You two going to tear strips off each other now?" Brad asked, throwing Trystan back into his chair. "If you hit Dax, he's entitled to hit you back and you know he could kill you."

"The bastard's drunk," Trystan complained.

Either his intoxication was obvious, or someone had phoned ahead to tell the brothers he'd been drinking all night.

"He'd still pummel your ass."

Was Brad protecting Trystan or sticking up for him? A fight was exactly what he wanted.

"Let him hit me," Dax said, "please."

"Where's the girl?" Brad asked.

The whole damn thing was a ridiculous show, it was obvious she wasn't there. "Gone."

"You let her go?" Trystan yelled and tried to rise again.

Brad pushed him back down with one hand, maintaining his focus. "That's a shame, Dax," he said.

"For who? Not for her," Dax said. "I wouldn't have watched him put a finger on her! She's long gone and won't be back here, never again."

"So what the fuck are you doing here, hmm?" Trystan asked. This time Brad let him get to his feet. "Why not ride off into the sunset with my fucking woman?"

"Your fucking woman?" Dax said, striding toward Trystan. "You don't deserve her. She would never be yours. You can't break a woman like Ivy, it's not possible."

"Because you couldn't do it?" Trystan spat. "You're a piece of shit."

Lurching forth, Dax got hold of Trystan's shirt in one fist and drew back the other. "No," came Mauri's voice from behind him. "We're gonna be civilized about this."

"Civilized?" Dax asked.

Mauri hated to get blood on the family carpet. He was happy for it to get on anyone else's if it increased his means or served his purpose, but he was a firm believer in not shitting on your own doorstep.

"Let him," Trystan said, shoving Dax who whipped around to growl at the squirt. "Let him hit me, I'll get the cops on his ass so fast—"

"You're gonna call the cops to this house?" Dax said and snickered. "Jesus, you're a fucking idiot. You call the cops on me now and you don't think I'll start singing the minute they get the cuffs on?"

"You'd go down, they'd never believe anything you said."

"They'd believe it. I've got more goodwill with the crew than the rest of you. If I start singing, I guarantee it won't be long before the choir joins in."

"Dax," Mauri said with a scolding tone. "You won't ruin the family for the sake of a woman, will you?"

"I know where to squeeze. Most of the guys would snitch just 'cause I asked them or because one of you treated them like shit. Anyone who wouldn't do it for that would be easily blackmailed or bribed."

"You're a bastard," Brad said.

Disliking his position in the center of their triangle, he began to move toward the wall. "No, I'm just done. I'm done being the lackey who fixes everyone else's mess and never makes any of his own."

"I'm disappointed," Mauri said.

"I don't give a fuck!" Pinning Mauri under a glare was liberating. He'd burst the dam; he could do and say everything. "I wondered how Bruno was so smart at that brainwashing shit. Now I know why, 'cause you've all been doing it, all of you, since the minute I got here. I don't know why I didn't see it."

"Why the fuck would my father care about brainwashing you? You're a piece of shit nobody! Bruno warned you," Trystan said, appealing to his father. "He's been saying forever we shouldn't trust Dax, and he was fucking right! He knew this would happen! You listen to Bruno about everything, everything but this, why the fuck would you—"

"He's his father," Mauri said. The room paused. Mauri took a step closer; Dax matched it in retreat. "It's true. Bruno is your father. He and your mother were together for years. The man you thought of as your father was just your mother's boyfriend. They didn't meet until you were two, but you were too young to… It doesn't matter now. Bruno is your father."

"No," Dax said. His back hit the wall; he hadn't been aware of moving. Glancing at Brad and Trystan offered no further answers, even Trystan had shut up and appeared just as shocked as Dax felt. "No, my father—"

"Your mother abandoned you with her boyfriend. We didn't know until years later. By then he'd already palmed you off on the fighting circuit. It took us a long while to track you down."

"No," Dax said. "Bruno fucking hates me; he's always fucking hated me."

"He wasn't keen on my plan to track you down and bring you into the fold. He resented your mother for leaving him, he still does. He didn't want anything to do with you then. I was always convinced that would change… unfortunately I was wrong."

Bruno still hated him, because Bruno hated his mother? No, that didn't make any sense, yet at the same time, it did. Why else would someone like Mauri be in a shitty back-alley club watching people beat each other? Dax hadn't been fighting that night, he'd gone there looking for a fight, and travelled in those circles. If Mauri wanted to find him, going to fights was the right way to do it. It was so long ago, and he'd been so young, his memory was blurry.

"Why are you telling me this now?" Dax asked, though the news was a shock, it didn't change anything.

"If you want the girl, you can have her," Mauri said with an impersonal air. "But you have to make things right first, she has to make things right."

"No fucking way," Trystan said. "She's my fucking—

”

"We'll find you another girl," Mauri snapped, revealing his temper in a rare public moment. "Plenty of them have disrespected you."

"It won't work," Brad said to his father. "You want Dax to have the girl then let him, but you know that Trystan will never let it be that easy. The animosity will build to resentment and—"

"That's why Dax is going to give her up, for one night."

"What?" Dax and Trystan asked together.

"You let your brother gain her respect and she can apologize for embarrassing him," Mauri said. "Then we can all move on."

Dax's attention slid to Trystan whose depraved smug expression tempted him to knock out a few teeth. "No."

There wasn't even a slim chance he would let Trystan have a night with the Minx, it wouldn't happen. More than that, Ivy wouldn't agree to it, which meant she'd spend the night being tortured, just like she'd predicted. She would never forgive him either, she'd said it herself.

Trystan would probably be satisfied after a night with Ivy. It would give him the superiority he craved, and it wouldn't hurt that he'd be getting one up on Dax in the process. While Trystan might be able to move on from that night, telling everyone he'd sampled Ivy, their marriage would never recover from it.

"This is reasonable," Mauri said. "You let him have a night—"

"With my wife?" Dax said, fixing Mauri under his scowl again. "Ivy is mine, every fucking inch of her."

Speaking with such vehemence brought acid to his throat and his gaze fell. She was out there, somewhere, he didn't know where, running for her fucking life, and he'd let her go. He had let her walk out, sent her out there alone. Where was she? Would he ever be able to find her?

Moving toward the door, a singular focus motivated him.

"Where the fuck are you going?" Brad called. "You

can't just walk out on this."

Dax stopped in the open doorway. "I'm through, with all of you. Leave me the fuck alone and I'll leave you all be. Hear me? We're through. I don't give a fuck about any of you, any of this. We're done."

Setting himself back on his path, he began to search his pockets for his keys. His bike was at the bar, but to find Ivy he'd need the car. He had to find her. Had to.

The cool air outside sucker punched him. Swaying on his feet, he squeezed his eyes shut. He needed to go home and sleep, but after that, she'd be his only mission. He had to find her and hope she would have him back, that she would trust him not to let her down again.

THIRTY-NINE

ONCE SHE HAD RAIDED Dax's storage unit, Ivy had enough cash to get her clear across the country. The ten grand Dax had given her at the beach house was still stashed in the lining of the ottoman in their walk-in closet upstairs at said house. On a clock, she wasn't going back for that money, not a chance. She didn't know if Bruno was there, or any other Stark men. Walking back into the lion's den would just be plain stupid, even for that amount of cash.

Everything she needed was in the storage unit anyway. The couple of grand she found would keep her going for a while. The car key in a boot in the corner of a closet was near a sports bag full of clothes. There were a few items of women's clothing too, which she would rather not wonder too hard about. She changed her clothes, got water and other supplies from the unit, then cranked the engine and set off across the country, trying not to focus on what had happened between her and Dax.

They were still technically married. If they were really broken up for good, they'd have to address that, but it wasn't like she was in any hurry to get hitched. Doing it with Dax had been impulse, one she didn't want to repeat anytime soon.

With no clear objective in mind she just drove,

stopping whenever the mood took her. She spent a week here and a few days there. The Starks could be looking for her, though she doubted they would expend too much energy on resolving the humiliating episode they would probably rather forget. But that was the great thing about being a drifter. It was tough for people to find you when even you didn't know where you were going.

Six weeks went by until she was stopped by an ocean. She'd driven from the Pacific to the Atlantic, not directly, via just about every direction, but had ended up staring into the blue. Standing looking out over the crashing grey waves, with Dax's car parked a hundred yards away, she sank onto the hard grassy ground beneath her and took a deep breath.

That was when the tears came. She sat on that cliff for hours wailing and staring, consoling herself about the love she'd lost and chastising herself for being pathetic enough to lose her heart in such a careless way. She cried for the humiliation of her kidnap, cried for every time Bruno touched her, cried for every time she wanted to give in and let them take the last of her, for every time she'd wanted to break.

She was human and had weakness just like everybody else. One thing she did not do was show that weakness without good reason. The tears came and went. She lay on the grass, emotions ebbing and flowing with the motion of the vast brine spread out beside her. It didn't make her feel insignificant as Dax once asked; it made her revere opportunity. Such a huge area teeming with life living in harmony, experiencing the circle of life, depending on each other to survive.

Yes, they were insignificant, but they were supposed to be. The meaning of life was to get up and carry on, no matter what.

No one was there to dry her tears. She dried them on her own and took another deep breath. It was time to start again. This time with a broken heart.

FORTY

DAX WOULD NEVER GIVE up his search for her but was beginning to wonder if it had any chance of success. Tracking where she went after leaving his apartment didn't take long. He picked up his bike from the bar and took it to the storage unit thinking the car would offer more comfort. He might end up needing a place to sleep and the car could carry more supplies.

But when he pulled up to the storage unit and pulled out his wallet there was no key. Smart girl. Ivy was the only one who could've accessed it. After busting off the lock, confirming the car was gone, and some of his stashed cash too, he knew she was alright, at least for a while.

Luckily, he had money in several places, and she'd only taken one bundle. At least he got some information, she was in his car and had a couple of grand to keep her going. After switching out the bike for the car before, he hadn't gassed it up. That meant she had to, so the first thing he did was trace which gas station she used and which direction she'd gone in.

From there the search was just as incremental. Every time he thought he'd found her, it would turn out he'd just missed her. He hit some dead ends and had to retrace his steps a couple of times. His misguided pursuit even took him on a few massive detours… kind of like the course of their relationship.

He'd gone clear across the country and still didn't know where she was. Contemplating where her journey would have gone next, whether she would've turned back to go west or taken another route, Dax pulled into a motel and asked for a room.

The woman on reception was older, maybe in her late fifties, with curly grey hair and pointed glasses that sat on the end of her nose. She gave him a check-in slip, which he filled out and returned to her, then he started digging in his wallet for a credit card.

"Oh, two in one week, that's funny," the receptionist said as she transferred the information from his slip into the computer.

He stopped, his thumb still in the pouch of his wallet pressed against his forgotten credit card. "I'm sorry?"

"Your last name, I'm saying we had another person in with that last name this week. Do you have family in the area?"

"What was her first name? Was it a woman?"

"I can't tell you that," the receptionist laughed and carried on typing, obviously oblivious to the fact that the information could affect the rest of his life. For a second, he thought about charming her, then remembered he was the least charming person ever. He considered threatening her but being arrested wouldn't help him find Ivy. So he adopted an uncharacteristic plan and told the honest truth.

"I'm looking for my wife," he said, hoping beyond all else that Ivy was using her married name, and this wasn't some huge coincidence. The receptionist stopped typing and peered over her glasses. "I made a mistake, in California, and she left me six weeks ago, seven now actually. I've been looking for her ever since."

"You followed her here? All the way from California?" the receptionist asked. "How did you know she would be in North Carolina now?"

"I didn't," he said. "Like I said, I've been looking for

her, and it seems I'm always half a step behind her. I need her back. I love her."

"You cheated on her?" the receptionist asked with an edge of displeasure.

"No," he said, desperate to ensure she didn't cast her own life prejudices onto him, tainting any glimmer of goodwill.

"Then what did you do?" she asked, removing her hands from the keys, and swinging her chair around to meet his eye.

Maybe the crone was just nosey, but he was asking for information, telling her the truth felt like quid pro quo.

"I let my father—" though Mauri wasn't really his father at all. "I let my family come between us and she knew I wasn't, that I wouldn't… I had to choose her on my own, she couldn't make the decision for me."

"And now the decision is made? You chose her?" He nodded. "That's a lovely story, Mr. Harrow, but I can't really do anything to help." Anger rose but didn't depressurize because she spoke again. "Ivy left here five days ago, she got a job, somewhere local and they fixed her up with a place to stay."

Ivy. Yes. She was using her married name. Getting a job implied staying put. She wouldn't have quit after five days. Though she didn't have the best of luck when it came to employment, maybe she'd lost the job.

"Can you tell me where? Did she leave any forwarding information?"

"I could lose my job if I gave you information like that," the receptionist said without contrition.

Who gave a damn about some crummy reception job? Concealing his tension wasn't easy. "Maybe we could talk about something else," he said, opening his wallet to flick through the bills inside, hoping for a reaction.

He'd been bribing people all over the country for information on Ivy, he'd give his last if it meant he finally caught her.

"Oh no, no," the receptionist said, rolling her chair back to her computer to finish inputting the details from his check-in card.

Another door closed. He bit his tongue to prevent himself cursing at the unassuming woman. It was dark outside though he didn't know the precise time. Needing to vent, any official, or unofficial, pick-up fights could offer an outlet. If he could find one.

"You've driven all the way from California?" the receptionist asked, finishing up with the typing and closing down his file.

"Yes," he said and groaned.

Ivy was somewhere nearby. Nearer than she'd been in a while. He couldn't believe he'd come so close.

The receptionist retrieved a key and came back to the desk, reaching for something else as she did. "That's a long journey for one vehicle to handle. Maybe your car could use a service, just to check everything is in working order, you know, before you carry on your journey."

With the room key, she gave him a business card, which he read. "Warner Autos?"

"They're the best in town," she beamed. "Local… you understand?"

The way her eyes locked onto his was deliberate. Her polished smile remained exactly where it was while she bobbed her head in the direction of the card. He wanted to leap over the desk and kiss her, not that he really did, but he'd never felt elation in his life. This was what genuine delight and relief felt like.

"I understand. They're open tomorrow?"

"First thing," she said. "Though they're busy, they'll fit in time for special customers, it's not too far from here."

"Maybe I'll take a ride over there in the morning."

"Like I said, the best in town. Who knows? Maybe after you see what they've got, you won't feel the need to keep on travelling."

"No," he said and exhaled, letting himself smile. "No, maybe I won't."

"Well, enjoy your stay, goodnight," she said and walked away to return to the novel she'd put aside when he came in.

One night's sleep and then he'd see her. He'd go over to the garage and find out what Ivy was doing there. Her job didn't matter though, what mattered was that he finally had the chance to lay eyes on her again.

FORTY-ONE

"WARNER AUTOS," Ivy answered the phone in the back office of the garage as was her job.

So far, she'd been getting on well with the owner, one of the busiest guys she'd ever known.

He didn't say much when she met him, but he hired her and gave her an advance, so she was going to work her damndest for him. Her job consisted of answering the phone, booking in cars, ordering parts, and basically just dealing with the day-to-day paperwork. It was nothing too taxing, but it made her feel needed because she was the only one dealing with the running of the place while Blaser Warner, the garage owner, was absent.

When she got the job, Blaser told her he managed the apartment complex next door and a unit had just come vacant. It turned out the place housed other employees of Blaser's businesses and those who worked for him got a discount, so she jumped at the chance of the cheap, modest apartment. Most of the men who lived there were scary as hell, or they would be if she hadn't dealt with her own share of thugs. The majority of them were ex-cons and they worked there at the garage or as security in Blaser's nightclub.

The only people residing in the apartment complex

who didn't work for Blase were his family members and their girlfriends: the only two women there at all. Ivy was the only female living there alone, but she didn't feel intimidated or scared. The Warners were decent men, and her door was secure, so she was fine.

This was her, starting a new life. On reaching over to hang up the phone after the call ended, the diamond on her finger caught a glint of light. Every day she thought about Dax and every day she thought about going back to him. She could just show up at his apartment, or at the Stark mansion, or at the beach house. But she didn't have any assurances he wouldn't turn her over to Trystan and his men.

One year. She had decided to give it one year. If he hadn't returned to her by then, it wasn't going to happen. That was her decision and she had to be firm in following through. She couldn't be weak and beg him to take her back, it had to be his decision to want her… or not.

"Ivy!"

There was nothing delicate about the auto shop guys. Although she'd only been there for a week, they were already warming to her, and her to them. If she could make it work, this could be a place to belong. The thing she'd always wanted most. At least she'd wanted it most until meeting Dax. Only then had she discovered what true craving was like.

Spinning around in her chair, she glanced through the Plexiglas screen framing the upper space between her back office and the outer workspace. Men worked on various cars and the radio played, but all of that disappeared when she saw the person next to the guy who'd called for her attention.

"Shit," she breathed and flew up out of her chair.

The mechanic next to Dax didn't look happy and they were exchanging words. Another mechanic saw and alerted others. If she didn't move fast, this could turn into a brawl.

Getting out of her office, she dashed the length of the building to dive in front of Dax. "I've got this, thanks, Pop."

The tall black man was terrifying to look at from afar but had never given her a cross word. "Dude says he's your husband," Pop said.

"Funny that," Ivy said. Groping behind her, she

snagged Dax's wrist. "I'll just… I'll take him out of your way."

Dragging Dax across the room, past all onlookers, she got him into her workroom and slammed the door, which was odd because that door was never, ever closed, except when the rest of the garage was.

"Dax," she breathed. "What are you doing here?"

"What the fuck are you doing working in a place like this?" he demanded, closing in on her. "Those guys out there are dangerous."

"No one is dangerous, Blaser assured me that—"

"Who is Blaser?"

"Blaser Warner," she said. "The owner of the garage, he gave me this job. He's a really nice guy and—"

Dax's palm slammed onto the wall at her back, startling her, boxing her in. "Are you fucking him?"

"Oh, God, that's where your head goes first? I haven't seen you for seven weeks. The last time I did see you, you were ready to feed me to the fishes and the first thing you ask me is if I'm fucking my boss?"

"Yes," he said with no shame or apology. Grabbing her hand, he jerked it up, squeezing her ring finger. "You're wearing your wedding ring and using your married name."

"So why would I be sleeping with another man?"

He frowned. "You've been faithful?"

"You haven't?" Tilting her head, she folded her arms and waited for his answer.

No space existed between them.

"I haven't had time to look at a fucking woman. I have spent the last seven weeks chasing your damn tail across the country. Why can't you stay put, woman?"

"I haven't found my place to belong yet. When I do, I will."

"Your place to belong," he spat out. "There's only one place you belong, and you've spent almost two months running away from it."

He caught hold of her face and hauled her up, forcing his mouth over hers. Although the kiss was unexpected that didn't mean she didn't want it. Opening herself to him, she leaned in and trailed her hands up to his shoulders

"That's right," he grumbled, crouching to hook his hands under her ass, boosting her from the floor.

Turning to the desk, he sat her down and leaned over to consume her mouth again. His fingers began to work the buttons on her blouse, though his impatient hand stopped its task to fondle her breast.

"Dax, I'm at work," she said, leaning away from the kiss, and turning to alert him to the transparent panel on the opposite wall. "And people can see us."

"Where's your boss?"

"Probably still in bed," she said. "He owns a strip club, so he hasn't been home for long. Why? What are you going to do? Find him and beat him until he fires me?" Smacking both hands onto his chest, she made him move and got off the desk to put some space between them. "Why are you here?"

"I thought that was damn obvious."

"You came here to get laid?" she asked, folding her arms again in an attempt to conceal the drawn-out pant of her breathing and the pebbles at the peak of her breasts that his kiss made ache.

"Yeah, I walked away from my life and chased you across the country because I needed a tramp to ride my cock." When he moved toward her, Ivy tried not to tense or back away. "Are you crazy, babygirl? I came here for you. You're out of options."

"Options?"

"I told you that you'd never be free of me. That if you left their prison you'd be stuck in mine. I'm not gonna let you escape again."

"You left them? What about Mauri? What about—"

"We don't have to worry about that anymore. I told them I was gone, that I was out, and I wasn't coming back."

"I thought you were going to make them see, make them understand about us, so that your life wouldn't have to change."

"I was wrong."

"Wrong?" she asked. When her shoulders loosened, her hands fell to her sides. "I told you that weeks ago. I knew they would never let us be together, that it would come down to a choice."

"A choice I've made," he said, bringing his hand to her face. "I went in there, to that midnight meeting…"

"What happened? How did you get out of there?"

"You don't have to worry about that," he said, cool anger crystallized in his irises. He tried to hide it with a smile and a swipe of his thumb along her jaw and up over her lips. "We're not going back there."

"They let you walk away," she said.

The smile on his lips twitched.

This wasn't over and he knew it as well as she did. Dax would either carry around the loss and betrayal of his supposed family for the rest of his life, or that family would track them down and do everything in their power to get him back.

"I don't need their permission to be with my wife."

"You shouldn't have come here," she said, shaking her head and looking away.

She started for the door, but Dax shifted into her path, blocking her exit, forcing her to look him in the eye. They were right in front of the window. The mechanics wouldn't be getting much work done while the drama was unfolding.

"You belong to me. I'll follow your tail for as long as I need to."

"I wanted you to follow me, to fight for me," she whispered. "I knew we weren't over, that I'd see you again. But if you can't let them go—"

He snatched her arm when she tried to get around him. "I've let them go. I don't give a fuck about them."

"You do," she said. "You have to admit what they did hurt you. You fought with me, Dax. You fought me so hard, you were convinced they'd let you be happy, that they would let you be with me. The fact they didn't… it changes everything about your relationship with them. They weren't who you thought they were. They didn't give you the respect that you—"

"What do you want?" he snapped, tossing her arm

away. "Do you want me to get the fuck out of your life?"

Sarcasm rolled her eyes. "Yes, I'm using this horrible situation as an excuse to dump you, tough guy. If I wanted rid of you, I wouldn't still be wearing my rings, would I? I wouldn't have used your last name every chance I got."

"Why did you do that?" he asked, edging toward her. "Because you wanted me to find you?"

"Yeah, because I love you and I want to be with you. But you can't resent me for—"

"They made their decision," he said, scooping his hands up under her chin to hold her head. "They got the chance to accept this, they didn't take it. Being with you was never a question for me, whether they wanted to be a part of it, that was the question."

"Dax—"

"Yes, babygirl, I love you," he said, answering the question she didn't get a chance to ask. "We are the same and the only place either of us belongs is side by side."

"It'll be tough, you don't have a crime syndicate to run around after anymore. You won't know where to fight and—"

"Are you kidding? I started my career not far up this seaboard. Anyone I don't know in the underground circuit isn't worth knowing."

Smiling, she shook her head. "Not much of a smooth talker are you, tough guy?"

"It's not talk you need from me," he said, lowering to lift her off the floor and take her to the closed door.

Resting her back against it, they were no longer in view of the window. "We can't have sex here," she said.

Closing his lips on her neck, he elevated her body. "Says who?"

The rasp of his jeans opening boosted her heart rate. "My boss. We need me to keep this job, I have a place to stay and—"

"He owns a strip joint," Dax said, looking her in the eye. "And a car garage."

"Yes," she said. "And manages the apartment complex next door. That's where I stay. I think he owns it."

"Lots of money, lots of lowlifes on the payroll," he said, indicating the men on the other side of the door. "He's a crook, Minx."

She'd been impressed by Blaser when she met him. He was sort of distant, which made her constantly curious about what he was thinking without saying. But he'd been kind to her, as had everyone else. Though none of that meant his business was legit.

"What does that have to do with having sex?" she asked.

"I'll find a way to persuade him into understanding."

And the smugness in his tone relaxed her. "You think you have some secret skill that he'll need? One that allows you to get away with screwing his employees while they're being paid by him?"

"You worry about the secret skills I have that *you* need."

He didn't need fancy tricks; she'd been fantasizing about being in his arms for weeks. Every minute they'd been apart, she dreamed of him coming after her to declare his love and devotion. Just like this. It didn't seem he would take no for an answer.

Her lips parted to release a yelp of hopeless desire and relief. The question in his eyes wasn't going to be answered in words. She joined their mouths and went straight in to seek out his tongue. Losing herself in the emotion and sensation of their kiss, she didn't consider the future, the past occupied her thoughts.

If their hand hadn't been forced by circumstance, they'd never have started a proper relationship. They'd have danced around each other, goading, and lying, neither willing to relent first and admit the potency of their desire. Just like in that Vegas alleyway.

"You're staying," she exhaled onto his lips. "This is your last chance, tough guy. If you let me walk away again—"

"Never gonna happen, you're my prisoner."

"Or maybe you're mine," she said, throwing her arms around him and locking their mouths together again.

The kiss got faster, more desperate, hungrier. His

hands on her body and his lips on her skin didn't alleviate her burning need. The thick length of his erection teased her, pressing the path of its intended raid outside of her body when it should be charging into her.

He had already opened his jeans, getting him out of his underwear was easy. Peeling her own aside, she was about to guide him in when his hands stopped roaming and he moved her away from the door.

Fearful he was going to take her to the desk, where they'd be on view, Ivy stopped all action and tried to speak. Dax's tongue passed her lips, muffling the words that were forgotten when he took them down to the floor.

Ivy had to give him brownie points. If he started pounding into her on that door, the noise would carry into the echoing cavern of the garage. Her colleagues would have a second-by-second performance that would render the radio obsolete.

Keeping them by the door, so no one could interrupt them, Dax laid her down. He pulled off his tee-shirt to stuff it behind her head before guiding the end of it around into her mouth.

"Things could get rough," he said and smiled. "You keep it down."

Spitting out the tee-shirt tail he'd intended to dampen her screams, she grinned up at him. "I have to make some noise. How else will they know how well-trained you are in pleasuring me?"

"I'm trained?"

"Yeah," she said. "You're the perfect husband now, my evil plan worked."

"Shame mine didn't. You're untrainable, Minx, and you still don't know when to keep that mouth shut."

"I know when to keep it shut, I choose not to."

"No one tells you what to do or how to be."

"That's right," she said, tightening her arms around his neck to bring his mouth close to hers. "But you've got a long time ahead of you to try, tough guy. You better use your time wisely."

"Oh, I will," he said, kissing her on the route to sating

her passion.

Fate couldn't be battled. Its plan may not always be clear, but everything turns out the way it's supposed to in the end.

TO BE CONTINUED...

Thank you for reading this tale!

If you can, please take the time to review.

~

Ask your local library for more Scarlett Finn
novels!

~

For all things Scarlett Finn
check out:

www.scarlettfinn.com

BOOK TWO

FIGHTING BACK

SCARLETT FINN

OUT NOW!